BOOKS BY MARILYN LUDWIG

SEARCHING FOR JULIETTE (2015)

"KUDOS TO MARILYN LUDWIG FOR crafting an intelligent, well-written mystery for young adult readers, which is also a good read for all ages. Set against a well-researched background of French-Canadian history, language, and political intrigue, her plot unwinds with many turns, right up to the end. I look forward to her next book." —Susan Throckmorton, author of *The Humply Rumply Beast: Poems and Papercuts*, and *They'll Be Back!* (www.papercuttings.waw.pl)

HASTE YE BACK (2015)

"IN THE RAPIDLY GROWING GENRE of YA books, Marilyn Ludwig's mystery novels stand out for their fast-pace and great writing. *HASTE YE BACK* is set in the British Isles and the flavor of the country is on every page, enticing the reader to want to see for herself. This is the perfect book selection for any reader, any traveler, of any age. I know I'll slip Ms. Ludwig's next book in my carry-on bag!" —Melinda Morris Perrin, author of *Prairie Smoke, Goldenrods*, and *Winterberries*.

THE SECRET OF KENDALL MOUNTAIN (2016)

"*THE SECRET OF KENDALL MOUNTAIN* IS a wonderful story that readers of all ages will enjoy. The young heroes, who are quite believable and relatable, are called upon to perform a daring rescue and solve a lingering mystery against the backdrop of avalanche season in the Colorado mountains. The setting is beautifully described, and the suspenseful tale is well-told and sure to satisfy." —Mike Manolakes, author of *Variation Seven, Strange Times, Living in the Future*, and *Dying in the Past*.

IT'S PERFECTLY SAFE ... THE RULISON MATTER (2016)

"MARILYN LUDWIG'S STORIES HAVE DELIGHTED me for over a decade, but the newest book *IT'S PERFECTLY SAFE* actually kept me up late reading (into the morning!) during a season I work seven days a week and that's a feat for any author. This historical fiction work has captured an event that many, including those of us who lived in the western U.S. at the time, had never heard about. Kudos to Marilyn for keeping the astounding use of an atomic bomb in our consciousness, and doing so with characters who arouse our curiosity, empathy, and who keep us turning the pages until we find out if they are safe." —Deb Wayman, owner Fair Isle Books, Washington Island, Wisconsin

"*IT'S PERFECTLY SAFE* IS A young adult novel based on atomic bomb tests of the Cold War era. Those tests resonate to contemporary fracking concerns. Marilyn Ludwig draws on early childhood memories to illuminate a landscape of mid-century isolated small towns in the Colorado mountains. At the center of the story is a fledgling teacher with two mysteries to unravel: one from her childhood and another forming the quick moving plot. The mysteries converge in a clever and exciting resolution. A reader quickly experiences a vivid sense of place, as well as a young woman's sense of self. This novel surpasses its young adult genre to appeal to readers who remember the 1950s and 60s, of which Marilyn Ludwig's description and details hit the mark." —Edward Searl, author of *A Place of Your Own*, *Around the Delaware Arc*, and the five-book series, *A Treasury of Poems, Quotations, and Readings*, among others

TRUST THE MAGIC (2016)

"*TRUST THE MAGIC* PULLS YOU under its spell on page one and does not let go! A story of family, coming of age, and a great mystery to boot, Marilyn Ludwig has once again spun a tale full of fun and enchantment, befitting the beautiful Prince Edward Island on which this story takes place. It is obvious that, much like Anne of Green Gables, PEI is Ludwig's spiritual home . . . and for a little while, she makes it your home, too.

Susan's journey of self-discovery and friendship is so full of honesty, it's impossible not to fall in love with her and the stunning island life Ludwig so thoughtfully portrays. Fast-paced with surprising twists, *Trust the Magic* is the perfect book for both new readers and for those of us who have spent a lifetime reading. A great addition to anyone's library." —Katie Jaros, author of *The Lost Souls Trilogy*

"A METICULOUS PLOT, A COMPELLING setting, and an exciting array of characters—these characterize *TRUST THE MAGIC*, Marilyn Ludwig's story of young Susan Olympia Slade and her great aunt's challenge to her to be adventurous, "trust the magic" and, ultimately, discover the fate of her daughter, Emily Rose, who disappeared over 50 years ago. Ludwig writes of a family's secrets, deception, and meanness that require her smart protagonist to delve into the past through portraits, letters, conversations, and her visions—with a little help from a brother, friends, and a particularly sad and restless ghost—to try to solve the mystery. Ludwig's love of Prince Edward Island is evident in her selecting it as the setting: beautiful scenery, including that along the Confederation Trail; sites reflecting her loved *Anne of Green Gables* series (also important to her hero); and a lighthouse/home Susan inherits when the story opens—all unite in the novel, providing the reader with an inviting dwelling place. While the story focuses on one teenager growing in consciousness and confidence, other characters, such as her lively parents, an elderly lighthouse keeper, two giggly girls who need a teacher, her friend Abby, her Aunt Bea, and an unruly cousin no one can understand, also enrich this delightful and wise novel, drawing the reader to them." —Sandra Duguid, author of *Pails Scrubbed Silver*

The
GEESE
That
WON the WAR

A Bletchley Park Novel

Marilyn Ludwig

Book cover and interior designed by Ellie Searl, Publishista®
Cover photographs by Marilyn Ludwig
Maps are in public domain

ISBN-10: 0996742247
ISBN-13: 9780996742245
LCCN: 2017903406

ZAFA PUBLISHING
Downers Grove, Illinois

For Nancy A. Friedlander
Dear Kindred Soul
Thank you.

The geese that laid the golden eggs but never cackled.
Winston Churchill
September 1941

The Prime Minister of England, describing the dedicated,
discreet code-breakers, who cracked Germany's Enigma Code
during World War II

The Enigma Machine

Map of Great Britain

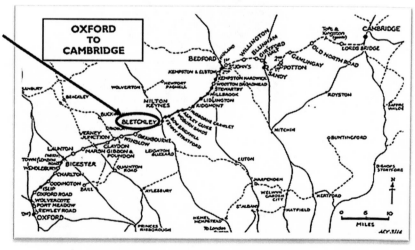

Rail Line from Oxford to Cambridge – 1940s

September 3, 1939
A grim date to remember

IN LONDON SIRENS WAILED. AT 11:15 AM the nightmare became real—perhaps inevitable. Hitler's intentions were clear. Germany would invade, and England must prepare. For War!

Coming attractions: relentless bombings, blackouts, rationing, evacuation, distrust, fear. But also incredible courage to search within—to find ways of accepting and enduring a new normal. At risk were loss of country and way of life in this small island nation. Survival rested in each person's hands.

While fifty miles north of London, only a brief railroad journey away in the working-class town of Bletchley, a grand manor house was spruced up, ready to do its bit. A few years earlier, thanks to visionaries such as Admiral Hugh Sinclair and geniuses like Allan Turing—men who anticipated the worst—preparations had already begun.

Black curtains, replacing lush maroon drapes of velvet, now covered the windows, but Bletchley House barely noticed the change. Black was in keeping with the mourning of the last two years. House had no way of knowing the new curtains had not been hung to honor Sir Herbert Leon, so long deceased, nor the more recently departed Lady Fanny. All House knew was loneliness, and it sighed as only an abandoned manor that has seen great glory can. Without Lady Leon, all sparkle had vanished—from the carved oak-paneled walls, Italian marble columns, glazed fireplace mantles, to the fixtures of nickel and chrome. Chandeliers grew dusty, most of the furnishings sold, and what little remained had become dingy and decrepit. What House missed most, though, was the glitter of people—clinking their wine glasses and teacups in the pavilion, their hushed flirting and giggles from twenty-seven bedrooms, followed by the sounds of rushing bathwater and the scent of French perfume. All this, and then sudden, total silence.

At first, House hardly noticed the difference. Judith still came each morning to draw the drapes and at end of day to close them. Then came the fight with George and everything changed. "It's not fair you should inherit when you don't love it." That was Judith.

"The terms of the will were not my doing. This place is an eyesore, a monstrosity. Tearing it down is a public service, and selling the land for development will be most lucrative."

"No, George, please. This is my home—not yours."

All was silent again. The black curtains remained closed, and the massive front door bolted shut.

Then one day, and for many days afterward, the door opened again, and heavy footprints muddied the tiled entranceway. Men invaded, different kinds of warriors, with measuring tapes and papers. Then more men came with long tables and more papers. Finally, another day, a woman and a man entered—by themselves—she, wearing a fancy hat with peacock feathers, excited and cheerful, he in a sober gray suit and dark tie, all business.

"Hugh, those griffins guarding the entrance are absolutely cunning."

House was shocked. Sir Leon's stately griffins—cunning?

"I'm sure you're right, dear, but do consider they might be suitable for scrap. There's a war on, you know."

"Hugh, if I hear that expression one more time . . . Well, I don't know what I'll do. Don't ever use it on me again. The only reason we're here is because 'there's a war on.' Please, Hugh, don't destroy the griffins. When this country prevails—and it will—what will we have won if our treasures have been turned to scrap?"

"Our lives, if we're lucky. Very well, Katherine, you know you always have your way with me. The griffins may stay for now. I do wish some of those pillars could be taken down to give us more space, but I suppose they're vital to the structure."

"Of course they are. Look around. This place has its own personality. Can't you feel it? And it is truly beautiful. Hugh, we must keep as much beauty as we're able. Why should we allow wicked people to destroy beauty, too?"

"The upkeep will be tremendous, but we'll attempt to do what you think best. I must tend to business now. My goodness, what an enigma of a house!" He chuckled at what seemed to be a private joke. "Well, that certainly suits the present situation." He walked off to the small room he thought might do for his office, leaving his wife behind to gaze and dream.

"A great pity all those ugly huts must be built on such magnificent grounds, but Hugh has agreed—although he may regret it later—to let me concentrate on this lovely home. Yes, a little waxing and polishing, and perhaps just a few handsome desks and settees. I shall insist on a decent bedroom, library, and sitting room for myself. It's a marvelous old house. It deserves to live. We all deserve to live."

House warmed to the sound of Lady Katherine Sinclair's gentle voice, so much like Lady Fanny's, repeating some of the very words she had spoken to Lord Leon so many years before. House knew it was not *just* a house. Not *any* home, but a manor, a grand mansion. It was Bletchley House of Bletchley Park, and it would soon live again.

PART ONE

Don't you know there's a war on?

CHAPTER ONE

ARRIVING AT BLETCHLEY RAILWAY STATION, Buckinghamshire, England, summer 1940—Bundles. Bundles of children whisked out of London, safely from the Blitz. Excited children. Apprehensive children. All kinds of children—laughing, crying, dirty, tired. Traveling alone, together, in schools. Bundles of adults—determined, proud, resigned, confused, some sworn to solemn secrecy as they turned right at the main road, walked a few hundred yards, and turned up a country lane—only to encounter forbidding fences, surmounted by harsh barbed wire. Finally arriving at imposing iron gates, giving the password to enter, not knowing what lay beyond. Bundles. Bundles of lists. Bundles of letters in pouches. And coming from everywhere, land, air, and sea, all going to the same place—Bundles and Bundles and Bundles of Codes. Top Secret!

Back in a small one-up, one-down flat in London, just off Tavistock Square, Sheila Bradshaw waited for the whistle of the kettle, signaling it was time to pour her goodbye cup of tea, so lovely even in the July heat. Some morning music would be grand, she decided. Turning on the radio, she found nothing but war news—on every station. Six of one, half a dozen of the other. She shrugged. War news was everywhere. At the chemist, tobacconist, green grocer, even church.

After accepting she would hear neither music nor good news, Sheila turned off the squawking box and stared at covered furniture and four suitcases. How would they ever survive on so few possessions? In the largest and heaviest, a Revelation suitcase, she had just managed to squeeze in one more item—a framed photo of her deceased grandmother. The beloved face resembled her own—a perfect oval with blonde fluffy hair, startling blue eyes, and a slightly crooked nose. Deceptively candy-box-pretty, hiding a toughness and resiliency that Sheila dearly hoped she had inherited. She supposed she should remove the photo, saving space, but the frame was a family heirloom. Something good from the past must go with her into the unknown.

She faced the truth. Home might not be there when she returned. At this point, she had to admit she didn't know if she would return, or rather, if she would want to. Roger wouldn't be a factor, which was a bonus. He had made that clear before he left. He had asked for a divorce, and Sheila couldn't think of a single reason to refuse him. Financially, life would become more difficult, but other than that, she felt nothing but relief. She supposed she should tell the children sometime soon. Gemma might mind, but she doubted the other two girls would care. Roger had never noticed them anyway except to scold—or even worse. She didn't want to think about it.

Such a comfort the tea, even though it was not her usual Earl Grey— that supply long gone. There would be tea at Bletchley Park, of course, as well as wherever they were billeted. After all, this was England; there would always be a kettle. And please God, may it stay England. Most likely the Hun would issue each of them a beer stein—at least to those still alive. She rubbed the back of her neck. Still weary, but there would be no more rest for her. It was time to leave.

"Reenie?" Honestly, what was keeping the child? "Reenie! We must hurry. Now!"

A big sigh came from the room fifteen-year-old Reenie shared with her two younger sisters. "Yes, Mum, I'm coming."

"Right this minute. Please, no more delays. Gemma and Pippa are playing outside, and the garden is in such a state of rubble they'll need to be spruced up again. Hurry. No telling how long it will take to get to Euston Station. The train will not wait for us."

"Yes, Mum," came an even louder sigh. Sheila rinsed her teacup and placed it on the drainer. She knew she should put it into the cupboard, but it looked at home—where it and the four of them belonged.

Maureen Bradshaw, called Reenie, grabbed Pippa's hand to keep the great nuisance from wandering off again. "Pippa, you must stay with me. Do you want to be hit by a lorry?" The scurrying crowds on the sidewalks and the snarled traffic made the London streets even more dangerous than usual. Panic was in the air.

Pippa gave Reenie a look of disgust. "I won't be hit. Mummy, tell Reenie I'm too big for her to order me around."

"Yes, Pippa, but twelve is also old enough to know when it's time to follow good advice. Do carry your own satchel and gas mask and help with little Gemma, whose legs are much shorter than yours. Please try harder."

"Yes, Mummy. You must obey me, Gemma. Do you hear? I'm twelve, and you must do everything I say!" Gemma wisely ignored her.

Reenie wondered when Mum would realize that something was seriously wrong with Pippa, who acted more like six-years-old than twelve. Such an unattractive brat—big and gawky, stringy brown hair, whiny . . . But Mum did nothing, not even listening to Pippa's teachers about correcting her behavior. Gemma, although two years younger, was much more mature. Gemma, a pint-sized version of pretty Mum, was no problem, but she would soon grow tired walking to the bus stop and waiting for a bus that might never come. Perhaps they would miss the train and go home again. She crossed her fingers.

Leaving London was pure folly in Reenie's opinion. When she and her sisters had been forced just the year before to vacate to the country, it had been a nightmare, and if it hadn't been for her firm refusal to part from them, she, Gemma, and Pippa would have been separated. Who knows what would have happened if a kind-hearted lady hadn't said finally, "Very well, I'll take the lot of them."

But it had turned out to be a false alarm. After the grim declaration on the radio, followed by terrifying sirens and everyone rushing to their assigned shelters, not much happened. For eight whole months, in spite of all the preparations, including evacuating hundreds of terrified children, there were no bombs, no invading Germans—at least not in England. So Reenie, her sisters, and many others returned to London. They called it the "Phoney War."

This was probably phony, too, although she'd heard there had been some bombing in outer London—Croydon and Wimbledon. Might be just a rumor, but what was true were the night-time raids along the South Coast— the English Channel, seaports, and coastal radar stations. Now that France had fallen, everything was bound to be worse. This time they had no choice. The government ordered them to evacuate, certain that the docks and Central London would be hit soon. At least they would all be together— with Mum. Reenie remembered the sight of her mother crying at the evacuation center. Parents weren't even allowed to see their children off at the railway stations. At least this was better than that. Anything was better than having to take care of her sisters alone. Anything was better than seeing Mum cry.

Determined, Reenie firmly pulled last season's straw hat down onto her short brown bob, so like her father's, and raised the sharp chin inherited from Gram. So far, Mum had not noticed the Tangee lipstick applied more liberally than usual. "Forward, girls," she ordered her sisters.

Davis Dailey grabbed his briefcase, gave a farewell nod to his office, and headed down the long, impressive hall of the math and science building of the University of Chicago, where he lectured on cryptology. The decision was final. He was tired of second-guessing himself and worrying about his fiancée's reaction. He could understand Barbara's feelings, of course—he had more than a few doubts himself—but he wished she would at least try to understand his point of view.

She had cuddled close, as she always did when trying to get her way. "If you'll just be patient, Davey. You'll get that promotion soon. I'm sure of it. Head of Cryptology and Cryptanalysis Research at the University of Chicago—what you've always dreamed of!"

"You may be right, dear," he had said yet again, "but there's a war on, and I don't know when this country is going to wake up and realize it's our fight, too." What he couldn't share was Eugene Bifford's letter, so secret it had come by courier directly from London.

"What about us?" He didn't have much of an answer for Barbara—at least not one that satisfied her. Now she was angry because she couldn't go to New York and see him off. He could hardly explain that he would not be sailing but flying in a chartered airplane sent just for him and a few others. He couldn't explain that even to himself.

"This better be good, Biff." Gene Bifford was a joker, of course, but he did have a serious side and was one of the smartest men Davis had ever known. Davis, Biff, and Brian—also called Buffer, an old childhood friend—had been students together at Oxford. Great chums, spending long hours in deep discussion, consuming more than a little ale at the Eagle and Child. All their friends had silly nicknames; his was Dally, not just a take off on his name, but also because he normally took his time in deciding just about everything—until now. At Oxford, Davis read history and literature for four years before determining his future lay in mathematics, finally returning home to complete his degrees at the Illinois Institute of Technology. Brian had embarked on a career with the U.S. Navy and seemed to be pleased with his decision. Davis wasn't sure what Biff was doing these days but thought the letter indicated he might be involved with British Intelligence.

> We need you, Dally. Go to New York's Idlewild Airport on 20 July, report to the main information desk at 19:30. Identify yourself, and you will be escorted to a chartered aeroplane. You will be met upon arrival in London. Consider this top secret.

Perhaps it was, although Biff had always leaned toward the dramatic. Biff ended by saying how sorry he was to hear about Davis's father's death, following so closely his mother's. That had been part of the attraction for Davis in accepting the odd challenge. Everyone was gone—except Barbara.

Ron Marks, who had the office next to Davis, appeared suddenly, interrupting his thoughts. "We'll miss you, Dailey. You've done good work here. Hope you're not making a mistake by leaving."

"Thanks, Marks. Time will tell. I don't know what good I'll be fighting the Nazis, but I'm going to give it my best shot."

"Not our war yet."

Davis had not recovered from his dismay at the U.S. proclaiming neutrality the previous summer, and few things made him angrier than Marks's expression.

"And when will it be our war? After Britain goes down in flames as well as France and Belgium? Would Dunkirk have happened if their supposed best friend had been fighting alongside them? Wake up! Hitler has declared his intention to invade Britain. He's calling it Operation Sea Lion. What makes you think he won't set his sights on us next? And when he does, who will be left to help us? Damn it, Marks, it is our war, and you know it!"

"Not our call, Dailey. Sorry you feel that way." He started to leave.

"Wait, Marks. Can you think of any reason I should stay and be a part of whatever is going on here?"

Marks seemed troubled as he and others in the department did any time Davis asked this question. "Not certain what you mean, Dailey, but good luck to you." He walked quickly out of the building, and that was that.

Davis shrugged. Screw you, Marks. Screw all of them! It was not his imagination that he was being excluded deliberately. Ever since he let it slip he'd read German poetry and history at Oxford and had spent considerable time in Germany, people had regarded him with suspicion. As if he could have known back then that a passion for Goethe, plus a few side trips into the works of the Italian Dante, would get him into trouble. So many times he had come upon clusters of people talking softly, until he approached. Once he thought he heard the word "Manhattan." What did Manhattan have to do with Chicago?

Well, at the moment, Manhattan was precisely where he was heading. He hailed a taxi for Union Station.

"What the hell am I doing in Fenny Stratford?" Catriona MacLaren awoke with a start, uncertain at first why she was in this small, spiritless room. Oh, right. I'm here because I wanted to get the hell out of Inverness. How strange not to have Gramps tell her to hold her tongue—that he had a mind to wash out her mouth with soap. Other than her grandfather, there was nothing much left for her back in Scotland, and maybe nothing here either. But it would be a change. At the great age of twenty-three, Catriona needed a change.

Gramps had not been happy with her decision. He lit his pipe and puffed ferociously. "England? Ye'll go tae England? The people cannae even speak English, and ye'll nae be able tae abide the food."

But Gramps couldn't afford to continue sending her to university, even if her term results had been stronger. Unfortunately, she rarely brought her head out of the clouds long enough to train for anything worthwhile. Hers was a world of numbers and deep thoughts, not for anything practical, especially in Inverness. For the past six months, she had been miserable, employed as a shop assistant in a mediocre haberdashery.

"There's a war on, Gramps," she said, kissing the top of his head. "The king wants us to do our bit."

"Not our war. I have nae call tae fecht with foreigners. Let London have its war without us."

Like so many of their countrymen, Gramps was determined everything should remain the same. Cat tried hard to convince him. "Gramps, not just England is in danger. Consider how close we are to the North Sea. Think about Scapa Flow and the Royal Oak." Germans had bombed the nearby Orkney naval base the preceding March, sinking the important battleship and causing the death of 834 men.

But Gramps just buried his head in his Herald, refusing to listen. Until one day—"Here's something to take yer mind off war, Catriona. On Saturday, the Daily Telegraph is running a puzzle contest at our own Station Hotel. If ye solve the puzzle in less than twelve minutes, ye'll win. It doesn't say what the prize is. Give it a wee try, lassie. Ye'll find it a change from trying tae figure out how Nessie can survive the cold waters of the loch."

"Honestly, Gramps. That Loch Ness project was a third form school assignment. I didn't take it seriously."

But Catriona never could resist a dare, and this new challenge sounded simple enough. She hiked into town at the appointed time, completed the puzzle in eight minutes, and scarcely gave it another thought. Several weeks later, fortunately when Gramps was dozing, she received a telegram.

Congratulations. You are a winner in the puzzle contest. Your country needs your service. Call the following phone number immediately. Tell no one. Top secret.

It was signed Admiral Hugh Sinclair.

"Admiral" Sinclair was clearly a fraud—possibly even dangerous. Curiosity tweaked, ignoring her warning conscience, Catriona consulted a former university professor. "I've heard of this," he said. "Let me investigate. I do know that Admiral Hugh Sinclair is a real person—a very important one—but did he actually send this?"

In short order, the professor got back to her. "The telegram was genuine, Miss MacLaren, and it is quite an honor. You are being asked to serve your country and, indeed, this may turn out to be a fine opportunity for you as well. Leaving your studies was most unfortunate." He looked at her sharply. "Truly, you must not tell anyone. Remember, even the walls have ears."

This meant not even Gramps could know. So she told him she had joined the Women's Naval Service, popularly known as Wrens, and he was not pleased. Actually, she *would* become a Wren, but only after extensive training at a place in England. Top secret—even from her, back then. What must remain secret from others was her present location. Her cover address was the HMS Pembroke V, as if she were a regular Wren on an actual ship.

Eight weeks later at her billet in the tiny, definitely land-locked community of Fenny Stratford, Cat gave a long lazy stretch. My, she was stiff. The mattress wasn't very good—stuffed with something quite dreadful, she feared. She forced herself to her feet and surveyed the cheerless room. It looked as if her bunkmate had arrived during the night, judging from a few foreign suitcases. The bed seemed to be made up even neater than when Cat arrived, and a note lay on the thin blanket. For her, she guessed. Who else was there?

I didn't want to awaken you from your slumbers. I'm sure we'll meet later and that in the future you will leave your possessions in tidier order. I've gone to survey the town. I'm a great walker. Edith Ferrar.

Edith Ferrar, a great walker, who didn't think Cat was tidy enough. Oh, bugger! How very English and proper. Catriona shared some of Gramps's disdain and distrust of the English. And so far he was right about the food.

What she'd sampled had been tasteless, and the language deplorable. But it was still English and, thus, better than German. First brushing her sandy curls, made wild by a restless night, and then applying bright red lipstick, she gave her reflection an infectious grin. She'd be okay, as the Americans said. She was Cat, and, when necessary, she had claws.

Leon Herbert Jessup wiped the gummy motor oil from his hands. He was filthy and truly needed a shower but would miss supper if he took the time. Repairing motorcycles and teaching new dispatch riders wasn't a bad job; the pay was even decent. The main thing was that he and his mother had been allowed to stay at Bletchley Park. Lee checked the spares on the cycle that had just been turned in: One valve complete with spring, washer, and cotter; one sparking plug; one piston ring; a tire repair outfit; a spare tube and spare belt; spare link and chain. Check. All set for its next mission, so now he was ready to eat—and ready to take another look at the cook's daughter, Reenie. Too young for him, of course, but there was no harm in looking, was there?

Bundles of people. Sheila Bradshaw and her three daughters, Davis Dailey, Catriona MacLaren, Leon Jessup . . . During the coming years, more than ten thousand people would arrive at Bletchley Park's GC&CS, Government Code & Cypher School, to involve themselves in one of the most top-secret missions the world had ever known. Some would only cross paths—but others would meet.

A letter home from
Catriona MacLaren, Wren
HMS Pembroke V
P.O. Box 22543 London

Mr. Douglas MacLaren
40 Ness Bank
Inverness, Scotland
15 September 1940

Dear Gramps,

Here I am—a full-fledged Wren, complete with cute uniform, neat hairdo, and only a hint of makeup. You would quite approve of me, all scrubbed and polished. I quite love my hat, monographed with HMS, a big help in keeping my unruly locks in place.

The girls I've met so far are a fine crew, and I'm making friends. You were right about the food—dreadful! They have such strange names for the most colorless messes: bangers and mash, toad-in-the-hole, bubble and squeak. And if you say a word of protest, you get that patronizing question, "Don't you know there's a war on?" But I suppose the English would find some of our delicacies odd, too. Except the scotch. They quite like that!

The only person I really don't care for is my bunkmate. She is exactly the way you described the English—as starched and tight as her bed sheets. In time, I may become used to her, but I doubt it. She never ever smiles and looks as if she dined on prunes and the sourest of pickles. Everything about me is wrong in her eyes, and while you might agree with those things, she has no right to scold. She doesn't love me. You do. "Messy, messy, Miss MacLaren," she scolds, in the most judgmental voice. I far prefer your "Damn it tae hell, Cat! Pick up yer bloody clothes!" I'm thinking of finding another bunkmate, but I'm not sure who to ask. Strict regulations, you know. I would need a better reason than—my bunkmate doesn't care for my housekeeping habits. At the moment, I am just an old tabby, who knows her place—not a feisty kitten with claws.

Gramps, one of the first things I had to do was sign the Official Secrets Act. It was most exciting, and I felt quite proud. What it means, though, is that I can't tell you very much—not even where I am. We have to post our letters in a special bin. I don't know what happens to them after that. You should post my letters in care of P.O. Box 22543, London. My ship is HMS Pembroke V. Don't worry, though. I am not in London, where many sections are in flames, or docked near the other cities that are being so heartlessly bombed.

I pray for you every night and morning, Gramps. I pray that you are eating proper food and taking the walks your doctor advised. I pray that you are lighting your pipe a little less often. The doctor could be correct about smoking being the reason you cough so much. Although I know I am where I should be right now, a part of me wishes I were seated next to you, sharing too many drafts, watching great puffs coming out of that old pipe, smelling that forbidden sweet tobacco.

Lovingly,
Your Pussy Cat

CHAPTER TWO

A FTER REMOVING HER SOILED APRON, Shelia Bradshaw washed her hands. Fortunately, her green cotton dress, though faded and old, was still tidy. Dinner over, dishes clean and stacked, but in a few short hours, it would all begin again. The work was exhausting, but at least she would remain with the children, although that was an exhausting task as well. Dear Gemma was pleasant and undemanding, Pippa, unrelentingly difficult, but no different from the way she was in London. But Reenie had been horrid since the day she enrolled in the special class for evacuees in Bletchley and discovered it was over-crowded and that all ages were in the same class. The teacher, understandably overwhelmed, was aiming her teaching toward the very youngest.

Perhaps Sheila could ask Mr. Dailey's advice about Reenie. He seemed to be in charge of staff—an odd position for an American, but not her place to question. Might there be some small job Reenie could do, instead of attending a school clearly not appropriate for her? But that wasn't the reason Sheila was sacrificing her precious free time to go to Mr. Dailey's office in Bletchley House; she had been summoned. Surely there hadn't been complaints about her cooking. She had received nothing but compliments from the men and women who'd eaten at the canteen, and although a struggle, she had complied with the stringent budget, managing to provide creative and diverse meals. Her appointment was for fourteen hundred hours, and it was almost that now. Sheila hurried out of Hut 2, without even grabbing her coat and hat or noticing how piercing the late September wind had become.

"Enter!" Davis Dailey commanded, sounding gruff and rude even to himself. He was tired of pretending to be, basically, an office boy and was anxious to do the work for which he had been trained. He was a cryptanalyst—not a spy or a catcher of spies. He had followed procedure as directed, signing the Official Secrets Act, and was now playing a part—appearing to wait to be fully vetted before receiving final security clearance. Sometimes he wished that his cover story were true or that he had never received the wire from Biff.

Once in London, Davis had been escorted outside of the burning city to a secret meeting in the unlikely-named town, Wormwood Scrubs. Biff was pleased to see him, but Davis soon learned he would be working with Americans, rather than with Biff and British Intelligence. Instead, his bosses were William Donovan, whom he had never heard of, and President Roosevelt. Office of Strategic Services, OSS, not MI5, would issue his orders, with the ultimate goal of forming a more advanced U.S. Intelligence Service to help prevent future wars like this. But his cover was at Bletchley Park, and his contact the brilliant mathematician, Gordon Welchman. Why, he was not yet certain. Surely he would be more useful working with Welchman and the others on that incredible gift from the Poles, the impossibly complicated Enigma Machine. He almost wished he'd stayed in Chicago. He shook his head, wondering. What have I gotten myself into?

Another knock at the door. "Enter," he said again, more graciously this time. A small, pretty woman, whose curves led his imagination astray, entered the room. Right. He checked his calendar. Sheila Bradshaw. Dilly Knox had asked him to talk with her. He hoped he wasn't responsible for the fear in those startlingly blue eyes. He rose to greet her. "Please be seated, Mrs. Bradshaw."

Sheila sat, but at the edge of her chair. Perhaps he would prove kinder than his voice. He was good looking, in an American devil-may-care way.

"Now, Mrs. Bradshaw, are you happy here at Bletchley Park? Do you like your position as," he checked his notes again and started, "cook? Are you really a cook?"

He gazed at her with such steady, intense brown eyes, she wondered if her stocking seams were straight. She was certain her nose was more crooked than usual and needed a good powder. "Yes, Mr. Dailey, and yes, I am pleased to be employed here. It's important for me to be with my children. And I hope . . ."

"Oh, don't worry, Mrs. Bradshaw. I didn't mean to alarm you. You've done nothing wrong. It's just that Mr. Dilwyn Knox has been looking over your resume and wonders if we might find other uses for your skills, although I'm sure you're a very fine cook indeed."

"Skills?" Sheila wasn't aware she had any.

Davis chuckled. There was something about Sheila Bradshaw he liked very much. He sensed that beyond her fragile appearance lay a great deal of courage, although perhaps it was waiting in reserve. No doubt Dilly Knox, who had a reputation with the ladies, was not all that interested in her "skills" but wanted another filly for his corral.

"Let's see, you were a typist, according to your resume, and you once worked for a bank, where you received sterling references. This indicates you are accustomed to being discreet. Both very good reasons why you might be of more value outside of the kitchen."

"Well, yes, at one time, I was a proficient typist."

Before she married too young and had children right away, Davis guessed. That seemed to be the case with too many accomplished women. "We desperately need typists at Bletchley Park," he said, "even more than we need good cooks. If you were proficient once, most likely you would get back your former speed in short order. Accuracy, for our purposes, is even more important than quick typing."

"Perhaps. I'm not certain . . ."

"You have a great attachment to kitchens, Mrs. Bradshaw?"

"Oh, no, Mr. Dailey, it's not that. I must keep my daughters with me, you see. Right now, our situation is ideal because we live right here on the grounds, where it is safe for my two youngest when I'm not able to supervise them. We were assigned a cottage so I can be at work very early every morning. What would happen to us if I took on a different position? Would we lose our accommodations here and be billeted in Bletchley or Fenny Stratford or even Bedford? I'm not certain I could do that. I would be forced to resign. As a cook, I am not actually a recruit."

"Ah, yes, I do see the problem. Let me check with a few people and get back to you. We'll try to work out a way for you and your daughters to stay in your cottage. Are you finding the school in Bletchley satisfactory?"

Sheila saw her opportunity. "It seems to be sufficient for the younger girls, but my Maureen, age fifteen, is discontented, and I am concerned. Reenie would be in her fifth form in London, where she was a fine student. Here, all of the children are in one room, and the teacher is having a struggle. Reenie wants to leave school and study on her own. And I thought, perhaps—I wondered if there might be some way she might serve here at Bletchley Park."

"She is very young, but it is something to be considered. I'll make some inquiries and get back to you. Thank you for stopping in."

Sheila knew she had been dismissed, but he seemed kind. It would be wonderful to leave that hot, dreary kitchen and take up something useful again—something that might lead to a regular income after the war. "Thank you, Mr. Dailey, I'm sure."

"Oh, Mrs. Bradshaw." He called her back. "Try not to worry. I will put in a very good word for you." He almost but didn't quite succeed in earning a smile.

He picked up the phone. "Mr. Knox, I think she'll work out fine, but we have a few matters to settle before she'll be able to accept the position. What? I see. Well, please keep me informed." That sly old fox, but for now, he was Davis's superior at Bletchley Park.

One would hope Dilly had more on his mind than the lovely, intriguing Mrs. Bradshaw now that the German Blitz had begun in earnest. After the successful Battle of Britain Day on September 15, all had gone downhill. Southampton, Bristol, Cardiff, Liverpool, and Manchester had taken massive strikes, causing devastating casualties. As for London—The Strand, St. Thomas's Hospital, Piccadilly, The House of Commons, Buckingham and Lambeth Palaces . . . The civilian death count was almost six thousand already, although he wondered how anyone could be certain of its accuracy. Germany, Italy, and Japan had recently signed a partners-in-evil pact, a Tripartite. What an unholy development! How much attention could anyone really give to the concerns of Mrs. Sheila Bradshaw? Dilly's Fillies would have to take second place for a while.

Lee smiled in satisfaction. After giving Reenie the eye, which she definitely returned, he had received brilliant news. She was to be one of his new pupils. Awfully young to drive a motorcycle, of course. He shrugged. Not his decision. If the bosses wanted Reenie on dispatch duty, it was up to him to make sure it happened. He would also see that they became friends, if not more.

He could use a distraction from worry. Sometimes he felt like a hired hand, but at least his disposition was better than his mother's. Mum had been bitter ever since George Leon, her uncaring stepbrother, had inherited Bletchley Park. It wasn't fair, of course. Uncle George had never lived at BP and didn't like the place. This had always been Mum's and Lee's home—he was even named after his grandfather, Sir Herbert Leon. But it had been Grandfather's will that had caused the problem. Oh, well, nothing to do about it.

Lee had considered signing up and going off to fight, but he didn't think Mum could bear it. She didn't approve of this war, and she had already been through too much. Soon he would be eighteen and might be called up, unless they thought he was more valuable right where he was. Ultimately, it would be the government's decision, no matter what he or Mum wanted.

Meanwhile, he'd look forward to working—and possibly playing—with his new student.

Entry from Maureen Bradshaw's Diary
30 September 1940

I am so excited! I am so happy! I scarcely believe my good fortune. Coming to this place might not be so terrible after all. After griping to Mum countless times, she finally agreed to ask someone about me dropping out of that primitive school, but what happened is a thousand times better! I want to record everything as it actually happened, so I won't ever forget a single moment.

This afternoon, I received a message to report to Bletchley House to see a man named Mr. Dailey. Mr. Davis Dailey, actually, which I thought ridiculous until I met him. He's American, and they do give their children odd names. I have decided, though, that it's a perfect name for a perfectly wonderful man. I love Americans!

And he is so handsome. Very tall and everything about him is a rich brown—wavy hair, sympathetic eyes. He's simply brilliant, except he's old, of course. Probably even older than Mum.

"Sit down, Miss Bradshaw," he said. I've never been called Miss Bradshaw before. I felt quite the lady. He even offered me a cup of tea, but I shook my head. I would have been certain to spill it. "I understand that you're less than pleased with your education at present." I nodded, still unable to find my voice. He gave me a lovely smile. "From what I've read in your school reports, I don't blame you. No challenge, is that correct?" I nodded again in agreement. "Perhaps, then, you'll be interested in my offer. How would you like to become a dispatch rider?"

"What!" I bolted out of the chair. It's fortunate I had refused the tea. "What did you say?"

He laughed. (He even has dimples!) "I think you heard me."

"Me? Riding a motorcycle?"

"It appears you are interested."

"Oh, yes!"

"It also appears you can talk. Well, you won't be operating a bike at first. You'll need to learn how. The Bletchley Park caretaker's son will teach you. It may take awhile, depending on how proficient you are, for it's not just a matter of learning how to drive. You also must learn to make emergency repairs, although you are rather young and won't be going far afield at first."

I thought I would just clamp on a helmet, strap on my gas mask, jump on and take off, but what Mr. Dailey said made sense. "What do I do until I'm ready?"

"Walk. We do need a messenger right here at BP—between the huts and Bletchley House. And I imagine you'll still need to escort your sisters to school each day and pick them up in the afternoon."

"I'll do my very best," I said.

He told me to return to his office the next morning to sign the Official Secrets Act (how mysterious) and that he would introduce me to my instructor. I thanked him and was about to leave when he told me to go upstairs to see a woman named Lady Katherine Sinclair, the Admiral's wife. "She is expecting you."

I did as directed, of course, but was sorely puzzled. Certainly Lady Sinclair had nothing to do with motorcycles. At the top of the stairs, an elegant, but oh, so kind elderly woman, at least as old as Gram, led me into her private library and sitting room. "Sit down, dear," she said, pouring me a cup of tea. She even put a little sugar in it.

Lady Sinclair told me that since I no longer would attend school, she would see to my education. She lent me some books and said, "I shall expect you back when you finish reading, and we will discuss them together. For a while, that will be your school, and I will be your teacher." I don't mind at all. I love to read, and I've always meant to try some of them, especially ones by Charles Dickens and Jane Austen. She also gave me a recent American novel, *Gone With the Wind*, which sounded most exciting. It will be great fun to talk about them with Lady Sinclair.

I left Bletchley House happier than I've been since before Father left. And that evening I received more good news. My mother will no longer be one of the over-worked, over-tired cooks, but a typist working in one of the huts. She should have more regular hours now and will spend more time with Gemma and Pippa, so I won't have to.

It was a grand day. I only wish I could tell my friends back home about it. Oh, well—they're probably not home either, now that the Blitz is a reality. I wonder where they are and if they are safe.

CHAPTER THREE

WORRIEDLY, SHEILA TRUDGED TOWARD TOWN, staring down at her feet. She should have known it would happen here, too. Moving away would not solve the problem that was Pippa. But for once she needed to face that problem. Chin up, she told herself, and suited the action to the words. A positive step already, she thought, seeing a Wren in the distance— a walking partner, as well as a possible reprieve from troubling thoughts. She rushed to catch up. While they had never been formally introduced, she did recall the woman's name.

"Hello, Miss Ferrar."

The woman stared at Sheila as if she'd been insulted. Her sour expression should have told Sheila she had made a mistake, but with the possible exception of Roger, Sheila was used to her friendliness being reciprocated. She tried again.

"I'm only walking as far as my daughters' school but thought the time would be more pleasant if I had someone to talk to."

"Oh, yes . . .?"

"You don't remember me, do you?" Perhaps that was the reason for the woman's odd behavior.

"You are the cook."

"I was," Sheila admitted, "but now I'm a typist. We met briefly at orientation. I'm not sure where you're stationed."

"No matter. It's not something we're supposed to discuss."

Sheila flushed. "You're right, of course."

"Ah, well, as long as you know it. Do you find the work interesting?"

"Not really, but I'm mainly improving my typing speed at the moment."

"Perhaps we can talk more about it another time."

What a peculiar person. "Well, as you just said, we're not supposed to discuss it."

"Correct. I was testing you. I must leave you now. I have an important meeting in Fenny Stratford, and I abhor tardiness."

"Don't let me keep you then. Cheers." Sheila watched as the disagreeable woman strode off, nose pointed heavenward.

At least most people at BP weren't like Edith Ferrar. Most were jolly and helpful. She had already made a few chums. She supposed Edith must be very good at what she did for her superiors to put up with her unpleasantness. There was something decidedly off about her. She was English, of course, but she almost acted as if . . . Sheila, what a ridiculous thought!

Meeting up with Edith had at least given Sheila a slight break in thinking about Pippa and the urgent note from the teacher. She was about to hear the same old things. Pippa doesn't pay attention, Pippa doesn't do her work, Gemma is a fine student, but what can we do about Pippa? Sheila knew all the questions; it was answers that eluded her. It was difficult enough in London when she could work with Pippa before and after school, although the situation was intolerable when Roger was around. He brought out the worst in the child and blamed Sheila for her lack of progress. "Such stupidity. Must take after her mother," he would say. She sighed, as she often did when she thought of Roger. At times his cruelty was more than she could bear. She shook off the thoughts. No time to think about Roger, other than to hope he would carry out his threat of divorce.

A discreet beep from an automobile sounded right next to her. She wondered how long she had been followed. Oh, it was that nice Mr. Dailey, driving a staff car, along with another passenger. He rolled down his window. "You seemed deep in thought, Mrs. Bradshaw. Didn't want to startle you. Care for a lift?"

"That would be lovely. It's chillier than I expected. Just as far as the school, though. I need to pick up my daughters."

The passenger door opened, and a young woman got out and offered Sheila her front seat. "Oh, no, the back will do just fine," Sheila said quickly.

"I insist. Mr. Dailey came to my rescue, too, so I can catch the next train to Fenny Stratford. You're Sheila Bradshaw. I've seen you around. I'm Catriona MacLaren, but most people call me Cat." She gave Sheila a sunny smile.

How refreshing after encountering Edith Ferrar. Sheila took the offered front seat while Cat climbed into the back. "I can tell by a certain something in your voice, Cat, that you're from Scotland. Whereabouts?"

"Way up north. Inverness. Have you been there?"

"No, I'm afraid not, although we did journey to Glasgow when I was a small child."

"Ah, the lowlands . . . Well, I will nae hold it against ye," Cat said, giving Sheila an impish wink.

Davis wondered when he'd have a say. He had had enough encounters with the new typist to wish they could be more than friends, but that ring on her finger didn't make it likely. You fool! She was Mrs. Bradshaw—he was Mr. Dailey. He couldn't see how he could change that and was certain he shouldn't try. "Oh, it looks as if we're about to have another passenger," he said, noticing a figure walking briskly along.

"Edith Ferrar," Sheila said. "I doubt that she will accept. She is a great walker and has no time for common folk."

"I agree. We share a room in Fenny Stratford. I'm planning to request a change, though. I'm not certain how much longer I can handle her disapproval."

"Oh, my." Sheila wasn't sure what else to say.

"Nevertheless, politeness dictates I must offer." Davis pulled to a stop and rolled down his window. "May I offer you a ride to the station, Miss Ferrar? If you're tired, it can be quite a jaunt."

"Nothing I can't handle," was her taut reply. "Excellent exercise after sitting all day."

"Well done. Carry on, then."

Edith nodded and picked up her pace.

Looking back, Sheila saw the strange woman watching them, almost with longing—a bleak expression on her troubled, lined face, as if she had made a grave mistake. What a disturbing individual. Sheila vowed to avoid her as much as possible.

Davis pulled next to the curb and watched Sheila Bradshaw depart. Clearly, she was worried, and he wished he knew her well enough to inquire why. Cat quickly reclaimed the front passenger seat. "What?" he asked, responding to her quizzical expression. "What are you so anxious to say, Miss MacLaren?"

"I don't think I should."

"Oh, go ahead."

"Nothing, Mr. Dailey. Nothing at all."

"Come on, don't be nervous. No cat and mouse games. Spit it out."

"Very well. I was just thinking you should mind your heart."

She missed nothing. His first impressions of her had been correct. "And I'm thinking you should mind your manners."

"I'm sorry," she responded pertly, "but I believe you know what I meant."

"I do and will take heed of your words, even though you are a very impertinent young woman."

Cat grinned. "That is what my grandfather tells me every single day, although his language is less polite."

Davis gave her a severe look. "You might be careful of that here. After all, loose lips . . ."

". . . sink ships," she finished. "Yes, I will be discreet."

He started the car again. "Rather than dropping you off at the railway station, would you have time for a cup of tea? There's something rather important I'd like to discuss with you. That is, if you're not in a great hurry to return to Fenny Stratford. There are later trains . . ."

"All that awaits me there, sir, is a poorly prepared meal at my boarding house, run by a woman who doesn't want me there, and a quiet evening saying nothing to my bunkmate, praying that she'll decide to take another walk in spite of the blackout. Well, you met her . . ."

"Indeed, and it would be hard to find two people less suited to each other. There's a tea shop right here in Bletchley that serves a decent cup and perhaps a cheese toastie, if you'd like to skip your unpleasant evening meal altogether."

As it happened, Cat did opt for the cheese toastie—and crisps and a biscuit and a fine cuppa. "This is the best meal I've had in England," she told Davis. "Thank you so kindly, Mr. Dailey."

"You're quite welcome, Miss MacLaren."

Being here with him was perfectly proper. In spite of his youthful appearance, he was far too old to be interested in her. Besides, she saw the way he looked at Sheila Bradshaw. Having a male American friend could be pleasant—especially one who drove an automobile, provided treats like this, and seemed as relaxed and casual as a Scotsman. But he didn't seem to be enjoying his meal. "You're not eating much," she observed.

Davis glanced at his toastie. "I'm having a difficult time adjusting to all the starchy meals. I would give a great deal for a salad right now, or even just an apple."

"Now, Mr. Dailey, don't you know . . ."

". . . there's a war on?" Davis grinned. "Hush, you cheeky child. Now for the real reason we're here. No, you haven't done anything wrong—as far as I know. It's about your saying you might be looking for different billeting, or perhaps just a different bunkmate."

"Yes, could you help make that happen?"

Davis shook his head. "No, and I plan to dissuade you from pursuing that plan. Instead, I would like you to continue to room with Miss Ferrar— to try to know her better."

"Oh . . . Why?"

"In the car, after we left Miss Ferrar, you whispered something— something you didn't intend for me to hear. Would you repeat it, please?"

"I don't remember," Cat said.

Davis looked around before continuing. The teashop was almost empty, and the few people there seemed engaged in their own concerns. It seemed safe to talk. "You do remember, Miss MacLaren. You said, 'Heil,' and Mrs. Bradshaw said she had been thinking the same thing. What I want to know is—why did you say it?"

Cat flushed, embarrassed. "I'm sorry. I really shouldn't have. It was nasty and very wrong of me."

"Possibly, but what could have caused you to say such a thing? Please give me your impressions of Edith Ferrar. It could be important."

Cat gave a great sigh, organizing her thoughts before speaking. "Well, it has to do with my grandfather being so prejudiced against the English. He didn't want me to come and gave me a long list of what he called English characteristics, everything from their superior attitudes to how they hold their teacups. He's a wonderful old dear, but I knew what he was saying couldn't be true—at least not of everyone. And then I met stiffer-than-stiff Edith, and she matched every item on Gramps's list. I can almost check them off."

"And the problem?"

"The problem is she doesn't seem real. It's almost as if she had been taught how to be an Englishwoman. Oh, I'm talking nonsense."

"I think you're making a great deal of sense. Go on."

"She is so English, rigid and robotic—such a practiced English woman, she could be . . . well . . . German. Oh, I'm sorry. That was a hateful thing to say. I didn't really mean it."

Davis shook his head, wondering how much he should disclose. "You did mean it, and it needed to be said."

He shouldn't tell her much. Not yet, anyway. On the surface, Miss Ferrar's records were commendable—proper schools, perfect scores, never any problems, seemingly—all very difficult to prove. Actual references unattainable—people not in the country—schools no longer in existence. Explanations giving reasons for everything, but nothing that could be checked.

Cat slowly sipped her tea, wondering when Mr. Dailey would get to the point. Clearly, he wanted something, but what that was remained to be seen.

Davis felt like a fool asking this young woman, an amateur, for help. But in a sense, weren't most of them? Rank amateurs attempting the impossible? Big mistake, thinking that way. He shook his head, considering the reason for BP's existence. What did his old muse, Goethe, say? *I love those who yearn for the impossible.* They needed to more than yearn for it. The impossible was what must be achieved!

Finally, Cat put down her cup. Patience was not her strong suit. "Mr. Dailey, why do you want me to stay with Edith Ferrar?"

"At present I can't reveal a lot, Miss MacLaren. Truly, I might just be following a hunch, but we need to make certain Miss Ferrar is exactly who she claims to be."

"So you want me to . . ."

"Keep watch on her as much as possible. Find out where she goes and who she sees. Pay attention if she talks in her sleep. Be on the lookout for letters or notes she may receive or intercept. Be a little nosy and poke through her possessions when you're able."

"You want me to spy on a spy."

"Well, perhaps on someone who could be a spy." He stood. "Your tea must be cold. Let me freshen it."

Cat's heart thumped frantically while she waited for him to return. She had come to Bletchley Park because she wanted to leave Inverness. She wanted to do her bit and maybe have a wee adventure. Studying cryptology and improving her typing were challenging enough. This seemed far more serious than anything she had ever intended. It did not sound fun. It sounded dangerous and at the same time, tedious. She was a Wren, though, and not in a position to consider refusing. Without saying it, Mr. Dailey had made that clear. She accepted the fresh cup of tea. "I don't see Miss Ferrar often, but I'll do what I can," she said. "How do I let you know what I learn?"

Letter from Davis Dailey to Barbara Castle.
6 October 1940

Dear Barbara,

I received your undated note and package today. I have no way of knowing how long ago you sent it. You might be surprised to learn I wasn't especially shocked. I was building up the courage to write something similar, so you actually spared me the concern I would have had about your reaction. I would not, however, have requested you return the ring.

You are correct that we have grown apart and that it could be years before we meet again. I am pleased that you're seeing Brian, who has always cared for you, and I wish you every happiness. I will remember the good times we had.

Truly,
Davis

CHAPTER FOUR

DEAFENING EXPLOSIONS, SHATTERING GLASS, LOUD disturbed shouts. Pippa awoke, trembling. "Gemma, Gemma, wake up! Something's happening."

"Whah . . ." Very little disturbed Gemma's sleep.

"I don't know. I think we're being bombed! Wake up now!"

"All right . . ." But another explosion that felt as if it were next to them prodded Gemma to action as she jumped out of bed shaking. "What should we do?"

As if to answer her question, Reenie dashed into her sisters' room. "Come girls, quickly. Into the cellar. Now!" Reenie grabbed a few blankets and shoved the two girls out of the room into the hall, where their mother joined them.

A piercing whizzing sound, seemingly even closer, sent them all scurrying down the stairs. Wrapping themselves in the blankets, they huddled together for what seemed like hours. Finally, Pippa and Gemma fell back asleep.

Reenie, snuggled against Sheila, no longer felt quite so grown up. "Mum, how will we know when we can go back upstairs?"

Sheila shook her head. "I don't know. Perhaps once it remains quiet for a long interval, I'll go check. Maybe there'll be a siren. I don't think anyone anticipated this happening here."

"They should have."

Sheila didn't disagree. Had they been discovered? What would happen if the Germans knew the purpose behind Bletchley Park? Now that she knew it, she realized the answer to her question was too dreadful to consider. In truth, she had never been so frightened, even during Roger's worst nights, but she couldn't let on. She put her arm around her oldest daughter, and they sat in silence until Reenie fell asleep, too.

"Mrs. Bradshaw? Sheila? Are you down there?" The cellar door opened.

"Mr. Dailey? Is it over? Is it safe to come up?"

Davis joined them. "All clear. Not too much damage. Hut 4 was hit and an old greenhouse no one uses. We got lucky."

"But do you think . . ."

"That BP was the intended target? No, we think it was a mistake. They probably were aiming for the Bletchley Railway Station and missed."

Well, that made sense, Sheila thought. Trains and stations were at great risk, and Bletchley's was so close to BP. "Was anyone in Hut 4? Anyone hurt?"

"No, thank God, and the damage was minimal. Now wake up the girls, and let's get out of here."

Sheila stood and offered Davis her hand. "Thank you, Mr. Dailey."

"You're welcome, Mrs. Bradshaw."

Cat had finally drifted off into a troubled sleep when a piercing light flashing through the window caused her to bolt straight up. What the . . .? Somebody ignoring the blackout? Seconds later—an ear-splitting roar. "We're being bombed? Edith, wake up! It's a bomb!"

Silence from the other cot. How could anyone sleep through such a racket? God, what was happening? How close was it? Shaking Edith roughly, she tried again. "Edith! Wake up! Now!"

"Bloody hell! What yar want? Blimey! Can't a body ever rest?"

Edith sounding like a Cockney? Cat would think about it later. She thrust the woman's robe at her and grabbed her own.

Understanding finally, Edith shook off her drowsiness. "Thanks, sorry I was so nervy," she muttered, before following Cat down to the improvised shelter in the basement to wait for the all-clear.

There would be no sleep for Cat that night, alone with her frightening thoughts. Not knowing was maddening? Surely there should have been an alert. Fenny Stratford was such an unlikely target, someone must have been caught off guard. What could be happening at Bletchley Park? She tried to engage Edith in conversation, but the odd woman, who for a few moments had seemed almost human, turned her back and pretended to sleep.

Fortunately, the light disturbed Lee before he could hear a weak siren far away. Then an explosion! Almost on top of him! Bugger! An attack! "Mum!"

Lee raced into his mother's room, where he found her crouched on the floor next to her bed, head down, whimpering. "Mum, for Christ sake! Get up! Let's get out of here!"

No response. Shaking, Judith continued her pitiful cries. "Fire," she wailed. "We'll die in the fire, too."

Lee hoisted her over his shoulder and made his way to the cellar. He knew better than to reason with panic. Mum had always been afraid of fire. She never took part in burning the Guy on Guy Fawkes' Day. Even when he was a little boy, an innocent match to light birthday candles caused her distress.

"You'll be safe, Mum. I promise," he soothed. "We'll be in a safe place soon."

Later in the cellar, once he had placed Judith on a mattress and covered her with a blanket, he thought about her fear of fire. Was that what made her so against the war? Fear, rather than being just another wacky conchy?

Nazi bastards! Way too close for comfort, in spite of what Davis had inferred to Sheila. No sense in frightening women and children even more. A long night ahead, Davis thought, awaiting orders from Admiral Sinclair, Major Denniston and, possibly, even Prime Minister Churchill.

True, the strike was doubtless a mistake, meant for the railway station, but it was a mistake that could have been disastrous. Brick kilns in and around BP stored large quantities of ammunition. Had any of them been hit, it would have meant curtains for all of them, including many far away, who were dependent on their findings at Bletchley Park. And it was only luck that Hut 4 was spared greater damage. That hut had been in use for processing naval intelligence. But what in the world had happened to the siren warnings? Too late and too feeble to do any good. Heads would roll over that, Davis thought. Thank God local fire watchers had been able to deal with the small fires created by the incendiary bombs.

Wires came in through the night and into the early morning, barking orders to whoever might be implementing them. Not Davis. Anti-aircraft guns were to be placed between Shenley Road and the railway, and all buildings of BP were to be strengthened.

Davis had already put in an exhausting, troubling day. That morning he had journeyed outside of London to Bentley Priory, top-secret headquarters for the Battle of Britain. There, he met with Eugene Bifford and others, who, while not upbeat, seemed determined to put on a good front. Indeed, that was the British way, especially for true Londoners. The city would survive, they insisted. It always had. After all, hadn't it come back from the Great Fire? Chin up—act unafraid. We can take it! Mistake to give comfort to the enemy. That was the advice given to citizens.

We can take it. For how long? Davis wondered if he could take it if he had lost all of his belongings and if home were only a corner, deep down underneath the Elephant and Castle tube station.

Entry from Maureen Bradshaw's Diary
12 October 1940

Tonight I got into trouble. At least I saw something I wasn't supposed to. I was told to deliver an urgent message to Hut 8. Because it was late, I walked over, but no one was about. I had no choice but to go inside. "Hello!" I called. No one answered. So I walked into a room where some men were gathered around a dinky little machine, which they covered frantically the moment they saw me. I recognized two of them, Mr. Knox and Mr. Turing, whom people call the Professor.

Mr. Knox turned red with anger. "You have no right to be here! Get out now!" I was shocked, partly because of his reputation for being a great joker, but mainly because I was scared to death! This was not one of his jokes.

Fortunately, the Professor came to my rescue. "Dilly, there's no need to frighten her. What do you want, child?"

Child? I would talk to Mum about allowing me to wear more makeup, in spite of the thirty percent tax. I'd remind her of the poster hanging in the canteen. *Make-up is cherished, a last desperately defended luxury.* After all, I would only be doing my duty by wearing it. Not that anyone could look stylish driving a motorcycle, although I couldn't wait for that to happen.

I didn't answer; I just thrust the papers at him and dashed out of the building, tickety-boo. As I left, Dilly screamed out, "Damn it, Alan! We lost it again! That foolish girl distracted us!" Everyone in the room groaned.

Honestly, such a fuss over a machine, not even as fancy as the typewriters at my London school. Wouldn't you think they'd worry more about all the bombs?

CHAPTER FIVE

LEE JESSUP FELT SWEPT UP by Reenie's excitement. Driving a motorcycle was a big responsibility, but she was behaving like a small child with a new trike, practically jumping for joy—not at all like someone just turned sixteen. "You need to settle down before I can possibly let you go," he said, smiling. Lately, this girl had improved his mood immensely, making more bearable the dark cloud his mother had become. Now if he could only convince himself to think of her as a small child.

"I'm ready, Lee, I promise. It's just I've worked so hard for this—with your help, of course."

"Just take it carefully. Now do your inventory. Go through your check list one more time, to make sure."

Reenie took her list and followed orders. "Starting with my gas mask. Yes, everything is complete. But don't I need a gun?" She had noticed that some dispatch riders carried one.

Lee grinned. "Hardly. You're going to terrify the civilians as it is."

Reenie decided not to dignify that remark. It was enough that she'd soon be off. She was tired of delivering messages from hut to hut—on foot. Exciting, of course, and she had overheard things that made her feel quite important—and scared, that one time. But now that she and Bletchley Park knew each other as much as possible, she was ready for action—ready to become better acquainted with the motorcycle and the surrounding towns. A real mission! "Tell me, Lee! Where am I going?"

"Only Fenny Stratford, for starters. But you'll find it far enough as a first outing. Here is the pouch. The address is inside this sealed envelope. I am not allowed to open it."

"You could easily do what I'm doing, Lee. Wouldn't you rather be a dispatch rider? I'm sure it's much more thrilling."

He shrugged. "Not especially. I enjoy having my own motorcycle and going wherever I like. And I don't mind teaching cute young things like you to ride or making the repairs when you mess things up." According to the government, his job was plenty responsible, and for him it meant he could keep an eye on Mum, who was becoming stranger every day.

"So you think I'm cute?" She attempted a flirtatious grin.

"Well, young, anyway."

Lee cleared his throat before resuming his role as serious teacher. "Attach the packet to the strap across your chest, the way you've been taught, and wear your armband—turquoise, the color code of the day. Be sure to show it to security on the way out and when you come back in. You best be off now. Good luck, and report in when you return."

With enough crisp October wind to make the ride exhilarating, Reenie whizzed down the road, autumn leaves just a blur of red, yellow, and burnished gold on either side. Briefly, she considered what it would be like in driving rain and snow but soon dismissed those thoughts. Plenty of time to deal with that when it happened. She tried to ignore the damage along the route—deep pits, dangerous unexploded bombsites. The town of Bletchley in the other direction had been hit badly, too, even Elmers School, the former Wren training center, was demolished. For the most part, she reflected, BP was a safe and splendid place to live.

This could change soon, all because of Pippa. The impossible child had been thrown out of school; the teacher couldn't manage her. Not that Mum could either, but if she didn't quit her job, who would watch Pippa, and how could they stay at BP? Mum had been transferred to Hut 8, now working alongside some very important people, including the Professor, Alan Turing. Although Mum would not go into detail, she more than implied that her job was important, too. Briefly, she had tried to talk Reenie into quitting her position in order to take care of Pippa.

Reenie decided not to argue about how valuable she was as a dispatch rider. She took a different stance. "That won't work, Mum. If I quit, they'll insist I return to school. They know the one in Bletchley isn't good enough, and they'll make me go all the way to Bedford. I'll have to find lodgings. How would that help anything?"

She had thought she'd won until Mum replied, "Very well, I'll ask my mother to come live with us."

Strict, rigid Gram, who surely wouldn't approve of anything Reenie did. She would especially not approve of her riding a motorcycle or of her growing friendship with Lee. "Why, he's almost two years older than the child," she would say—"practically a man." She couldn't prevent either motorcycle or Lee, but she could make Reenie's life unpleasant.

"Bloody Pippa," she muttered, glad for the roar of the motorcycle keeping anyone from overhearing—not that there was another soul on Watling Street. But she had to admit that poor Gram, stuck all day with Pippa, was not someone to envy. Poor Pippa, too. Without school, Pippa would learn even less than usual. Oh, forget your worries, she thought, suddenly bursting into song. *We're Going to Hang Out Our Washing on the Sigfried Line.* Such a fun, peppy song with lots of verses to help make the miles fly by.

All this wind and unaccustomed exercise—suddenly she was parched. A tea break in Fenny Stratford before making the delivery was in order. She now had the address in her pocket and had determined her goal was on the other end of the town. As long as she kept the pouch fastened securely to her body, there would be no problem.

The teashop was cozy and old-fashioned, incongruous with Reenie's outfit and means of transport. But she gave the waitress a sweet smile. "A cuppa and a jam tart, please." At nine pence, she couldn't do this often. She crammed an almost empty wallet back into her pocket. Everything was becoming so expensive.

"May I join you?" A woman Reenie had seen around, one even sterner than Gram, gave her what looked like a fake smile. Reenie hadn't even noticed her entering the shop.

"I—I don't think I know you," Reenie stammered. She really didn't desire company.

The woman took the chair opposite. "But I know you," she said playfully. "You are the youngest dispatch rider at Bletchley Park. I work there, too, but my billet is here in Fenny Stratford. My name is Edith Ferrar."

"How do you do?" Reenie wished she'd go away.

"I'm sure you must be exhausted after your long ride," Edith said, "and I see you still haven't delivered your pouch."

Why did she mention the pouch? How did she even know about it? "I'm just taking a short break," Reenie said.

"I'd be glad to make the delivery. It could be our little secret, and perhaps I could purchase another cuppa and a biscuit for you."

Bribery? Was the woman crazy? Reenie should report Miss Ferrar, but then she would have to admit her detour from the mission. "Thank you, but I'll just follow the rules."

Edith's face changed from forced pleasant to mean. "You've already broken a rule and may be certain I'll report you for putting pleasure before duty."

Somehow, I don't think you will, Miss Ferrar, Reenie thought, as Edith stormed out of the shop.

"More tea, miss? Yours has grown cold."

"Thank you, no," Reenie said. In truth, her treat had been spoiled. She was about to leave when another person entered. This person she recognized—Catriona MacLaren.

"I won't keep you long," Cat said, indicating that Reenie should sit back down. "I noticed that you were talking with Edith Ferrar. A friendly conversation?"

Reenie squirmed. "No," she admitted.

"Please tell me what it was about."

"I . . . I don't know if I should say anything," Reenie said in a soft voice.

"It could be important. You seem afraid. Of Miss Ferrar?"

"Not exactly." Reenie paused to find the right words. It was hard to confess. "I . . . well, I made a mistake. Instead of completing my mission first, I stopped here. Miss Ferrar threatened to report me—when I wouldn't do what she wanted."

"She very well could—she's certainly the type—but what did she want?"

"To deliver my pouch for me."

My goodness, Cat thought. How blatant! What was going on? "I wouldn't worry about her reporting you. She would be in far more trouble than you. But I'd appreciate it if you not tell anyone else about Edith Ferrar's behavior. Come to me if anything more happens. I will pass on the information to someone qualified to deal with it."

"I will. I promise."

"Off you go then. Better complete that mission before it starts to rain. And perhaps not make the same mistake again."

Cat watched Reenie through the window as she started up her motorcycle. Then she recorded the event carefully in her notebook. The notebook was filling up quickly. Too quickly. It was all quite curious.

From the writings of Leon Herbert Jessup
A Poem

The War Poets
by Leon Herbert Jessup

The War Poets speak of
wasted youth
rotting flesh
towns ground into dust.

They write of standing tall
falling with courage
words beating news
of mourning
of glory
creating songs of pride for England.

The War Poets speak
but never of those left behind
the namby-pamby ones
staying only
and because of
Mum.

CHAPTER SIX

FOR THE FIRST TIME, SHEILA almost wished they were back in London, not just because her mother was now living in the cottage, making Sheila feel as if she were a child again. It wasn't Mum's fault, of course; she was just being a mother. Sheila might not want her there, but she couldn't both care for the children and work—especially now that she had her new assignment. Her assignment . . . She was overwhelmed by the gravity of what she had learned.

The Enigma Machine. After encountering this bewildering gift from Poland, Sheila knew she would never again be the same. She had entered a world most people didn't know existed—one centered on an innocent-looking contraption, resembling a small typewriter with many keys and lights, housed in a wooden box. She had learned of the harm it was doing, as well as the harm it would still do if experts failed to decipher its many meanings. How could something so ordinary in appearance have so many billions of possible combinations, with the goal of destroying her country and its allies? And who would ever guess that her German language classes in secondary school, even though she had reached A-levels, plus her rusty typing skills would make her a player in decoding the tiny monster? Of course she wouldn't be using the actual Enigma Machine, but one of its many replicas. It was every bit as confusing, she thought.

Not that Sheila was alone, of course. She'd be working with other women on an eight-hour rotating shift. Mum was willing to be flexible, thank goodness. Sometimes Sheila thought she should have remained in the kitchen, but once she had accepted the assignment and had learned about Enigma, there was no turning back. Mr. Dailey had made that clear. England was her country, and she had an obligation to do her bit as she was told. It was also clear that she had received the recommendation because of Mr. Dailey. "I trust you," he said, "and I believe you will be careful and diligent."

Davis Dailey. The rumor floating around was that he had recently broken his engagement to an American woman. Could be idle gossip, of course, nothing to do with Sheila, but she could tell he was attracted to her. "And what about you?" she whispered. "What do you think of him?" At the moment, she was grateful for his kindness, if not for the assignment. Beyond that, she refused to think. She was still married and had a great many responsibilities. So that was that.

Mr. Dailey had started calling her Sheila and suggested she call him Davis or Dave, but she wouldn't. That would step up their relationship to another level. He seemed to be involved in a number of activities, interviewing candidates in his office at Bletchley House, as well as working in Hut 6. She was not to know what he did there, and he wouldn't know what she did in Hut 8. Everything, he explained, was on a need-to-know basis. Well, it was sobering enough knowing what *she* was going to do, and it was best that they not work in the same location. That would prevent anything too personal from developing. Sometimes, though, she wondered from his comments if he knew more than she about Hut 8's Enigma Machine.

Cat was beginning to find this amateur spy business impossible. How could she trail Edith, relying only on her feet or public transportation, and continue taking classes at BP to improve her typing skills? She hoped to find something conclusive soon, so she would be allowed to move on to a different task. Faithfully, she made her reports to Davis Dailey, who seemed appreciative, telling her to stay on the case. Cat was starting to question whether or not Edith knew she was being followed. At times, it seemed as if

Edith were playing games—the mouse to her cat—as if she were pretending to be a spy, a spy who wanted to be caught.

Davis read over her report. "This is most interesting, Miss MacLaren." She wished he would call her Cat but didn't feel bold enough to ask. "So you think she wants you to follow her. My, she is leading you on a merry chase." He chuckled, and then stopped when he noticed her bristling. "I do think you are making progress. Just keep at it."

"Is there something else I might do as well, Mr. Dailey? While she's at work, for instance?" She was not permitted to enter Edith's hut and was tired of taking incessant walks around the lake waiting for the woman to reappear, although sometimes she was joined by the dispatch trainer, who was pleasant enough but never had much to say.

"Do? Well, I don't know. Let me think about it. I don't think I can free you up to take more classes. You might miss something important. Finding too much time on your hands?"

She nodded but didn't try to explain. She had never been solitary, enjoying the company of people—many people. They didn't have to be mates, just someone to talk to, perhaps to have a dram with or a cup of tea. Or go to parties. There were parties here—which Edith never attended.

Dailey smiled at her but said, "Carry on, then," which seemed to be his signal that their meeting was over.

Cat stood. "Edith will be going for lunch now."

As soon as she left, Davis read over Cat's notes again before adding them to Edith Ferrar's growing file. "So you slipped into Cockney, did you? You are not what you seem, Miss Ferrar, but who or what are you?" He glanced at his watch. Oops! It was late. Time for his meeting with Gordon Welchman.

At the canteen, Cat noticed Edith sitting at a table as far away as possible from everyone else. She seemed to be writing in a journal. Oh, why not? Cat grabbed her tray of food. After all, we do share a room, and I did rouse her during the bombing. "May I join you, Miss Ferrar?"

Quickly, Edith stashed her journal into her bag and pulled out a book, covered so Cat couldn't detect the title. Her answer to Cat's question was an ungracious grunt.

Cat surveyed her unappetizing one-color meal. "My goodness, the food here is getting worse every day." No response. She couldn't stay there—she just couldn't. She looked around the room for other possibilities. The young dispatch rider was sitting alone at another table, looking as lonely as Cat felt. "Well, you're obviously busy," she said. "I'll find another place to sit." Edith didn't bother to respond, so Cat picked up her tray and moved.

"May I join you, Miss Bradshaw? You look as if you could use some company. I know I could." Cat was rewarded by the most genuine smile she'd received since arriving at BP.

"Oh, please, and do call me Reenie. Everyone does."

"And I'm Cat, although few people here call me that."

"I thought I saw you sitting with that woman."

"Well, I was, but it didn't go as planned. And that woman, Edith Ferrar, is my bunkmate."

"Oh, no! You poor thing. And I thought living with my sisters was bad. You must be terribly lonely."

"Yes, I am," Cat admitted, "but you must be, too, riding around the countryside alone."

"Sometimes, although I do like my job, and my dispatch instructor is ever so nice."

Cat detected all the signs of a crush and wondered if she looked the same when she mentioned Davis Dailey. Fortunately, there hadn't been many occasions to mention him. At least she was old enough to realize it was only a crush; she was certain to get over it soon. "Both of us have solitary jobs that we're not allowed to talk about."

"Yes, but that's true of most people here. I can't complain. I'm also studying literature with Lady Sinclair, and she's simply lovely."

"Speaking of lovely, so is your hair. You must have cut it since I saw you last."

"Yes. I don't really like it, but it's much easier to handle now. Lee calls it the cap under the helmet. He says it makes my eyes look huge."

Lee must be the name of the motorcycle instructor. Odd, Cat had found him rather close-mouthed during their encounters.

Soon, Cat and Reenie were sharing stories of back home—especially humorous ones that made them laugh. Before she was halfway through her meal, Cat saw Edith rise and clear her tray. Out the window, she saw her leaving in a direction opposite Hut 4.

"Oh, dear. I'm afraid I have to leave quickly, Reenie. I lost track of the time."

"But your food . . ."

". . . is horrible. The last cook we had was much better."

Reenie smiled. "She certainly was."

Davis drove the staff car to his billet in Bedford, wondering how in the world he would break it to her. Commander Denniston had sent word. Sheila would not be allowed to remain at Number Two Cottage Stable Yards. It was needed for people who were instrumental in running the place—cleaning, cooking, taking care of the grounds, pigeons, and equipment. Judith Jessup and her son Lee would stay. Mrs. Jessup actually owned her cottage, purchasing it with an inheritance from her mother, and was essentially serving now as groundskeeper for the property. Shocking that, considering her heritage. Lee, of course, was doing vital work, repairing motorcycles and training new dispatch riders. Davis feared he hadn't done Sheila any favors when he requested her transfer, although she was becoming proficient on the Typex machine. Even the Professor and Dilly were pleased with her work, assigning her to top-secret Hut 8. Sheila's mind was sharp, and at the rate she was going, she might end up interpreting codes.

As you would be, Davis, if the U.S. had entered the war or if you hadn't let yourself be caught up in an assignment way over your head. The German Luftwaffe was now focusing its attention on bombing coastal towns and airfields—at all times of day and night. Davis belonged in a hut, intercepting, deciphering, analyzing, distributing . . . But instead . . . Well, he supposed it was understandable. It would seem odd for an American to be working along with Hugh Foss, Alan Turing, and Dilly Knox. At least Welchman kept him up to speed. "Your time will come," Gordon kept assuring him.

He sighed. Back to Sheila. He should relate the news to her that very day, but perhaps he'd stall a little longer—try to come up with some pleasing options. The least he could do was help her find a suitable billet in Bletchley, close to Gemma's school. Farther than that would create an almost impossible hardship on her and the girls. Look, old man, you don't seem to mind making life difficult for other people. How many times had he heard, or even said himself, "Inconveniences are not a deterrent." The uncomfortable truth was that he was losing his objectivity. Although he would have ended his engagement to Barbara anyway, he was beginning to care for Mrs. Roger Bradshaw. He hoped Dilly Knox, who claimed all attractive women, hadn't noticed—or anyone else, especially Sheila.

Entry from Maureen Bradshaw's Diary
19 October 1940

Terribly disturbing news today. We are to lose our cottage and must find quarters in Bletchley or Fenny Stratford, or even as far away as Bedford. It has something to do with Mum not starting work before the sun rises because she's no longer a cook. We'll make do, I suppose, as long as Gemma can go to school. I doubt if there's billeting left in Bletchley. Each day, more and more people are arriving, all involved in their small bit of secrecy.

Gram living with us has turned out to be a fine thing. She manages to control Pippa, who keeps Gram so busy she never has time to boss me around. Actually, Gram seems to approve of me lately. I never really had a chance to know her before. We may turn out to be good friends.

When I think about moving, I must admit, but only here in this diary, that my biggest disappointment will be to no longer live next door to Lee. We'll still see each other when he checks over my motorcycle, but it won't be the same. I suppose my assignments will be different, too. Most likely, I'll be driving to various listening posts and bringing pouches to BP, rather than being stationed there. I simply will be a messenger and won't feel like such a part of Bletchley Park.

Lee will forget about me, since he's older, even though all the girls in fifth say we mature faster than boys. Right now, he fancies me, too—I can tell. It's not one-sided. And I am good for him. He seems sad most of the time, but whenever I come along, he brightens right up. I don't know yet what's bothering him, but it may have to do with his mother. Every now and then, she comes by the stables when I'm there, and she's always angry and unpleasant.

She's the only person I know who is against this war, but I don't think she's a conscientious objector, a conchy. It's more than that. Lee told me she's still bitter about not inheriting Bletchley Park. Her stepbrother, who never lived here and didn't even like it, was the principal heir. This seems wrong to me, but at least she and Lee are permitted to stay.

shouldn't even be thinking about our problems or about Lee. I just
_arned that my old schoolmate, Paula, and her entire family were killed in
the Blitz. I used to be jealous because her mum refused to send her away
from London. I was so immature back then.

Gram is calling. Must stop.

CHAPTER SEVEN

"REENIE, LUV—YOU HAVE A caller."

"Coming."

Reluctantly, Reenie put aside her diary, although truthfully, she didn't have much more to write. Writing or even thinking about Paula was too troubling. She managed to open the door just before Gram did. Reenie preferred that no one enter her room. For the first time since she could remember, she had privacy. Most likely, that would change in their next billet.

"Who is it, Gram?" she whispered.

"A fine lady indeed," Gram whispered back. "Dressed ever so grand. A bit above our station."

Reenie smiled. "Lady Sinclair. She's my teacher."

"Well, she's waiting for you in the lounge. Have you been applying yourself to your studies?"

"I have, Gram. There's nothing for you to worry about."

"Shall I put on the kettle?"

"That would be nice, thank you." Reenie would prefer that Gram be somewhere else, just in case she *had* done something wrong.

Lady Sinclair gave a look of elegance to the plain rather shabby room. "Lady Sinclair, welcome," Reenie said.

"Reenie, forgive me for intruding. An important matter just came to my attention, and I thought we might discuss it. Do sit next to me."

"You could never intrude, Lady Sinclair. I owe you so much."

"And I you, my dear. You have no idea how much teaching has brought the spring back to my step."

But would she continue studying with Lady Sinclair if they had to move? "My grandmother is fixing refreshments. She's thrilled at the chance to play hostess, so please accept the tea. It's rather nasty, but not as dreadful as the slices of the national loaf she'll serve with it, although there might be a bit of raspberry jam."

Lady Katherine chuckled. "I'm becoming accustomed to that dreadful loaf. Perhaps when the war is over, I'll find it preferable to good bakery buns and scones. I shall accept your grandmother's hospitality with pleasure."

"Thank you." Reenie sighed in relief.

"Now let's talk before we're interrupted. I'll need to discuss the situation with your mother as well, once she's on break. I had an unexpected caller today—Mr. Davis Dailey, the American gentleman, who first suggested you continue your studies with me."

"He's been very kind to us."

"Mr. Dailey is concerned that you may have to leave this cozy cottage because of your mother's new position. Because he recommended her, he feels responsible for your dilemma. He also told me that one of your younger sisters is no longer enrolled in the school in Bletchley."

"Pippa. Her teacher wasn't able to handle her or to really teach her anything. She gets along well with Gram, though."

"Mr. Dailey suggested that I might give it a try—teaching her, too, I mean."

"But . . . but I don't see how that would be possible if we move. We might not even find a billet in Bletchley."

"That's where I enter the picture. I have a certain amount of pull with my husband, as well as a few others. Mr. Dailey thinks I might be able to find a way to keep you in the cottage—if I said I wanted to teach Pippa as well as you and, perhaps, even young Gemma."

"That would be wonderful, but do you think it's possible?"

"Admiral Sinclair does like to please me. First, we must have your mother's approval."

Before Reenie could say anything further, Gram interrupted. But it was just as well. Reenie was tongue-tied by this unexpected generosity. It would be quite wonderful if they remained in the cottage, but she was puzzled. Why were they being singled out this way? There was nothing special about the Bradshaw family. Surely there were important people, vital to the running of BP, who should live at the cottage instead. Perhaps Mum would understand.

Gram was both flustered and pleased when Lady Sinclair insisted she join them. "I haven't had a proper tea in ages," Lady Sinclair insisted, "and do, please, call me Katherine." Gram did a double take at the suggestion. Someone in that class wanting to be addressed by her Christian name? She had never heard of such a thing!

"Well, I wouldn't mind a cuppa, although I wouldn't call it a proper tea—certainly not like in the old days."

Soon the two women were comparing their lives, finding much in common, including a passion for knitting and the theatre. After promising to show Janet, as Lady Katherine immediately began calling her, some interesting patterns and telling her they should think about forming a knitting club, Lady Katherine Sinclair said goodbye.

"She's just like us," Janet proclaimed, "and a *real* lady, not just one with a title."

Reenie was relieved Gram needed to fetch Pippa at the children's playground. Now she would not be tempted to tell her about Lady Sinclair's strange offer. Reenie needed to talk with Mum first.

In Hut 8, Sheila was far too busy to worry about family problems. Somehow, they all dissolved once she entered the cold, dank room, where she spent a minimum of eight hours a day. She had mastered using the Typex, a larger replica of the famous Enigma Machine, and was often asked to train new recruits, who were always disappointed when they discovered they would spend their shifts typing jumbled, meaningless letters. Sheila was starting to find the work fascinating, though, and had had some successes that pleased her superiors. And she'd made a few friends—women of all ages, whom she rarely encountered outside of the hut.

That day, she was training a new girl, Christine, who couldn't be much older than Sheila's friend, Catriona. She sat Christine at a large table, holding what looked like an over-sized typing machine. "This is your station," Sheila told the startled girl. "I'll explain how it works; you'll soon catch on." Next to the Typex was a tray of messages. Sheila removed a message and placed it on the tray above the keyboard. Then she showed Christine how to select the proper drums and to plug up the board. "You just start typing whatever you see on the message."

Christine stared. "But it doesn't make sense!"

Sheila smiled. Every girl she trained had repeated the same words. "No, it doesn't—except sometimes. After awhile, you'll identify patterns. Note that all the letters are in groups of five. Type them exactly as you see them. Yes, it is boring most of the time, but it can become fairly exciting. You're here, not only because you can type, but also because you have some knowledge of the German language. If you see a word you recognize as German, raise your hand immediately, and someone will come to check."

Christine looked disappointed as many had. But never Sheila. She had grasped immediately that her work was crucially important, and she certainly preferred it to laboring in the kitchen canteen. If a recruit seemed especially upset or started to complain too much about the ensuing boredom, it was certain to be noticed and reported. It would not do to have a display of dissatisfaction infecting the rest of the women.

Sheila patted Christine's shoulder and gave her an encouraging smile. "You get started now, and I'll return often to see how you're progressing." She pointed to another table not far away. "That's where I'll be, doing the same work as you."

"You're doing the same thing? I thought you were a supervisor—my boss."

Sheila shook her head. "No, I'm a beginner, like you. I've just been here a little longer. We're all learning, and we all become supervisors to new girls and help each other as much as possible."

Sheila took her place, grabbed the next message, which she inserted into the Typex, and began a relentless search for a buried key to open doors that might end the nightmare sooner. That was the hope that kept them going.

A letter from Catriona MacLaren
25 October 1940

Dear Gramps,

I'm thinking of you, beginning to prepare for winter. Where I'm stationed— somewhere in England—it's still beautiful, crispy late fall, but in Inverness, there must be more chilly days than warm now, and soon the gales will be strong enough to blow you into the loch and out to sea, just as it did the Orkney chicken farmers' flocks. You'll be sitting in your old chair, with your father's Clan MacLaren rug wrapped around you, puffing your pipe, watching the rising sparks in the fireplace. Do put out at least one fire before you fall asleep.

Right now, even with the winds, your life seems more sensible than the one I've entered. I almost wish I were there. But if I were, no doubt I would be complaining— never appreciating what I had. I needed to leave to know that, Gramps. I'm starting to grow up—starting to realize I could have made better choices. I'm also beginning to find out how I might apply myself once this terrible war ends. More important, I'm learning what kind of person I want to be, as I meet people I admire and others who have shown me, unexpectedly, what the enemy may look like.

I'm frightfully busy, doing work I wish I could share with you. I am hopeful, though, that my present assignment will be over soon.

Don't worry about me, Gramps. In my next letter, I'll be your foolish Cat again, sometimes with sheathed claws, sometimes not. But always loving you.

Your Catriona

CHAPTER EIGHT

ATELY, CAT HAD BECOME AWARE of a change in Edith's tactics. Her billet mate seemed chatty—sometimes friendly, almost humble—and she had stopped all of her futile complaints about Cat. Perhaps she and Mr. Dailey were wrong about Edith, Cat hoped, or that the strange woman's games were finally over. She had seen a different side of her the night BP was mistakenly bombed. That person seemed real.

Because of Edith's improved attitude, Cat put more of an effort into being tidy. She made her bed, and then surprised herself by sweeping underneath both beds. The broom offered a reward as it pushed out a paper that must be Edith's. "What's this?" she scolded. "So Edith, ye mak the boorach, too? It seems I'm not the only messy one." Cat was about to throw the paper onto Edith's desk, when she remembered Mr. Dailey's suggestion and decided to read it instead. An address that seemed familiar, close by in Fenny Stratford, and a poorly written draft, with many cross outs and substitutions. A crude attempt at a ransom note—this went beyond silly games. "If you want to see your little darling again, you will follow my orders." That was all.

"Looks as if you'll be late for your meeting with Mr. Dreamboat, old girl," Cat told herself, putting the paper into her brown leather bag. She would make her apologies to Dailey, but she needed to check out this address, and fast.

No wonder it seemed familiar, she thought, as soon as she stepped into town. It was the newsagent's, right next to the teashop she often frequented. The "For Let" sign she had noticed previously in the newsagent's front window had disappeared. Nothing strange or suspicious about that, but she supposed she should check it out—using the considerable gifts of gab and charm that had served her almost too well in the past. The newsagent was an elderly man named Angus Campbell, who seemed lonely and in need of a little chatting up.

"Aye, I did have a wee flat," he said. Oh, joy, not only was he alone and lonely, but he was Scottish. "But I let it tae a lass just the other day —a Wren like yersel', but not sae bonny or friendly."

"I believe I ken who that was," Cat said and described Edith. Mr. Campbell confirmed the identity. "Ye might be surprised I'm asking," she said. "but the woman is billeted with me, and I'm nae too pleased. I need tae know if she plans to leave me stranded."

"I ken what ye mean. Ye'll be doin' fine without her, lassie, so dinnae fash yersel'."

Cat was able to learn more about the flat, how large it was, and when Edith planned to take possession. She took note that it had a separate entrance; it was not necessary to go through the shop to reach the small apartment. Then she engaged the man in a lively chat about Inverness—he was a Highlander, too—and they both admitted to a wee bit of hamesickness. She bought a newspaper and used some of her precious ration points to buy a small bag of boiled sweeties. Promising Mr. Campbell she'd return often, she left the shop and hopped on the bus for BP.

Co-commander of Bletchley Park, Alistair Denniston, gave Davis Dailey the news. "Frankly, I'm shocked, Dailey. With your background, I thought you'd be working along with Knox, Foss, and Welchman. Your credentials are certainly as impressive, but it seems higher-ups have pulled rank. So, that's your assignment. What do you think?"

"Truthfully, Commander, I'm disappointed." Dailey thought he did a good job of seeming surprised, although he'd known almost from the beginning what would happen.

"I suspected you might be. Pity you don't have any choice."

"I realize that, but I thought I had been brought here because of my cryptanalysis background and because I can read German. Surely not because of any knack for espionage. I thought I was vetting volunteers until my own screening was complete."

Denniston shook his head. "That's what I thought, too, but it seems you were too clever by half. The names you flagged as being problematic were right on target, and your interview notes have been outstanding. Many people have remarked on your ease in talking with people. Yankee blab, no doubt, but still . . . Foss and Dilly, for all their charm, don't have what you have— sociability. Of course, the Professor will never come down to earth long enough to have a normal conversation with anyone."

"Alan Turing must continue exactly what he's doing," Davis said. "We need him to keep on thinking and making his figures." Neither men stated what was on both of their minds. Until the Americans entered the war, Davis was in an untenable position.

Denniston excused himself, promising to keep searching for an opportunity for Davis to join the codebreakers.

Good luck with that, Davis thought. Admiral Sinclair, the head of MI6, not to mention Wild Bill Donovan and President Roosevelt were responsible for where he was now. He wondered if he'd ever be able to reveal his role in all this. Well, in that regard, he was no different from the lowliest typist at GP. They were all sworn to complete secrecy, possibly until long after the war ended. Even Denniston wasn't aware of Davis's secret meetings with both Alan Turing and Gordon Welchman, and not even those men knew about Davis's trips to Wormwood Scrubs—or fighter command headquarters, Bentley Priory. Fortunately, there was good news there, for a change. The RAF had proven to be superior to the German Luftwaffe. All Ultra intelligence derived from Enigma decryption and other sources agreed that the Battle of Britain would soon end. Hopefully, whatever came next would not be as grim. Back to work. Davis opened his messages for the day.

"Gemma. Gemma Bradshaw. Over here, child!"

Gemma recognized the woman. She worked at Bletchley Park and certainly looked respectable enough. Gemma knew not to talk to strangers, especially those who didn't look respectable. She approached the woman just outside the school gate. "Hello. Were you calling me?"

"I'm Miss Ferrar, Gemma. Your mother asked me to fetch you because Reenie is running late. She'll meet you at my place as soon as her dispatch duty ends. We must hurry to catch the bus."

Gemma knew better, of course. All she needed to do was follow the orders she'd obeyed her whole life—to never go anywhere with a stranger. But Reenie was late, and Gemma was tired of waiting. It might be different if the other girls on the playground were friendly. But after all, Miss Ferrar *was* in uniform and said the right things, so Gemma followed the new set of orders and hurried.

From the writings of Leon Herbert Jessup
An Essay
30 October 1940

Autumn in Bletchley Park, truly the most wondrous time of year in my favorite spot on earth. I walk around the lake, chatting with the gaggle of wild geese, throwing them a few illicit breadcrumbs. Even they can tell the national loaf is nasty; they honk their displeasure. "Don't you know there's a war on?" I scold them. "You'll fare no better here, and probably nowhere else in England, either. If you think you can migrate all the way to America, you're welcome to try." They seem to understand and accept my offering.

For these infrequent moments in time, I ignore the ugly huts, containing great secrets I may never know, and think back on my idyllic childhood when we lived in Bletchley House, not at Number One Cottage Stable Yards. The stables then were filled with purebred stallions, and I was the envy of all my classmates as I rode the esteemed, beribboned Black Thunderbolt to school. I don't remember my grandfather very well. Perhaps a wisp of memory—being seated on his lap, bounced on his knee, surrounded by the ever-present clouds from his thick cigars. Were they real memories, or something Mum or Grandmama Fanny related? I do remember my grandmother and miss her still, although she died over three years ago. She often read my little bits of verse. "Someday, Lee, you'll be a writer," she said. Perhaps, Grandmama. After I'm called up, after I survive, after the war.

Meanwhile, I breathe in the crisp air, commune with wild geese, and appreciate that I remain here—at home.

CHAPTER NINE

"MUM, THIS IS SPLENDID! I can't thank you enough!" Sheila whirled around, showing off the black taffeta skirt, once worn and tired, destined for the dustbin, now covered with sparkly silver beads and buttons.

Her mother beamed with pride. "I got the idea from one of the *Make Do And Mend* pamphlets. It's chockfull of helpful hints."

"And this gorgeous silk blouse! Wherever did you find it?"

"An old one of mine, considered a little old-fashioned now, but I thought it would add a dressy look to the skirt."

Sheila planted a rare kiss on her mother's cheek. "It's fabulous. You're fabulous."

Janet blushed. "One more thing—for these cool evenings." She opened her bottom dresser drawer and pulled out a black, heavily beaded woolen shawl.

"Mum! That was Grandmother's. Are you certain?"

Janet nodded. "She would have wanted you to have it. I've been selfish holding on to it for so long. Now, you are certain to be the belle of All Hallows' Eve."

Sheila laughed. "Well, it's just a little get-together, but there will be music and dancing. Oh, you are a luv! I am looking forward to it."

Mum, Gram, or Janet, as she was known to her many friends, gave an inward sigh. Sheila's plans had put an end to hers, but she had been brought up to believe children came first. Because of that heel of a husband and difficult children of her own, Sheila had had a challenging year and clearly needed someone to care enough to make sacrifices for her.

Janet had become involved with a group of entertainers at BP. They were having a meeting that night to select the next play, and Janet wondered if there might be a part for her. As a girl in secondary school, she had participated in theatricals and thought it might be amusing to try again. There could be some older character roles. No matter. Perhaps the turnout would be poor because of the dance, and the meeting would be rescheduled.

Looking at Sheila, Janet decided the sacrifice was worth it. Sheila certainly glowed. Could a man have put the roses on her cheeks? The kind American, for instance, who had shown such interest in her? Unlikely. Sheila was seldom interested in kind men. Of course, Janet shouldn't even be hoping for such a thing. Her daughter was married—hopelessly stuck with Roger, definitely an unkind man.

"Where are the girls?" Sheila asked suddenly. "I'd like to show off a bit."

"Pippa is reading with Lady Sinclair," Janet said, "and Gemma and Reenie haven't returned from Bletchley."

Sheila glanced at her wristwatch and frowned. "So late? It's seventeen hundred hours." Sheila no longer had to make the mental leap from regular to Navy time. Since being at BP, it would not have occurred to her to say five o'clock.

"They do seem to be running late," Janet said.

At that moment, they heard the downstairs door bang shut, followed by rushed footsteps coming their way. "Mum! Gram! I couldn't find Gemma! She wasn't there!"

Just as Cat entered the gates and pulled out her identification pass, she bumped into Sheila Bradshaw and daughter Reenie about to leave the premises. One glance at their faces told her they were not embarking on a routine trip into town. "Trouble?" she asked.

"It's Gemma," Reenie said. "I went to fetch her at school. I was delayed, but she knows to wait for me. She wasn't there. She'd simply vanished. I asked a few of the children still waiting on the playground, and one girl said she saw Gemma talking with a strange woman. 'Very proper,' was how she described her. The girl didn't know if they'd left together."

"She must still be there," Sheila insisted, "and becoming quite worried. We must hurry."

"It's probably nothing but a harmless misunderstanding," Cat said. "The kind of thing that happens between children and parents all the time. Still . . ." The schoolgirl's description, very proper, along with the damning note under Edith's bed, sounded an alarm. She had a troubling hunch, and she'd learned to pay attention to those hunches. "We need to see Mr. Dailey immediately," she said.

Reluctantly, obeying because of the authority in her voice, Sheila and Reenie followed Cat, who didn't turn back to see if they were behind. "Wait here," she ordered, when they arrived at Bletchley House. "I'll be right back."

Davis read the latest updates from his source in London—concerns about Italy's invasion of Greece, casualty figures in Manchester—and then the message just for him. He whistled. There it was—proof that although she was probably not a spy, Edith Ferrar was at the very least a dangerous nut-job. All of her records had been skillfully fabricated. She must have had money to make that happen, he reflected, as he reached over to answer the intercom that might have been buzzing for some time.

"Miss MacLaren? Send her right in." No doubt his assistant had a good reason for her delayed appearance.

Cat was amazed Mr. Dailey responded so quickly to her update. Her hunch was so ridiculous that she expected an argument. Maybe it was because she mentioned Sheila, Cat thought, with a pang of jealousy. He rang immediately for his car and as soon as the driver parked next to the stately griffins, he took the driver's place and indicated to Sheila she should sit in the passenger seat. Cat shook off her resentment and climbed into the back with Reenie.

"Wait!" They all watched as Davis's secretary dashed to the car. He read the note she handed him, nodded, and then started the motor. "We have no time to waste," he said.

Sheila was becoming increasingly impatient. What were they doing? Unless it had something to do with Gemma, couldn't it wait? Of course she appreciated the ride, but if Cat hadn't stopped her, she might have been there and on her way back with Gemma by now. Poor Reenie looked terrified, but there was no need. Reenie just hadn't looked hard enough. Sheila had trained her children well. Gemma would not have gone off with a stranger.

Then, to Sheila's dismay, Davis headed in the wrong direction. "Mr. Dailey, what are you doing? Turn back! Gemma must be frantic by now!" But Davis kept on driving, ignoring her.

Cat took pity. "Sheila, please be patient. I have good reason to believe"— actually, Cat didn't have a good reason; just a strong suspicion—"that Edith Ferrar took Gemma. I think I know where they went, and it's in Fenny Stratford, not Bletchley."

Sheila felt her face grow hot as an unaccustomed rage swept over her. "That is absolutely ridiculous. Turn back now! Gemma doesn't even know Edith Ferrar. Besides, she never would have gone with anyone so unpleasant."

Davis reached over and patted Sheila's hand, which she withdrew quickly. "We must go ahead, Sheila . . . Mrs. Bradshaw . . . whether or not you think we're doing the right thing. We have only Gemma's interests at heart." In addition to getting a certain sick woman far away from Bletchley Park, he thought. The note was proof that Ferrar had tried to contact a known Nazi spy. Fortunately, a British agent was able to intercept the message. The foolish woman wasn't a spy herself, more like a wannabe-spy. All of her documents were falsified. The real records showed a sick and dangerous pattern of always seeking attention. The sooner she was out of commission, the better, whether or not Cat's hunch about Gemma was correct.

Following Cat's directions, Davis parked around the corner from the newsagent's store. "Maybe you should stay here and let me go in," Cat said.

"This is absurd!" Sheila was almost shouting. "I demand an explanation right now!"

"Very well," Cat said. "No, I don't have proof that Gemma is in the upstairs loft of the newsagent's, but I do know Edith has secretly rented the place, and she dropped a very suspicious note in our room that I found quite accidentally. I have a strong feeling she was the proper stranger who took your daughter."

"I don't like her either," Reenie said. And I don't trust her, she thought. "But why would she kidnap Gemma?"

"Kidnap!" Sheila explained.

"That's what it's called." Davis was losing patience. "You've established a relationship with the newsagent, Miss MacLaren. Go talk to him, and come for us when it seems right."

Cat jumped out of the car and kept on going. She did not want to discuss the matter further with Sheila, although she couldn't blame the distraught mother. Mr. Campbell was pleased to see her and had news as well. She returned quickly to the car.

"Come on," she said. "The newsagent will unlock the door for us. He was thinking about going up anyway. He says there's been some odd banging on the pipes."

Soon, Gemma was safe in her mother's arms. "Mummy, the bad lady tricked me. She locked me in." Suddenly, Gemma fully realized what had happened to her and began to cry. Then Sheila started crying, and so did Reenie. Cat and Davis gave each other bemused but relieved looks.

"May I use your telephone?" Davis asked the newsagent. "It's just local."

Mr. Campbell looked at Cat for confirmation.

"Aye, Miss Ferrar's awa i the heid," Cat said. "Mentally unstable," she translated for the others, while Mr. Campbell nodded and Davis left to call Bletchley Park Security.

Cat wondered if she'd die of stress, waiting in her now-single billet for word from Davis Dailey. Finally a message arrived, asking her to join him at The Eight Bells in Bletchley that evening, saying he would drive her back to Fenny

Stratford afterward. What might she do while waiting? A shower, perhaps, if there was any hot water, or even a nap, if she settled down a bit.

Or go through and pack up Edith's possessions. A brilliant idea! All thoughts of shower and nap abandoned, Cat's first inclination was to fling everything on to the floor, just for spite. Oh, grow up, she told herself. Instead, try to be useful. Look for evidence.

She was surprised by the prospective "date" with Dailey. Surely he was not required to give her any information. Her short-lived career as a fledgling spy had come to an end. Soon, she would be assigned a hut, where she would type for eight hours and, with luck, eventually decipher codes. That had been the purpose of that silly crossword puzzle, hadn't it? To show her aptitude? Funny, after all the excitement today, even code breaking sounded rather tame. But what did Dailey want? She toyed with the idea—for about three seconds—that he might want to see her. No, he still had stars (or smoke) in his eyes for a certain married mother of three.

First, Cat opened Edith's heavy, but empty, standard Revelation suitcase, intending to pack the clothes from the dresser. The items couldn't be more refined and uniform, everything folded or rolled just so: stockings, knickers, vests . . . She unfolded and unrolled to be sure nothing was hidden. Finally, under a shockingly flimsy dressing gown—"My, Edith, how daring of you; how very improper"—Cat discovered a notebook. Should she? Oh, why not? Dailey had told her to snoop; it was just contrary to her upbringing. Cat stretched out on her bed, opened the notebook, and out pounced the sick woman's thoughts.

> *From the Casebook of Edith Ferrar*
> *30 September 1940*
>
> *Feeling nattered. Unsatisfactory day, filing unimportant papers. Waste of valuable time.*
>
> *Security clearance taking too long. Why? Records in perfect order. Sheer incompetence.*
>
> *Patience. Persevere. Mistakes made. Do better. Fortitude.*
>
> *Note forward tarts accepting automobile rides from men. They will end up with more than a ride and be open to suggestions. The men vulnerable, too. The most powerful lessons are often learned the hard way.*
>
> *Be friendlier with Dumkopfs, even cooks. Sources of information.*

No doubt she was one of the *Dumkopfs*, Cat thought, but she imagined Edith must have been referring to Sheila, who had been a cook at one time. She skimmed over to see what Edith might have said about the way she dropped character during the bombing at BP on 4 October. Nothing. Possibly too embarrassing? This next one was most amusing.

> *7 October 1940*
> *They're all fools, especially Sherlock MacLaren. Does she think I'm not aware of her feeble attempts to follow me? But at last they're noticing. They see that I am important. Which side will approach me first? Three possibilities. I don't care which.*

"Sherlock MacLaren? Och! That's guid!" But what did Edith mean by the rest of the entry. What sides? And then Cat was not amused. What followed next was serious and frightening.

> *15 October 1940*
> *The child's name is Gemma, daughter of that dizzy blonde, who should have remained a cook, and the sister of the nowty, hoyden dispatch rider. I've found the perfect location, private, no one will suspect. Biscuits, a puzzle, and an old Beano comic to keep her occupied. Not long until I receive the important position so deserved.*

Chilling, but not a lot of information. Clearly, Edith was not a spy but wanted very much to be one, if she didn't receive what she considered an important post at BP. And Cat had been correct for some time. Edith was trying to be such a proper Brit she would actually seem unbelievable. A bizarre plan, even for these strange times.

Cat turned to the back pages. There she found lists of what Edith thought she should do and how she should behave. She certainly wasn't German. There were columns of German translations of common English words, as well as a pronunciation key. *Learn to think in German*, she'd written. Also were Edith's drafts of possible ransom letters. Basically, a later draft said Gemma would be returned if Edith were given an assignment in Hut 8. *I'm willing to start with something small, as long as I can rise to the top quickly. You'll find me invaluable.* She signed her own name, not even pretending someone else was the author. No, Edith was not a spy, but she was definitely crazy—and dangerous. There was enough craziness in the world right now; Bletchley Park could afford only the sanest of the sane. Curiously, the drafts were badly written—spelling, grammar, punctuation— by someone poorly educated. Perhaps Dailey would give her an explanation after all, seeing as how she was providing valuable information.

Cat found drafts of other letters as well—attempts at blackmail. These were preceded by a list of letters or initials.

> *R.B.—possible German spy*
> *S.T.—German contact?*
> *J.—Soviet sympathizer. Might have important contacts.*

There were several pages of these cryptic notations.

Edith's efforts at writing a form blackmail letter were similar. Whoever received one should realize Edith knew all about the person's activities and would report this treason unless a meeting were arranged to discuss matters advantageous to both. She gave dates and possible meeting places and instructions on how to respond. A hollow tree in the woods? Cat shook her head. Edith must have fed herself on a diet of cheap spy novels before coming to BP. Possibly no notes had been sent, but Dailey would want to determine if such a tree existed. The initials might be more mad ravings but must also be investigated.

Almost time for the train to Bletchley. Cat put the notebook into a satchel and opened the small closet. She'd pack all of Edith's clothing and leave the suitcase for someone to pick up. On the top shelf she made one last discovery. A Beretta pistol and ammunition! Cat whistled. "Why, Edith Ferrar, ye are as deep and dirty as the River Clyde."

Trembling, not touching the ugly object, Cat wrapped one of Edith's vests around the gun before adding it to the satchel. She didn't believe it was loaded but was uncertain how to find out. She must be very careful, she thought, as she headed for the Fenny Stratford Railway Station. Most likely, she would arrive at the pub first, but the train had its own schedule—it did not follow Mr. Dailey's.

After receiving the once-over from the locals, it took some pluck for Cat to remain in The Eight Bells. She was the only woman there. Avoiding all the interested eyes upon her, she retreated to the doorway and stood waiting. Why had her boss picked such a place? The town of Bletchley was populated mainly by employees of the railway or brickworks, and the Eight

"Sounds like you'll be very busy."

"Yes, but I'll have help. You, Miss MacLaren."

"Me?"

"Yes. I hope you won't be too displeased, but your next assignment will be to work with me. I'm to continue my present job, investigating people's backgrounds, and I've decided you have skills we can use. Your abilities would be wasted as a typist. People talk to you, and you have excellent instincts. Without your efforts, Edith might not have been captured as soon, and who can tell what harm she would have done? What do you say, Sherlock MacLaren, or perhaps Watson? Will you be my assistant?"

Cat looked into Davis's eyes and nodded, almost shyly for her. She had been thinking that a typing position would be very dull indeed, and she had also been feeling low about no longer reporting to Mr. Dailey. Like it or not, the crush was back.

Davis stood and grasped Cat's hand. "Now, I don't know about you, but I'm freezing my backside off. What do you say we give The Eight Bells a chance?"

While Cat sipped her ale, Davis had a few more words. "It's about time that we progressed to first names. You may call me Davis or Dave. For the most part, Cat, you'll work in my office, where people will assume you're one of my secretaries. My real secretary will be part of the cover. Fortunately, everyone at BP is used to discretion."

"Maybe not everyone," Cat said. "Those are the people we must find."

"True. Oh, good timing. I wanted you to meet someone, and here she is. She doesn't seem any more pleased than you with this masculine mecca."

Cat looked up and saw a young woman, who bore a strong resemblance to herself—short curly reddish-brown hair, hazel eyes, a few too many freckles sprinkled on her nose.

"We could be twins," the stranger said, giving Cat a wide smile when she reached their table. "Well, maybe not, but sisters." She extended her hand. "Hello, I'm Millie Hanson, and I understand you're looking for a new bunkmate. I am, too, and I have just the place for us right here in Bletchley."

Letter from Lady Katherine Sinclair
to her husband Admiral Sir Hugh Sinclair
By private courier
3 November 1940

My Darling Hugh,

You will be pleased to hear, my dearest, that you were correct. It always pleases you to be correct. I am fitting in well at Bletchley Park, and you were wise, after all, to insist on my staying. Whether or not you will approve of all I'm doing is another matter altogether. I believe you envisioned my being a grand lady of leisure, sipping tea (weak and nasty as it is these days) and reading fine works of literature. Did you really think I could be satisfied with such a useless life? It seems to me odd that what endears men to their intended while courting is the very thing they wish to change once they're married. But that is a thought for another day. Now for the important news.

Hugh, I've become a teacher! I always wanted to teach, you know, and my library makes a fine little classroom for my few pupils. My school started with just one student, young dispatch rider, Maureen (Reenie) Bradshaw, a bright young thing who could not endure the lack of challenge afforded in the class provided in town for evacuees. Reenie is now reading Dickens, Chaucer, and Austen with me—quite wonderful for both of us. I am brushing up on my French with her, and we are tackling maths together. Then came her sister, Pippa, who seems to be afflicted with some kind of retardation and was expelled from the school. This, by the way, I consider shocking. I do not understand why adequate education can't be provided for all children, no matter what their innate abilities might be. Pippa requires much patience and understanding, but working with her is worthwhile.

I worry about what the future holds for her, but that is certainly true for all of us.

Now the youngest sister, Gemma, will come to me as well. The child was traumatized by a recent event, and her mother wishes her to stay close by. I do not know the details, which seem to be a matter of security. She was abducted by a crazy person, now thankfully incarcerated. Gemma is a delightful ten-year-old, eager to learn and to please.

The little family lives at Number Two Cottage Stable Yards. It looked as if they might lose their billet, which would have created a dreadful hardship for them in this time of many hardships. But a satisfactory solution has been found, enabling them to remain. The girls' grandmother, Janet Hill, has taken over early morning kitchen duties from the girls' mother, who now works as a typist. This will allow the family to remain in their cottage, close to the canteen. Janet most certainly will become a great friend, once I convince her to stop treating me like her "betters." If there is one thing I hope this war accomplishes—other than breaking down barriers for women—it's removing our bloody class system. Sorry, dearest, I do know how you hate to hear me use foul language.

Soon I may have another student, the young man who repairs motorcycles and teaches new dispatch riders. He and his mother have lived here their whole lives. You remember them, Hugh. His mother is Sir Herbert Leon's other child, the one who did not inherit the estate but does own Number One Cottage. Her son, Leon, is quite fine. He wants to go to university and become a writer. I've offered to assist him, and he is considering. He seems greatly troubled by something. Perhaps in time I'll learn what it is.

Our community is growing and starting to thrive. We can't be secrets and gloom all the time. Other people are starting classes and clubs. Janet is teaching Make Do and Mend groups, helping the women do just that. Both of us have joined BP's theatrical society and are sewing costumes made from whatever we can find (I believe I spotted an actor wearing the chintz curtains that used to hang in one of the cottages). Another group of ice skaters is looking forward to the first freeze on the lake. Dances in the canteen after hours are a common occurrence, and while taking on chaperone duties, I've detected a few romances. Most importantly, I'm hearing a great deal of laughter. May the war never permanently take away that!

I feel very sorry for people who are alone—for whatever reason—having to deal with this war by themselves. Better that they be in service, either officially or as volunteers, both men and women. Everyone "just mucking in and getting the job done." Here at BP, we are a team, and it makes all the difference in the world in keeping up our spirits.

You, of course, are always on my mind and in my heart. I miss you, my darling, and have faith that you are keeping safe and well. I long for your next visit, when your arms will be around me once again.

Your loving Katherine

CHAPTER TEN

L EE TRIED TO EXPLAIN. "SOME of my writing is private, Reenie. I don't want to share it."

"You don't have to show her everything." Reenie sighed. "If you want to be a writer, Lee, shouldn't you start by writing things people can read? What are you hoping? That you'll be discovered after you die?"

"I don't know what I want," Lee admitted.

"Well, you do know you want to go to university. Lady Sinclair could help make that happen. Don't forget her husband is an admiral as well as a lord. You're afraid of conscription, and maybe they can help prevent that, too."

Lee stuck out his chin. "I'm not afraid. I'm not a coward."

"Of course not. It's not the same thing. People who aren't afraid of fighting in this war are bloody fools."

"Language!" Mrs. Jessup, showing her everyday troubled face, entered the stable garage just in time to hear Reenie's proclamation. "In this case, though, I agree with you. No one should be fighting."

"That's not what I meant," Reenie muttered, but Lee's mother had swept out the door again and didn't hear. "Why is your mother so against the war?"

"Who knows? I'm through trying to figure her out. But what did *you* mean before, Reenie?"

"Lady Sinclair explained it. I think I understand. She said only fools aren't afraid. Cowards are afraid but find ways to avoid the situation. Brave people are afraid but go on in spite of their fear. You are one of the brave ones, Lee—I'm sure of it. But we need you at BP, taking care of motorcycles and training riders. If the government keeps you here, I say, bloody swell!"

Lee grinned. "Nothing like combining British foul language with American slang. But you've convinced me. I'll work with Lady Sinclair. Now let's check out that motorcycle so you can be on your way."

"Aye, aye, sir."

"Will I see you at the dance tonight?"

"Perhaps, if you'd like to see me there."

They smiled at each other. No other words were necessary.

The November wind chilled Reenie to the core as she headed her motorcycle in the direction of Station IX. Bletchley Park, of course, was Station X, which looked mysterious when read, but actually meant it was the tenth site acquired by MI6 for wartime operations.

She was running late, not just because of encouraging Lee to study with Lady Sinclair, but also from trying to answer Lee's questions about what had happened to Gemma. Now he knew as much as she, which wasn't much. Miss Ferrar was arrested, and all of Bletchley Park had heard her swearing and carrying on when she was whisked away. Gemma was shaken but fine. Sheila, though, was a bundle of nerves and could scarcely manage having her daughter out of sight. Gemma was not at all pleased by the turn of events—leaving her school friends and being subjected to so much unaccustomed adult supervision.

The dance. Would Reenie be allowed to go? She should have explained to Lee that it all depended on Mum's and Gram's plans. If Mum were going to the dance and Gram had her dramatic society meeting, Reenie most likely would be on sister duty.

But unknown to Reenie, something had happened to cure Sheila's frayed nerves. Jubilantly, she whirled around in a full pearly-gray skirt, feeling like a princess. Bless Mum for creating it. And bless her, too, for agreeing to watch Pippa and Gemma so both she and Reenie could go to the Guy Fawkes dance. Because of the blackout, there would be no fireworks or burning of the Guy again this year, but they would still have a lovely evening. She could tell that Reenie's main interest was seeing her motorcycle instructor, Lee Jessup, which was fine with Sheila. He was a nice lad. What difference did it make if he was a bit older? These were war times, and there seemed to be different rules for everything. She looked into the mirror and admired her glowing, happy face. Different rules—even for her now, and she intended to flirt outrageously and dance with anyone who asked. Or she might be terribly modern and do the asking herself, for she was young, young, young—in spite of having three daughters. Ready to live again!

The reason for this burst of pure happiness? A letter—a glorious love letter from Roger! The best love letter she had ever received from him. Sheila grabbed the note and gave it a huge kiss, her lipstick leaving a perfect bright red print. Roger had fallen in love with a nurse, and they were having a hot, steamy affair. In actual words, he said he no longer loved her and had been able to contact a lawyer in London, who was beginning divorce proceedings. "Oh, Roger," she sang. "Do stay in love. Stay in love forever!" The only thing better would be for the enemy to shoot him down. That thought stopped her. She couldn't be as cruel as that, could she? She gave a brief thought to this before deciding. Oh yes she could! To keep from accusing herself of being unfeeling, she opened the letter again. Roger wanted nothing to do with the girls, except Gemma, perhaps, someday—if his intended approved. The nerve! He was a cruel father and husband. She almost felt sorry for his poor nurse. Almost.

Roger said she would be entitled to half of their possessions, although he planned to keep the flat. With any luck, the Blitz would destroy his precious flat. But which half of the possessions would he pick? Her grandmother's china and silver, her jewelry? He might. Maybe even the family photos if he were in a vindictive mood. How might she retrieve them? She was certain Lady Katherine, who had become Mum's great friend, would allow her to store the items in Bletchley House, but Sheila wouldn't be able to transport much by train. She would ask Mr. Dailey for help. That was an excellent idea because he often had use of a large staff car. He would be thrilled to be asked—she hoped.

Sheila shook her head. Davis was becoming a problem, and she should be ashamed of herself for using him. She did like him but not in any romantic way. He was attractive enough, but too safe, too boring. She liked men who were more exciting and at least seemed as if they could be dangerous. Like Roger? Be quiet, she told that inner, annoying voice. Not like Roger, but maybe like Roger used to be. She would flirt with Davis and ask for his help but would not let him suspect that she and Roger were no longer a couple. And she would start calling him Davis to his face. She supposed she would have to forego other men and dance just with him. That would be disappointing. Perhaps he would be busy and not attend. But you can't have your cake and eat it, too, that voice scolded.

Janet laid out her knitting supplies. Tea was set to brew, and she had managed to bake some biscuits that didn't look too unappetizing. Babysitting had become more appealing now that Lady Katherine had agreed to come and share the duties and even help Janet prepare for her audition.

She heard Sheila singing upstairs. A silly pop song everyone seemed to love these days— *Yes, we have no bananas.* Such foolishness! Of course they didn't have bananas and wouldn't for a long time. And they hadn't arrived at BP in time to plant "string beans and onions, cabbages, and scallions." Didn't they know there was a war on? And what, pray tell, was a Long Island po-Tah-toe? Janet shrugged. She supposed the song wasn't any more foolish than ones she sang as a girl. She burst into a suddenly remembered one. *Laugh! I thought I should've died—Knocked 'em in the Old Kent Road.* She, her sister Grace, and friend Helen used to love to sing that.

The Old Kent Road. She guessed that song wasn't funny either. From what she'd heard, the Blitz had badly damaged that area of South London, and from all reports, East London had been obliterated. But she must proceed with the tasks that were hers. She glanced at the watch she had inherited from Grace. It was time to retrieve Pippa and Gemma from the playground.

Lee examined his wardrobe. Just one clean pair of trousers would do the trick. Mum seemed to have given up doing laundry, not that he blamed her. He was old enough to do his own chores. The problem was a lack of time or interest—until now. A welcome message from Reenie, saying her mother and grandmother had approved of his escorting her tonight, triggered this sudden interest in clothing. This dance could be exceptionally grand, taking place in the Bletchley House ballroom, where he hadn't been since he was a child and allowed, along with children of invited guests, to peek at the grandeur through the upstairs banisters. For just an instant, he permitted himself to mourn his grandmother. Reenie's Gram was swell, but no one could ever match Grandmama Fanny.

Back to the trousers. This pair wasn't too shabby; it seemed clean. All the shirts had frayed cuffs but folding them in such a way would make this white one work. The hot water allotment for the day had been used up, but if he scrubbed extra hard with lye soap, he should be able to remove most of the oil—even using cold water. Reenie was certain to look beautiful, and he meant to do her proud.

"Mum, you've used all the hot water!" Reenie shouted. "How could you?"

"Sorry, dearie, I didn't mean to. I'm sure you'll clean up just fine."

Honestly. What had gotten into Mum? Like magic, her mother had stopped fretting about Gemma and was behaving younger than Reenie—like a schoolgirl herself. Oh, well, she couldn't possibly be as happy as Reenie. Her first real date with Lee!

Even though it was cold for early November—only twenty degrees— Reenie had become hot and sweaty. She had covered many miles on her motorcycle, newly christened Oscar. So many people required messages and pouches delivered, including Mr. Dailey and, curiously enough, Catriona MacLaren. She had been trained not to question anything, though, and just carried out her duties. It didn't help that Oscar broke down three times, but thanks to Lee, she was able to make the repairs without much difficulty.

Mum peeked into Reenie's bedroom. "I'm really sorry, dear. I wasn't thinking."

"That's all right, Mum. I understand. It isn't fair, though, that you are going to look prettier than me." Sheila's delighted smile made Reenie think she had said the right thing, for once. And she couldn't begrudge Mum her happiness. After all, Reenie was on cloud nine herself.

"How do I look?" Cat carefully examined her bunkmate before applauding.

"Like a picture. Almost as good as me." Both wore refurbished outfits they had created in Janet Hill's Make Do and Mend class. Cat's dress was rose red while Millie had changed a faded lifeless skirt into a billowy blue cloud. A white pullover and dark blue velvet jumper, covered with tiny rhinestones completed the ensemble. Living in Bletchley, so close to BP, made it possible for them to socialize.

Cat had won her own private Welsh Sweepstakes when Millie had come along. In their free time—although they didn't have much—they were inseparable. And although their resemblance was startling, they had discovered no link, no relationship anywhere. Cat was pure Scot while Millie came from Cardiff, Wales. For both of them, it was as if they were roommates at university, talking late into the night, confiding in each other about everything—well, almost everything. Cat had yet to admit, aloud anyway, her feelings for Davis Dailey. Since they never would be reciprocated, better for her to remain quiet. But it was good to have a friend, especially after living with crazy Edith.

Their flat in Bletchley, while not glamorous, was a tremendous improvement over the room in Fenny Stratford. And they had their own small kitchen, where they shared expenses, took turns preparing dinner, and were good sports when one of their meals proved unsuccessful. Both declared Millie's Welsh rarebit and Cat's attempt at mock haggis truly awful.

"Do you suppose anyone will ask us to dance?" Millie asked.

"If not, we'll dance with each other." Cat determined to have a good time, with or without a certain man.

Sheila's heart dropped when Davis entered the ballroom. Oh, well, widespread flirting must wait until the next dance. Recruiting Davis's help was more important than her social life. She couldn't take a chance Roger would be granted leave and steal her possessions. Some of the things were valuable, and she knew better than to trust him. Sheila forced a warm smile. "Davis, I'm so glad you've come. I was worried you wouldn't be able to."

Davis blinked. At last, she'd called him by his first name, and she certainly seemed pleased to see him. What had changed? No matter. He was thrilled it had. He had begun to think he was wasting his time. You are, you fool, he told himself. You keep forgetting she's married. Happily? He wondered. Well, it wouldn't be the first time he'd opened himself up for heartbreak. "Care to dance?"

Reenie buried herself under the covers, more for privacy than for heat, although her bedroom was freezing. *I've got my love to keep me warm,* she sang softly, and then giggled. Well, maybe someday. But for now—her first kiss! Lee had brought her home and kissed her. It hadn't been the kind of kiss you see at the pictures; she thought it might have been his first time, too. But it was a start—a wonderful, glorious beginning!

Letter from Janet Hill to Helen Price
8 November 1940

My dear Helen,

I'm sorry I have not been able to write sooner. As you know, I am taking care of my grandchildren in order to free up daughter Sheila for war work. We are doing well, although I am unable to disclose where we are living.

The children are thriving, under the tutelage of a fine lady and a new friend of mine. Although young, Reenie is also involved in the war effort, as well as keeping up her studies. We were not surprised that the local schoolteacher wasn't able to handle our Pippa, but the troubled child is doing much better with private instruction and much patience. Darling Gemma seems to adapt to almost anything, although a difficult situation, which I am not at liberty to relate, made us decide that for now school was not the best fit for her, either.

We have heard nothing from that son-in-law of mine, and no one here seems to care, although Gemma does ask occasionally. Sheila and Roger should never have married, although I cannot find it in my heart to regret my three granddaughters. He is a domineering man, who must have his own way in everything. I try to talk to Sheila about him, but she acts as if she's been conditioned not to speak. Or perhaps she just feels it's none of Mum's business.

As for me, I haven't been this content since before Gerald died. Helen, you'll never guess what I've done. Oh, you could guess the Make Do and Mend sewing classes I've been running for the ladies, but the other activity will take you back to our school days. I've joined a local theatre group, not just sewing costumes, but also acting! Me, your friend Janet, after all these years! Auditions will be held soon for Mr. Wilde's wonderful play, *The Importance of Being Earnest.* I fancy myself as Lady Bracknell and hope the casting committee is bitten with the same fancy. Goodness knows, I'm large and loud enough.

I think of you often and pray that you and your family are in good health and spirits. Perhaps when we're together again in your lovely Chelsea parlor, playing many rounds of faro and bridge, we'll all have stories to tell. You'll serve Earl Grey tea, and I shall make my famous Dundee cake, using plenty of eggs, butter, and sugar. And this dreadful, dreadful time will be over.

We are busy preparing for the second Remembrance Day of this terrible war. I have been blessed so far in not knowing any of the poor boys who have lost their lives. I realize it's only a matter of time until I do.

All of my best to you and yours,
Janet

CHAPTER ELEVEN

T HE BLETCHLEY HOUSE CHAPEL FILLED quickly, solemnly, for the second Rembrance Day service since the war had begun. Sheila took a seat in the front row between her mother and Lady Katherine. That should discourage Davis Dailey. She could not trust herself to remain unsentimental on such a day. "Everything looks grand, ladies," she said. Both women beamed at her.

Janet and Katherine had worked tirelessly on shining the woodwork and arranging bouquets from the gourds, squash, and wild grasses that grew around the lake. Janet, seeing that Katherine knew every bit as much about cleaning as she did, finally forgot Katherine was a great lady and welcomed her as a dear friend and equal. Whether or not that would be the case after the war ended, remained to be seen.

The congregation rose for "I Vow to Thee My Country." Had it had ever been sung with such pride, filled with so much emotion? That was Cat's question, anyway. Someday she would ask Gramps what it was like for him, singing the famous hymn, written during the last year of the Great War. Perhaps he was less of a contrary Scot back in those days. Here, there were no dry eyes when they sang,

The love that never falters, the love that pays the price,
The love that makes undaunted the final sacrifice.

Cat hadn't made any sacrifices yet. In many ways, her life had improved dramatically. But she shuddered. Others were enduring far more than their share.

She pulled herself together. It was her turn to speak. She walked proudly to the pulpit and recited by memory the beloved poem written by fellow Scotsman, Lt. Col. John McCrae, words now partially engraved in stone outside Eilean Donan Castle in Dornie, a tiny community she and Gramps had visited often. For this occasion, she allowed herself just a wee touch of a brogue, realizing that many would hear and see a different side of her.

In Flanders fields the poppies blow
Between the crosses, row on row . . .

As Cat returned to her seat, she noticed Dave's look of admiration. She wished it meant more. Oh, he trusted and respected her. He even liked her. But he looked at Sheila with his heart in his eyes. Silly schoolgirl with a crush. He was way too old for her, not even from this country. She must stop all this nonsense. Besides, this was Remembrance Day; she had no business thinking about herself. She wished she had been nervy enough to sit next to him, though. He was by himself and looked somewhat lost and alone.

Reenie smiled at Cat as she passed her in the aisle. She often forgot Cat was from Scotland. Maybe someday she would visit her there. Cat was becoming a special friend. Not as special as Lee, of course, who was her greatest friend. She worried about Lee, who seemed to grow gloomier each day. If only he would confide in her. She knew he was concerned about being called up, since his eighteenth birthday was approaching. Mainly, he didn't want to leave Mrs. Jessup. No, he wasn't a "Mum's Boy"—something else was wrong. If she were Lee, she would be eager to get away from the bitter woman, who never had a pleasant word to say to anyone—especially Reenie. If their paths crossed, she glared as if to say, "What are you doing here?" or "You stay away from my son." Well, now that Reenie was sixteen, no one should object to their age difference.

Reenie tried to concentrate on the service. It had been deeply moving so far. Lee had wanted to read his essay about the Christmas Eve truce during the Great War, but he was not allowed to because it portrayed Germans as real people. Then he wanted to recite Yeats's "An Irish Airman Foresees His Death." That was turned down, too, for a similar reason Reenie didn't understand until Lee read a line: *Those that I fight I do not hate; those that I guard I do not love.*

Lee wasn't a conchy. He believed this war was necessary. His point was that there were good and bad people on both sides. Well, Reenie wasn't sure she agreed. Accepting that all British people should hate all Germans was a simpler, easier way to handle all that was happening now. She would need to think more about Lee's opinions. She wanted to please him, and besides, he was smarter and older than she.

It was hard knowing what to believe now. So many things were considered unpatriotic. Ever since September, the Blitz had decimated the entire country. No longer a "phoney war." Reenie wondered if their home in London had been bombed. Sometimes, even here, they had to seek shelter in the Bletchley House or cottage cellars because of bombs landing too close. Some of the huts now had underground facilities, and all the windows wore giant Xs of tape to prevent shattered glass. Anti-aircraft guns had been placed along the roads, mainly near the railway station and tracks. Residents knew which buildings were actually disguised pillbox bunkers. Although sturdy enough to withstand extensive shelling, some were meant to resemble run-down filling stations or shabby additions to adjacent structures. Inside might be machine guns, emergency lights, or observation areas. Would they fool the enemy? Reenie wasn't sure, but having them there did gave her comfort.

Oh, it was Gram's turn to do a reading. The chaplain's short sermon had been just fine, mainly about the risks of appeasement—and they bowed their heads to honor Neville Chamberlain, who had died a few days before—but also about the dangers of seeking vengeance. "We must not answer cruelty with more cruelty," he said. Exactly what a chaplain should say, Reenie thought, even though people weren't in the mood to listen. But the best part of the service was seeing and hearing people she knew: Cat's poem, that wonderful tenor from Wales, and now Gram. Reenie was proud of her grandmother, who had found purpose, almost a new life at Bletchley Park, and was acquiring a reputation as a skillful character actress.

Davis had been trying, by staring hard at the back of her head, to get Sheila to look in his direction. No luck, though. He hoped he was only imagining she was avoiding him. Ever since they returned from London, after making several trips, she had been aloof. He had used up his personal allotment of petrol for November, and the month wasn't even half over.

Now the automobile must be driven for business only. Sheila had been gracious and grateful up to and on the actual day, and truly, he hadn't minded helping her pack way more than he expected—or lifting heavy objects and hauling them up all those staircases to the Bletchley House attic. So many possessions you would think she never planned to return to her home near Tavistock Square. Well, the square itself had been bombed, with looters now hard at work, so no doubt she had acted wisely. But was she ignoring him, or was he being overly sensitive? Probably she was just absorbed in the service as he *should* be.

Having people from all over Britain speak or sing was a fine thing, he supposed, but he was feeling left out and uncomfortable. He had been invited but had declined to share something from his country. What could he say? Perhaps something about Armistice Day back home? It had been a federal holiday for two years now. He could quote Woodrow Wilson—"On the 11th hour of the 11th day of the 11th month." No, Wilson's words would only draw more attention to the present and what wasn't happening in America. At least a few days ago Franklin Roosevelt had been overwhelmingly elected for a third term, bringing Congress along with him. The moral effect of this was heartening to the Allies. After all, Germany, Italy, and occupied France had been predicting and hoping for Roosevelt's defeat, even though Davis didn't think Wendell Wilkie would have been a pushover. He was a good man, too, but it was the wrong time for a new administration.

He sighed. When would the U.S. wake up and join the struggle? He almost wished something would happen to force the president's hand. Almost, but not quite. Funny, he had been treated as an outsider back in Chicago, his home. And while he wasn't treated that way here, he didn't really belong. He felt alone and incredibly lonely.

The service came to an end. Davis rose to join the congregation in singing "Jerusalem," a hymn he didn't understand but one that stirred all Englishmen.

> *Nor shall my sword sleep in my hand,*
> *till we have built Jerusalem*
> *in England's green and pleasant land.*

He shrugged. Most of William Blake's poems didn't make sense to him. He knew the music had been added to the lyrics during the last war. Briefly, he wondered what enduring songs would come out of this one and watched as Sheila left the chapel, without looking back at him even once.

Essay by Lee Herbert Jessup
Assigned by Lady Katherine Sinclair, 19 December 1940

A Christmas Memory

When I was a child, encouraged by my grandmother, I thought Bletchley Park was Father Christmas's headquarters. My mother approved, though not because of any strong religious leanings on her part. Perhaps she thought the fantasy would help make up for my father's desertion when I was only three and Grandfather Leon's death when I was five. I have no memory of my father. Mum won't talk about him, and I've always thought there was some mystery about why he left. I do recall being unhappy when Grandfather died, although sometimes I don't know if I actually remember Grandfather Leon or just the stories Mum and Grandmama Fanny told about him.

At Christmas time, Bletchley House—our home—outdid itself. The front entryway was filled by a giant spruce, which stretched from the mosaic tile floor all the way to between the beams of the lofty ceiling. I was not allowed to climb the tall ladders necessary to decorate the immense tree, but I did accompany the groundskeepers to one of our forests and helped select and chop it down. And I was permitted to decorate the lower branches with the paper chains and ornaments I created myself. Each year, I consoled my mother when she was certain we'd all burn in our beds because of someone forgetting to extinguish one or more of the lit candles. In addition to a long lighter, my grandfather had designed a candlesnuffer that could reach the tall branches, even from the floor. Mum fretted, making many trips downstairs, just to be sure, before I, young as I was, finally coaxed her back to bed.

Grandmama Fanny kept Christmas lively and happy even after Grandfather was gone. We still strung popcorn and cranberries, hung ornaments passed down through the generations, and used the famous candlesnuffer. And my mother continued her yearly tradition of worrying about a renegade fire.

My most memorable Christmas occurred when I was eight years old. Uncle George, Mum's stepbrother, made one of his infrequent visits. It didn't take long for me to idolize him, especially when he asked me what I wanted for Christmas. "A train ride." I sighed with longing. Long before motorcycles, trains were my passion.

"Done," Uncle George declared grandly, not giving Mum or Grandmama a chance to protest. "You and I, young Leon, shall travel by train to London to do our Christmas shopping."

Mum started to object, but my shouts of joy stopped her. She knew I would have considered her crueler than Scrooge if she had denied me this treat. She reached for her purse. "If he is going shopping, he will need a little money."

"This will be on me," Uncle George said.

It was obvious Mum didn't care for George, and even Grandmama seemed troubled. I had thought it considerate of him to inquire so often about Grandmama's health, but Mum did not like it one bit. "For mercy sake, George, look at her! She is the picture of health. Why don't you ask about me? I would tell you that Leon and I are finally recovering from nasty cases of the croup." I coughed delicately, backing up Mum's lie without knowing why.

The big day arrived about a week before Christmas. Uncle George and I sat in first class! The black steam train traveled from Bletchley Railway Station to Old Smoke, as we used to call London. I exclaimed and commented on everything I observed out the window and asked so many questions he complained I was giving him a headache. But I could tell he didn't mean it. He was having a good time, too.

In London, he announced we would have our lunch in a department store, and then do our shopping. "Harrods?" I asked, not knowing anything about the famous store, but it was the only one I'd ever heard of.

"A bit pricey," he said. "We'll go to Selfridge's on Oxford Street. I know the owner. I will introduce you to Mr. Selfridge himself."

We had a grand luncheon of steak and kidney pie. I was too full for dessert but had a small dish of chocolate ice cream, just because I could. Mr. Selfridge came to our table. He greeted Uncle George like an old friend and even shook my hand and called me Mr. Jessup.

Then we shopped for presents. I bought a bottle of "Evening in Paris" cologne for Grandmama and a diamond bracelet for Mum. Well, I suppose the diamonds were actually rhinestones, but they sparkled enough to suit me. "Anything else you think might please them?" Uncle George asked.

"They both like books," I said. We rode the elevator, another big adventure, to the top floor. I had never seen so many; it was like the biggest library in the world. I selected a volume of poetry for Grandmama and the latest Edgar Wallace spy novel for Mum. She would say she didn't approve of novels, but I knew she would devour it in private. Then Uncle George bought me a new adventure book for boys about an air pilot named Biggles and told me I could read it even before Christmas. He took me to the giftwrap counter, where soon my gifts were finely wrapped, ready to be placed under the tree.

I chattered so much when we returned home, Mum was probably telling the truth when she pleaded migraine and escaped to her room. The next morning, after making more inquiries about Grandmama's health, Uncle George left.

The day before Christmas, we received a message that a large parcel awaited us at Bletchley Railway Station. We had no idea what it might be, but the groundskeeper harnessed one of the horses to the cart and invited me to come along.

The parcel was for me—from Uncle George. And to this day, it was the finest present I've ever received. A gigantic electric train set! So long it encircled the Christmas tree! I scarcely glanced at the jumpers, socks, and books from Mum and Grandmama—although I did notice with surprise that they preferred the drawings and childish poems I'd presented to the elegant bracelet and perfume. For the first time, I didn't help Cook make mince pies and current buns. That Christmas was about my train and nothing else.

I still have it carefully packed away in the attic of our cottage. My stalwart train continued its circular jaunt around the Bletchley House tree until Grandmama died three years ago, and I saw Uncle George again. He had been my hero for such a long time, but that came to an end when I saw him finally get his wish from that long-ago Christmas. Grandmama's health was no longer good.

Wishes today are both simpler and more complicated. They are certainly less unique, for everyone I know, approaching this Christmas 1940, has the same wish. God willing it will come true.

CHAPTER TWELVE

C AT CHECKED OFF ANOTHER SET of initials on her list—copied from
Edith Schmidt's notebook. She had been able to clear half of them so
far. Another dozen to go. It had been a laborious effort. Two were German
sympathizers, although not actual spies. Only because an opportunity hadn't
arisen, Dave told her. They had been imprisoned for safety reasons. During
peacetime, this would not be legal. "Many things we're doing would appall
us normally," Dave said. "Such is the pure evil of war."

Cat knew Dave was thinking of the annihilation of Coventry on the 14th
of November and of the wild rumors spread about this tragedy. Surely, it was
just talk. Surely it would have been prevented if at all possible. They looked
into each other's eyes but said nothing. Verbalizing their suspicions would
be too painful, if not treasonous.

The two of them, now comfortably on a first name basis, had made
many trips into the forests surrounding Bletchley Park, sometimes together,
but usually on their own. They had yet to discover a single hollow tree. Cat
thought it might just be one of Edith's flights of fantasy—it was too much
like a John Buchan novel to be real. But Dave told her they really had no
choice, even though all predictions were for one of the worst winters ever.
The end of December had been unusually damp, and even these early days
of January were dull and wet, with both rain and heavy snow. The easterly

winds were so bitterly cold and fierce Cat wondered how her friend Reenie and the other dispatch riders were able to complete their missions. Cat hadn't heard a word of complaint from Reenie, though.

Nightly bombing raids in London were becoming unbearable as entire neighborhoods were decimated. Cripplegate, the area between St. Paul's Cathedral and the Guildhall, Patermoster Row—the list seemed endless. Amazingly, St. Paul's survived the firestorm. Worst of the whole war were the last two days of December. Reports stated that 1400 incendiary fires in London's commercial center had gutted the City, and over 15,000 civilians had been killed. The death toll couldn't be accurate, Cat thought. Not that high. Perhaps the figure applied to all civilian deaths in 1940, not just the end of December. Lady Katherine hadn't even returned to her London home for Christmas. Her husband forbade it—simply too dangerous.

Meanwhile, Cat was learning more about the work at BP. Dave had required her presence at a meeting led by Admiral Sinclair and Gordon Welchman. Hugh Foss, Dilly Knox, and Alan Turing were also present. Sitting by herself, like a wee mouse in a corner, she heard for the first time about the Enigma Machine and the Bombe the Professor and Gordon Welchman had invented, as well as why cracking the codes could mean the survival of the British Empire, if not the entire world. "Even one undiscovered Nazi agent could destroy GCHQ—Station X," the Admiral said.

Then, to Cat's amazement, another mouse—a rather large one— appeared from the shadows of another corner. Prime Minister Winston Churchill crossed to the table. "I can't emphasize enough the importance of what you are doing," he began. In an odd way, those working here at BP were blessed. Relatively safe with definite tasks to complete that might make a difference. Having little time to think was a blessing, too.

As risky as it was, Cat did travel to Inverness for Christmas and Boxing Day. Lonely-sounding letters from Gramps had convinced her she was needed. Millie's parents and sister had fled Cardiff to stay with relatives in America, shortly after the relentless German bombing of Wales in September. Her Robert was posted somewhere far away, so Millie was pleased to accept Cat's invitation. The Glasgow train, leaving from Bletchley Railway Station, was so crowded and uncomfortable, both girls felt safer traveling together. Conditions on the local train taking them the rest of the way from Glasgow to Inverness were even worse. They sat, huddled together, sitting on their suitcases in a crowded smoker. Finally, coughing with eyes red and achy, they arrived in Inverness, only to find the town especially bleak, bathed in the total darkness of the whole country. Normally, Inverness would be in winter mode, but now it lacked even sparkling fairy lights to brighten the gloom. The wind forced Cat and Millie to cling to each other as they made their way to Gramps's small house on the Ness Bank.

Inside, though, Cat felt the last months roll off her back. The warmth and comfort she had known her entire life were exactly what she needed. The worn sofa, dear, tired stuffed chairs, the wood-burning fireplace with framed photos on the mantle of parents she never knew—all took the war and BP farther away than mere miles. Gramps and Millie took to each other immediately, as Cat was certain they would. There was something to be said for the Celtic connection.

Gramps, to Cat's surprise, had changed his mind about the war and was now eager, following every battle with zeal, even posting pins on a large world map, especially the coastal areas up and down Britain. No more disdain for the "auld enemy," England. The reason, Cat discovered, was all that was happening in Orkney. As she had tried to explain to him earlier, the security of the North Sea was crucial. Over a year had passed since the HMS Royal Oak had been sunk by a German U-boat at Scapa Flow. Gramps had scarcely acknowledged it back then. But one of his cronies was now in charge of the construction of permanent barriers to prevent further invasion.

The First Lord of the Admiralty, now Prime Minister Winston Churchill, had ordered the construction, and Churchill was one of Gramps's few heroes. "Italian prisoners are doing the heavy work," Gramps said. "Get them busy on something tae benefit *us*, for a change. Puir bliddy weary bastards that they be. But a fine idea by Mr. Churchill." If only Cat could tell him she had seen the great man in person.

It was good to see Gramps active and involved, talking with enthusiasm about the meetings he was attending. "Aye . . . I'm thinking of joining the Home Guard, as soon as I'm certain the wind won't blow me well awa'."

The wee holiday ended too soon and with promises to return, Cat and Millie returned to BP on 27 December. On New Year's Eve, they attended a party at Bletchley House, hosted by Lady Katherine. A quiet affair—cheap ale and crisps, leftover Christmas Crackers, with the usual foolish party hats and jokes—but the few friends who attended took comfort in being together, joining hands to sing the song beloved to all Scots, *Auld Lang Syne.* Happy New Year, 1941. What indeed would the new year bring?

Reenie and Lee attended the New Year's Eve party together. Because of the lack of time and opportunity, they had had only a few dates since their first dance. Lee made certain of the location of the mistletoe and led Reenie there before the critical time—before anyone else could claim the space. Gram stayed home with Pippa and Gemma, where they would have their own party, and she would study her lines after they went to bed. Gram had been disappointed at not being cast as Lady Bracknell but was now quite content with her small role as Miss Prism and with her increased involvement in the Bletchley Park Dramatic Society. "My part is most amusing," she said, "and won't take up all my time." Reenie had no idea where Mum was. A party, but where and with whom, she didn't know. She was hoping it might be with that nice Mr. Dailey, but Cat said no, Mr. Dailey was away at a conference.

Davis's Christmas was spent alone, wandering through bombed out streets in London before spending the night in a West End, determined-to-stay elegant hotel. That could be a way of describing much of London, he decided. Determined to stay, well, perhaps not elegant, but, at the very least, normal. In spite of daily as well as nighttime raids, traffic continued to flow, people went shopping, and ladies still fed pigeons in what was left of Trafalgar Square. At first, he thought the citizens seemed to be anaesthetized. Then he realized he was seeing a raw courage that was infectious. Just witnessing people carrying on made him stronger, ready to face whatever lay ahead.

Davis had come to town early because of meetings taking place, beginning the next morning. He had been ordered to a top-secret location in London—the Cabinet War Rooms, where life and death decisions hung in the balance. The meetings turned out to be mainly Stiff-Upper-Lip, No-Comfort-to-the-Enemy affairs, but thrilling none-the-less, as he learned more and more about the harrowing desert offensive in North Africa, where most of the land fighting now centered.

But soon, Davis grew uncomfortable fielding off so many questions about why the U.S. hadn't entered the fray. He was hardly in a position to speak for his country. "After all, *I'm* here," he wanted to say. He was just as relieved to be off on his next mission, as difficult as it might prove to be.

Davis had decided to visit Edith Schmidt (aka Ferrar) on the unlikely chance he might learn more about the curious initials in her notebook. This meant a railway journey to an isolated asylum in Northumberland, where he would be met and then escorted by an agent stationed in the area.

A turn-of-the-century horror movie was Davis's impression of the grim, desolate red brick mansion, which had once housed five hundred lost souls. "Abandon all hope, ye who enter here," he said softly.

"Pardon?"

"Dante."

Agent Bill Herriot shrugged, appearing to wait for an explanation that didn't follow.

Davis knew that the armed forces were now in charge of this building, as well as the adjoining one that served as a TB sanitarium. "Other than TB cases and wounded soldiers, who lives here now?" he asked Herriot, as they waited for a guard to unlock the high metal gates.

"Nutters like the one you're going to visit, and people possibly too dangerous to be set loose. Your woman is not the only case from Bletchley Park."

"Oh?" This was new to Davis.

"You didn't hear it from me—a bit of a gossip. One of our majors, a married gentleman, had an affair with one of your workers at BP. He was caught in the act, so to speak, and was transferred. The poor woman went off her head and acted in such a bizarre fashion, she became a security risk. She lives here now. You might hear her yelling for her lover."

"How tragic," Davis said, looking sharply at Herriot. Surely the agent didn't know anything—wasn't trying to offer him a cautionary tale. Besides, his relationship with Sheila definitely hadn't advanced to an affair. He was certain that no one, except perhaps Sheila, suspected his desire.

As they walked down the gloomy corridors, he noticed several men and women seated on chairs or on the floor. They stared straight ahead, silent and expressionless. In the distance, though, he could hear groans, screaming, and the loud voice of a woman, calling out a name—a name he recognized. Why, he had met that major but hadn't given it much thought when he was no longer there. Often, Bletchley Park seemed like the revolving door in a department store. People continually came and went. One never questioned. Outside of your own little circle, secrets were to be kept intact.

A guard unlocked another gate and escorted Davis to Edith's cell, leaving Bill behind in a unheated waiting room. "Quite the madam, this one," the guard told Davis. "You've got a quarter hour." He gave him a whistle. "Any problems, blow. I'll be right outside."

Edith Schmidt sat on her cot, writing furiously in a new notebook, which Davis would need to confiscate. She looked slightly worse for wear, but was obviously making an effort to stay tidy and clean in spite of difficult circumstances. There was something about her Davis admired, even though he didn't like or trust her. "Edith," he whispered. She looked up, and there was madness in her eyes.

"Excellent," she said. "You've come at last. I'm ready to report to work. How may I help?"

Edith had no idea what she'd done. Did she even realize she was being held against her will? It was best for Davis to play along. He pulled a copy of the list of initials from his pocket and held it out. "We're very interested in your research," he said. "Will you tell me more?"

She smiled. "Ah, yes." She patted the cot, indicating Davis should sit next to her. "Yes, that represents weeks and weeks of diligent effort. What do you wish to know?"

"Names, of course. Names to match the initials."

"That would be telling. Perhaps we'll wait until I return to Bletchley Park."

She wasn't as gullible as he had hoped. What approach might he take? He must tread cautiously, he decided, naming some people who had been cleared. "I believe you made a mistake with them."

"They were only hunches. You did not give me proper time to investigate."

Davis gave additional names. "Those people are German sympathizers, who have now been imprisoned."

"Well done, Mr. Dailey. I'm gratified to hear that."

"But the initials K.S. The only person those initials fit is Lady Katherine Sinclair. Surely you don't consider her a suspect."

Edith glared at him, her eyes cold, angry, dangerous. "And why not? All that money, all that power, all that charm? What better cover?"

Envy was what Davis read on her face. He did not believe for a minute that Lady Katherine was guilty of anything. "What about this one letter—J? Would you give me just a hint?"

"All you need is J, and that's all I'll tell you."

"What about the hollow tree? Does it really exist?" The look she gave him said he had made a mistake."

"I repeat. I have no more to say. Let me pack while you order our car brought around."

"Very well. I'll fetch the guard." Davis blew the whistle, and the guard rushed in immediately, worry on his face. "Miss Ferrar needs time to pack her bags," he said, nodding to Edith as he left the room.

"Say, what was that about?" the guard asked. "She ain't going nowhere. She don't have no bags."

"I know that, but who can tell what Miss Schmidt thinks or knows?" Davis gave the guard his card. "Please remove her notebook and have it mailed to me at this address. It's probably worthless, but we can't take a chance. I doubt that I'll be coming back."

No trains were scheduled for the rest of the day, and there were no places to stay in the nearby town of Stannington. Herriot, who seemed disappointed Davis was not going to return the gossip, drove him to a hotel in Newcastle. He'd leave from the larger railway station in the morning.

In spite of the war, Sheila's holiday had been joyous, more fun than in years, culminating in a New Year's Eve party at the Bedford Hotel—with a brand new man! But the party lasted longer than anticipated, and both she and Peter, who also worked at BP and was billeted in Bedford, had consumed far too much champagne. No more trains were running, and Peter surely couldn't take her to his billet, so there was nothing to do but book a room at the hotel. It is doubtful that Sheila would have remembered anything about their night together if Peter hadn't refreshed her memory the next morning

and on into the early afternoon. Finally, she insisted on catching the train for
Bletchley. Peter escorted her as far as the Bedford Station and in a quiet
corner gave her one more passionate kiss. Neither was aware of another train
arriving from the north, or of a man, who watched them from his window
in stunned disbelief.

"Happy New Year, Davis," he whispered to himself.

Letter from Wren Millie Hanson to Ensign Robert Evans
3 February 1941

Dearest Robert,

It has been such a long time since I received word from you, but I feel you must be safe for I would certainly know in my heart if you weren't. Possibly we're having problems with mail delivery. With all that is happening, this must be expected. I dearly hope you had some joy over the holidays. Will we be together this time next year? Surely we'll be back in Cardiff, at church singing in the choir—and planning our wedding.

I am keeping busy as a Wren, fighting, too, in my own small way. Like you, I'm unable to say where I am. It's all terribly secretive, but I am happy thinking I'm doing my bit, too.

I now have a peach of a billet mate, and it's made all the difference. Her name is Catriona (Cat for short), and we've become great friends. Because I had no place to go for the holidays, Cat came to my rescue. We traveled by train all the way to Inverness and spent a subdued Christmas and Boxing Day with her delicious grandfather, who lives on the Ness Bank. The weather was frightful, but we were able to journey to Urquhart Castle in Drumnadrochit, where most of the sightings of the Loch Ness Monster have been. Cat laughed each time I was certain I spotted the beast. But you can't help it, really. The water of the loch is dark, so full of peat, and the waves mysterious and strange. No one with an imagination would doubt the truth of the legend.

I pray with all my heart that you are safe. Whenever a siren goes off here, I wonder what it's like where you are. Whenever there's a commotion in the village about how a single leg of mutton might be divided among all who want it, I wonder what you're eating and if you have enough. You need to know that no matter how far away you are or how long we're apart—or even what condition we are in once it's over, I'll always be waiting for you, my love.

Your Millie

CHAPTER THIRTEEN

SHEILA LED A TRIPLE LIFE, at least that's the way it seemed to her. She had become almost schizoid in her ability to keep the three lives straight. From talking to the women she worked with, she knew this was not unusual at BP. In Hut 8, although physically and mentally uncomfortable, she had never felt more involved or worthwhile. Her work using the Typex machine and training recruits was the most serious undertaking she had ever encountered and indeed was a matter of life and death. Every time the enemy prevailed, she and her co-workers felt it as a personal blow. They were forced to accept the agonizing truth that they had failed at finding the daily key to crack the code in time. Sheila was certain, though, that no victory, such as the recent British forces' advancement into Italian-held East Africa, could ever seem as sweet anywhere than at Bletchley Park.

But, oh, the discomfort! So far, February of 1941 had been raw: rain, snow, bitter cold. Then a warming trend, followed by a return to the deep freeze. Everyone Sheila knew seemed to have the sniffles or worse. Conditions in the huts were miserable. Frigid— icicles hanging jaggedly, even from the inside eaves. Day after day, without any regard for fashion, Sheila wore her heavy brown sweater, a woolen cap covering her ears, and a pair of Morlands' lined boots. After long shifts, working in lighting that would be judged insufficient in a cave, she grew pale. Often, the hardest part of the job was not physical. Tasks were so dull, monotonous, and soul draining that motivating others became difficult. Sheila rarely allowed herself the luxury of self-pity. Instead, she tried to keep up her fellow workers' spirits, as well as her own. "Just think," she would say, "you could be the ones to unlock Rommel's plans in Tripoli."

That was one life. At home, her least favorite place, she was still Mum to her daughters, although, thankfully, they seemed to need her less and less. Reenie had become quite the young lady— sixteen and in love. Sheila didn't mind at all. Sixteen and in love was an enviable place to be. Gemma and even Pippa were thriving under Lady Katherine's instruction. Pippa had begun to read simple books, making progress each day, her behavior greatly improved. Gemma was a darling, as always. But there was Sheila's mother. She had avoided Janet as much as possible since New Year's Eve when she had stayed out all night. Janet stared her disapproval but said nothing except, "I hope you're being careful."

Sheila listened. She certainly didn't want more babies. "It was just that one time, Mum. It will never happen again." And so far it hadn't. She and Peter went to parties and pubs, but she always made arrangements with girlfriends billeted in whatever town the event was located, bunking the night with them if she drank too much. She made her arrangements clear to Peter ahead of time. He didn't like it but was accepting it—for now. Sheila knew he was just waiting for her to lose her resolve.

Well, she wouldn't. In her third life, she was a girl again, having a wonderful time—flirting, dancing, and wearing lots of make up—more fun than she had ever had. She might not stick with just Peter. After all, other men seemed to fancy her, too. In the midst of all this, divorce papers had arrived from Roger, and the happy event would take place in a matter of days. That it was happening so quickly made her wonder when he had started the process, but she didn't really care. Sheila thought another trip back to London to examine the contents of the flat would soon be in order. Although truly unkind of her, she would resume using her feminine wiles on Davis. He had seemed rather cold to her lately. Probably her imagination. He must be terribly busy, although she knew from Gemma that he occasionally visited Lady Katherine. Well, she would go ask him as soon as her shift ended. If she waited for good weather, it might be too late.

"Enter." Davis had been engrossed in the records of a newly captured Nazi spy from Station VIII, who had worked for a short time at BP. He hadn't meant to sound so unfriendly. "Enter," he repeated, more gently, and Sheila entered the office. Cat, seated at another desk, quickly left the room.

"Mrs. Bradshaw, what can I do for you?"

Mrs. Bradshaw? Not her imagination, Sheila thought, wondering if flirting would still work. "Mrs. Bradshaw, Davis? I thought I was Sheila."

"Sorry, I have some important work that needs my attention. What might I do for you?"

Sheila felt even less sure of herself. "I—I was hoping we might motor back to London. I've remembered more things in my flat that should be brought here, and I would so appreciate your assistance again. Perhaps we could even have a bite to eat somewhere?" This was dreadful. She felt her face grow hot; most assuredly it had turned red.

He shook his head. "I'm very sorry, but I will be unable to get away for anything but business for some time. You'll need to take the train or find another friend."

The way he said "friend" . . . He knows, Sheila thought. My God, he knows! "Well, thank you for all you've done," she said.

"You're welcome. Now I have some papers that need attending to." She had been dismissed.

Well, that was harsh, Dave, he thought. He felt like a brute, even though she clearly had been using him. But he thought of his visit to Edith and the story of the major and his ladylove, who was now a lost soul in an institution leading only to death. *Do not give in too much to feelings. An overly sensitive heart is an unhappy possession on this shaky earth.* He hadn't thought of that quotation since Oxford days. Goethe always did have his number. Davis was lonely, often certain he was drifting, but . . . I will not become romantically involved with anyone until this war is over, he resolved. He even thought he meant it.

It was unfortunate Cat hadn't stayed in the office. Her day would have been better if she had. Her feelings had intensified to the point she no longer fooled herself. She didn't have a schoolgirl crush; she was in love with Dave. On rare occasions, it felt absolutely grand, but most of the time it was miserable. She consoled herself. At least we work together and are friends. At least I have that.

She finally confided in Millie, who said, "Stay pleasant, be patient, and wait. I believe his infatuation with the lovely married lady will end, and he'll see the person who has been by his side all along. Besides, from what I've heard, Sheila Bradshaw's reputation is not all it should be." While Cat didn't believe Millie entirely, she did cherish a small ray of hope.

Cat was due for tea with Lady Katherine, her friend, but also one of Edith's supposed suspects. Cat could find no evidence of Lady Katherine Sinclair being anything other than what was apparent—a privileged English woman, married to a peer and admiral, strongly against the German regime, and totally loyal to her country. Communist leanings? Unlikely, considering her background and class. However, every innuendo on Edith's list had to be checked out, but Cat had decided Edith's direct hits were simply a matter of luck. More often, Edith had just pointed an envious finger at people she didn't like. Today, Cat would close the investigation on Lady Katherine. The accusation was vindictive nonsense.

At Bletchley House, Lady Katherine was in full hostess mode, wearing a purple velvet skirt, a silk blouse, and a black, lacey jumper. The mahogany sideboard, with silver tea service and tray, laden with biscuits, crumpets, and even a small amount of jam, matched its mistress in elegance. The room was warm, comfortable, and so very England-before-the-war. A reprieve from war concerns was most welcome. On everyone's mind these days were Germany's upcoming invasion of Greece, as well as Bulgaria, allowing the Nazis to use its land as an attack base.

Lady Katherine's other guests were Lee Jessup, Janet Hill, and her granddaughters. Cat didn't mind their presence. In fact, she rather liked Sheila and her relatives. It was Dave's interest in the woman that she minded. Cat sat back, sipped her tea, hoping to enjoy the chatter.

"How are your rehearsals progressing, Janet?" Lady Katherine asked.

"Very well, I believe. I do hope you all plan to attend the performances."

"Even me?" Pippa chimed in.

"Especially you, my pet."

"I've been so busy lately, I've lost track of all the happenings," Cat said. "When is the production, Mrs. Hill?"

"Opening night is the 7th of March, running two weekends."

"I'm certain we'll all find time to come," Katherine said.

"I think what you're doing is splendid, Gram," Reenie said.

"So do I," Pippa chirped.

"Me, too," Gemma echoed.

Everyone laughed and accepted another crumpet. They relished this brief return to small talk.

"Are you having a difficult time making deliveries in this weather, Reenie?"

"I was, Cat, at first. My skin was practically raw from the cold. I was beet red and hurt so much. But Lady Katherine gave me some special cream, as well as many lectures on how to take better care of myself."

"Well, I must say it worked. You are glowing with good health."

Reenie smiled shyly at Lee, and all could guess that she gave him some of the credit for that glow.

Lee smiled back. So far, he hadn't said much. He seemed to be enjoying himself, though, in spite of being surrounded by the opposite sex.

"Are you making progress in your writing, Lee?" Janet wondered.

"You'll need to ask my teacher." He changed the subject quickly. Lee never liked talking about himself. "Pippa, would you like some war work, too? I have something you might do."

"Me? Really? But what about Gemma?"

"I have war work already," Gemma said. "Gram is teaching me to knit."

"No, this job would be for Pippa, with Reenie and me helping just a little. The weather is too nasty now to send out our carrier pigeons, but it is very important they stay healthy and well fed, so they will be able to resume their duties in the spring. Will you help feed and take care of them, Pippa? I think you could handle it."

"I would love to," Pippa breathed. "When may I start, Lee?"

"Right after our tea would be fine, as long as it's okay with your grandmother."

Janet nodded and smiled. Such a fine lad! Too bad he had such a distant mother—not that Sheila was much better these days.

Lee stood. "After I walk Pippa home, I'll meet you at the lake, Reenie." BP's sizable lake offered a wealth of spare time possibilities in all seasons. Now frozen over, some skaters attempted tricks, but most just wobbled along, trying not to fall. Lee, who had lived there all his life, was accomplished on the ice.

Reenie gave Pippa a worried look, which the girl managed to interpret correctly. "My friend Margie is coming over," she said proudly. "We will have plenty of our own things to do, Reenie."

Pippa received a relieved hug for her efforts—and rare praise. "I'm proud of you, Pippa," Reenie said.

Lee and Pippa entered the area of the stables, which housed the pigeon loft. The pigeons, property of MI6, were taking a brief respite from their duties behind enemy lines. Lee gave grand introductions to the indifferent birds. "This is Mary of Exeter."

"They all have names?"

"Absolutely," Lee told the excited girl. "Say hello to Lord Montgomery, Sir Winston, and Miss Beatrix Potter."

Pippa giggled with delight. "I wish I could name some, too."

"The next time we receive a new flock, I will make sure you're in charge of naming. But you must give them important ones. They deserve it." After showing her how to feed the birds, Lee allowed her to proceed by herself. He wouldn't tell Pippa he didn't like pigeons—dirty lot that they were—but he could understand their appeal to a child. "They are an important part of the war effort," he told her.

"I think they're cute," Pippa said. Mary Exeter fluttered, signaling her objection. "I'm sorry, Mary Exeter. You're not cute; you're beautiful. What kind of war work do they do, Lee?"

Lee picked up a message capsule and showed Pippa how it could be strapped to a pigeon's stomach. "These pigeons carry messages to agents, even into enemy territory, and then they bring messages back. Often this saves people's lives."

"What about the pigeons. Isn't it dangerous for them?"

"It is. Sometimes they come back injured, so we have to call in a vet to repair a wing." Wisely, Lee didn't tell her they didn't always return—that often they were shot down. "We're giving these pigeons a short winter break, but they'll soon begin work again."

"Do you put the messages on them? Do you know what the messages say?"

Lee laughed. "Oh, no, and neither will you or the pigeons. The messages are top secret. I do strap on the capsules and wrap the pigeons securely so dispatch riders, such as your sister, can deliver them safely to pilots who will drop them by parachute."

"Reenie transports pigeons?"

"She does indeed. Now let's go, so you'll be home when your friend calls."

Pippa insisted on saying goodbye to each one of the dozen residents of the aviary.

And then she surprised Lee with an unexpected hug. "I will be good at this job, Lee. Thank you for giving it to me."

Cat returned to the office, where she opened a file, made some notations, and handed them to Davis. "With your permission, I'm closing this investigation," she said.

"Lady Katherine Sinclair, Admiral Sinclair's wife. I agree. A waste of time and politically quite dangerous, but you had to check it out."

"I know, but every time we clear someone, I feel I've helped an innocent person—even if they don't know about it. That pleases me."

"And we've caught a few."

"Yes, we've caught a few. When must we return to our silly find-the-hollow-tree game?"

Davis sighed. "Soon, in spite of this miserable weather. I'm about to tackle the initials N.W. as well as a dozen new recruits." And fulfill a difficult assignment from Wild Bill Donovan, he added silently. "What's next on your list?"

"The letter P. That's it. I don't know whether it's a first or last name, or male or female. Is it Patience, Patrick, Petula, Peter, Prudence, Perry, Paul, Patricia, Prunella . . . Or how about Phillips, Parker, Price, Powell . . ."

Her job was tough, too. "We're both looking for needles in haystacks." Davis watched as Cat removed a small duffel bag and a heavy winter jacket from her locker. "Heading for someplace special?"

"I am. I'm about to make a fool of myself—on skates."

Davis brightened. "Ice skating! I'm rather good at that. Any idea where I could pick up a pair?"

"There should be some available to borrow at the boat house until you can get your own. You might find some for sale in Oxford."

"I'll try to join you there later—if you don't mind—at the lake, I mean."

Cat managed to hide her excitement. "The more the merrier."

Davis watched her leave. Cat had become a good friend, as well as a capable assistant. Very attractive, but so young—surely no threat to his anti-romance resolution. It might do him good to have some fun for a change.

Back to Donovan's assignment. Davis and the others were to write to President Roosevelt, urging him to do everything possible to bring U.S. forces into action. Davis was certain he was too low on the totem pole for FDR to pay him any heed, but there was no arguing with the adamant Wild Bill. Davis sighed. He was far more comfortable with numbers than words. Perhaps a greeting, a brief reminder of the one time they'd met, and a few words so he wouldn't feel guilty. Davis would tackle the rest later.

> *Mr. President, as you well know, most of Europe has fallen to an evil greater than any mankind has ever known. "Peace in Our Time" now looks like a whimsical mirage. Only brave Britain stands strong in the West, but one of the reasons it keeps courage is the conviction that its greatest friend will soon do the right thing.*

It was a start. Davis wished he could ask Cat's advice. He felt sorry for the poor president, whom he felt certain already agreed with him. Roosevelt had too much to deal with. The U.S. was rampant with saboteurs and spies, and while he, Donovan, and the rest were working to form an organization that would detect enemy plots before they reached U.S. shores, it was going to take time and would not be possible until there was peace in Europe.

He shrugged, locking the letter into his desk drawer. He was only one man, and for now this man was going to show folks a thing or two about ice-skating.

Pippa Bradshaw
Writing assignment from Lady Katherine Sinclair
Final copy, with spelling and grammar corrected, written neatly in her best handwriting
3 March 1941

My Funniest Moment at Bletchley Park
By Pippa Bradshaw

My funniest thing at Bletchley Park happened at the lake. My friend Margie and I sneaked out of our cottage when Gram and Gemma didn't notice because they were knitting again.

We were a little sad because no one invited us to go ice skating, so we wanted to find skates in the boathouse that were our size. But they were all too big! We were going to go back home, but Margie said we should spy on the skaters. So we hid behind some bushes and pretended they were Nazi spies, and we were Nazi hunters. The skaters were so funny we stopped being spy hunters and just watched. They were terrible skaters! Everyone was falling down! Reenie was the worst of all. Lee wasn't terrible. He even did a few tricks. Then Mr. Dailey came along. He's old, so no one expected much, but what a surprise. He was wonderful! He did jumps and flips. He should be in the Olympics, if they ever come back. Everyone's mouths were wide open. We all cheered for Mr. Dailey. It was my funniest moment at Bletchley Park.

Gemma Bradshaw
Assignment from Lady Katherine Sinclair
Final copy, written in her best handwriting
3 March 1941

The Funniest Thing at Bletchley Park
By Gemma Bradshaw

Once in September when it was still warm outside, Pippa and I were going home from the playground. We heard loud splashing in the lake. People were swimming. We went to see who it was. A bunch of men were jumping up and down in the lake and laughing so loud. They had no clothes on! Pippa and I started giggling. We laughed all the way home and told Gram, but Gram didn't think it was funny. Then Pippa said the men were fruits, and I laughed even harder because that was such a silly thing for her to say. How could men be apples or plums or bananas? Gram didn't laugh. She got very angry and washed Pippa's mouth out with soap. Pippa made a terrible face and spit and spit and spit. I felt sorry for her, but I still thought it was the funniest thing I ever saw at Bletchley Park.

CHAPTER FOURTEEN

REENIE WAS SORTING OUT THOUGHTS in her diary—how could she convince people to start calling her Maureen, instead of the childish nickname?—when Mum knocked at the door. Uh-oh, she looked serious. Disturbing conversation ahead. Reenie supposed she should be grateful for any communication at all. It was a rare thing lately for them even to be in the same room. But there she was, sitting on Reenie's bed, a sure sign that it wasn't going to be just a talk—but *A Talk.*

"Did I do anything wrong?"

Sheila put an arm around her and grinned. "I don't know. Did you?"

For a minute, it felt like old times—when Reenie was younger and the two had had good times together.

"No, Reenie, you haven't done anything wrong. In fact, I don't know when I've been as proud of anyone. It's about me. Something I need to tell you, and something I need to ask."

"Sounds serious."

The first thing didn't come as much of a surprise. "Your father and I are divorced. The final papers came today."

Reenie wasn't as troubled as one might expect. Her father had stopped being a part of their lives even before the war. He never acted as if he approved of any of them, especially Mum and Pippa, Sometimes he seemed to like Gemma and her, although she wasn't convinced. "I'm sorry to hear that, Mum. I'm sure we'll be fine, though." Reenie wasn't positive she believed that, but it seemed the right thing to say. She wondered where they would live once the war was over. Everyone said it would certainly end soon, but she couldn't see any signs of it happening. She might be all grown up by then. Well, as long as I can be with Lee and my family, nothing else will matter, she thought.

"Yes, we *will* be fine." Sheila smiled, but then looked doubtful. "I should tell Pippa and Gemma."

Mum sounded hesitant—almost as if she were consulting her as some kind of authority. Reenie considered a second before responding. "They never ask about him. Maybe wait until they do? Don't give them reasons to fret."

"That's what I thought."

"Was that what you wanted to ask me?" Sheila looked uncertain, and then so uncomfortable Reenie started to get nervous. "Mum?"

"No, I . . . I need some advice, but I don't know if you'll be able to talk to me about it. It could be secret."

Reenie laughed a little. What a strange world this had become when a daughter couldn't talk to her mother because she had been sworn to secrecy. "Well, why don't you just explain, and I'll let you know if I can or can't."

"It's about Edith Ferrar."

"I don't know anything you don't."

"Someone—I don't remember who, maybe Mr. Dailey—said she tried to pry information from you."

"Oh, that. Cat MacLaren probably told Mr. Dailey."

"Cat? She's Mr. Dailey's secretary. Why would she know?"

"I'm not sure, but I think she could be more than a secretary." Reenie told Sheila about stopping for tea before completing her first assignment, Edith's absurd request, and Cat's intervention. "I learned a lesson that day. I never take breaks before my mission is complete, and I never talk about it, either."

"So Miss Ferrar tried to get information from you. Something like that is happening to me." Sheila confessed she was seeing a man named Peter but assured Reenie it was not serious.

Reenie had doubts about that. If it weren't serious, then why were there so many nights Mum didn't come home? But she wouldn't feel right about asking. Mum had a right to her private life. Even though she was old—thirty-three—she was still pretty.

Then, to Reenie's horror, Sheila went on to say that Peter kept trying to pry information about her work in Hut 8. For certain, Reenie didn't know what happened there, although she had seen that silly machine. But she knew Hut 8 was important; after all, that's where Alan Turing and Dilly Knox worked. "Did you tell Peter anything, Mum?"

"Absolutely not."

"Shouldn't you report this to Mr. Dailey right away"

"Oh, I don't think I can do that."

"You're frightened, Mum? Of Mr. Dailey? Why?"

"I can't explain, Reenie. I just don't feel right telling him."

"Then maybe Cat can help. I'll go with you."

"Well . . ."

"You don't have a choice, Mum. It's too late. You told me, so now I know, too. If you won't say anything, I'll have to. It's my sworn duty. If Peter is innocent, he'll be cleared."

"Very well, Reenie. We'll go together. You've really grown up during the last year."

"Then do you think you could start calling me Maureen?"

Sheila gave her daughter a warm embrace. "That sounds like a fine idea."

Millie left Hell Hole, the workers' nickname for Hut 11, thoroughly exhausted and discouraged. The late night shift was the worst. None of the shifts were pleasant, of course, but this one was the hardest to bear. Her back ached, she was hungry, and she craved daylight and a facial and a manicure and a proper hair cut and—Oh, she shouldn't grizzle, considering all that Robert and others might be facing this very minute. She wondered where he was and only hoped he wasn't one of the many soldiers headed for the Balkan Front. At the moment, though, it was difficult to feel sorry for anyone but herself. She envied Cat, who worked normal hours and would be sound asleep when Millie arrived home, and then out and about while Millie slept.

To be honest, her real problem was the difficult time she was having operating the Bombe Machine. Nothing like the Polish cream puff dessert it was named after—but a scary, room-sized contraption, with crossing, confusing cables. The goal of every shift was nothing more than to control time—to identify more quickly the settings of those intercepted on the Enigma machine—to speed up code breaking. One of the things that made the late shift, beginning at seventeen hours, so heartbreaking was to experience failure practically every time midnight came along, and the Germans changed the settings again. At least when working an earlier shift, you thought someone coming after you might have a chance of succeeding.

Back at the flat, much to Millie's surprise, Cat was awake, drinking tea, and looking as wretched as Millie felt she herself must. "My, you're up early," she said. "Big day?"

Cat yawned. "More like the end of a big day. I just got in. Ah could sleep on the edge ae a razor, as Gramps would say."

"Painful. Anything you can talk about?"

Cat shook her head, and the girls smiled at each other. Soon they were asleep, dreaming their individual top-secret dreams.

Cat's day had been her most stressful since Edith Ferrar was arrested. It started when Reenie Bradshaw and a very reluctant Sheila came into the office and asked to speak to her alone. Dave was at a meeting, so this was not a problem. After considerable prodding on Reenie's part, Sheila told of her experience with a man named Peter. Odd that Sheila seemed loath to tell Dave, but Cat didn't think it wise to question it.

Peter. The P referred to in the notebook? If only Edith had provided a second initial. "What is his last name, Sheila?" Sheila hesitated. "I promise to be discreet, but really, I must know."

This was a very different Cat. Reenie might be correct that Catriona MacLaren was more than a secretary. "It's Cole," she said. "Peter Cole."

"I'll make certain Mr. Dailey receives the information," Cat said.

"Will I learn what happens?"

"I don't know. You did right by coming, Sheila."

As soon as Reenie and Sheila left, Cat pulled Peter Cole's file and began examining every item. His vetting was not complete. Meanwhile, his job was delivering food supplies to the canteen. She wondered how he happened to be selected. Not much to go on from his records. Sometimes she despaired of the haphazard way people arrived here. Such as yourself? What had her qualifications been, other than a few years at university and doing well on a crossword puzzle? Winning a crossword puzzle contest and now hunting for spies. What a crazy world and war!

"Peter Cole. I haven't had a chance to check him out," Davis said, when he returned mid-afternoon. "Anything in the file?"

"Not really. A University of Liverpool student until the war started. He did spend some time in Germany when he was younger, but that isn't proof of anything."

"True. So did I." Davis paused before coming to a decision. Then—"Call the university right away," he ordered. "We need more evidence before we bring him in. And, I hate to say it, but in a few hours we're going for another walk in the woods."

Cat groaned but wasn't actually displeased. Getting away from the desk for a while would be a treat, and she enjoyed Dave's company. He hadn't seem surprised Sheila was seeing another man—not that she should take any comfort from that—but she did anyway.

The University of Liverpool—not the easiest place to reach. The bombing Liverpool was receiving rivaled London, with civilian deaths almost as great. Since the previous August when 160 bombers had attacked the city, there had been more than fifty raids. Practically everyone at BP had donated generously to the recent blood drive for Liverpool and other port cities on the West Coast. How the University was still functioning was, frankly, something of a miracle.

After many attempts with a frustrated telephone operator, Cat finally reached an admission officer, who fortunately ran an orderly system and was able to give a quick report. No Peter Cole had ever registered. Cat put on her heaviest coat and pulled on waterproof boots. It was time to join Dave for another tramp in the woods, in search of a hollow tree that might not exist.

"Not registered? I can't say I'm surprised," Davis said, as they entered one more of the many woods surrounding BP. "I've found other things about Cole that disturb me. My sources have discovered his last name is Kohler, not Cole. Hard to be more German than that."

Cat shivered. "Then why have you chosen this moment for our wild goose chase?"

"The moment chose us. We were getting nowhere, Cat, so I sent out teams of investigators to search. My men were given orders to report their findings but not to examine the contents of any hollow trees they might discover. One team found two. A few men are waiting for us now; they'll escort us."

"And then we can stop doing this?"

Davis grinned. "But I thought you were enjoying these little strolls."

"Well, sometimes, if it's not too frigid. Lately, I prefer trying to stay upright on the ice, watching you loop the loop."

Ahead, a man stood at the edge of the woods waiting for them. "Sorry we're late, Williams," Davis said. "You look frozen to the bone. Let's make this happen as quickly as possible."

"I didn't mind waiting, Mr. Dailey, but I sent Agent Gates home. His wife is poorly."

"Let's be off then."

A quick search of the first tree revealed nothing. But the second—"Pay dirt!" Davis yelled.

"Pay dirt?" Cat and Agent Williams exchanged puzzled glances.

"Sorry. Old gold miner talk."

"Is it something like 'Hit the jackpot?'"

"Exactly." Davis pulled out five envelopes from deep inside the hollow tree. He took a quick look inside one. "We'll read these later." He shook the agent's hand. "Thank you so much, Williams. I'll call on you again, if I may."

"My pleasure, Mr. Dailey."

Back at the office, Cat and Dave had a quick cup of tea before delving in. "No names," Dave finally said in disgust. "Notes but no names."

They had read all five messages. Two just told Edith to go to Hell. The other three agreed to the pub meeting places, the Beard and Bard in Bedford or the Frog and Nightgown in London, and dates, all taking place after Edith had been arrested. Davis sat heavily at his desk. "The Frog and Nightgown was on the Old Kent Road in Southwark. That whole area is gone. We'll try Bedford, but what a long shot! We're on another goose chase, Cat."

Cat grinned. "You're giving me quite an education in American slang, but it's not such a long shot after all. Actually, we've hit pay dirt again."

"Oh?" He looked hopefully at her.

"Handwriting, Dave. No names, but we've got handwriting samples of everyone at Station X and all the other stations in England as well. And we've got Edith's initials. Let's see if we can match Herr Kohler's handwriting with any of the messages."

Davis stood suddenly and gave Cat an enormous hug—like a brother, perhaps, but still . . . "Cat, you are a wonder," he said.

Much later, Cat knocked on Sheila's cottage door and found her in a ragged dressing gown, with her hair in huge rollers. Without makeup, she looked old, Cat gloated inwardly. "May we talk freely?" she asked.

"Yes. Everyone's asleep. What have you discovered?" Reluctantly, Sheila offered tea. Asking was just standard British hospitality; old habits died hard.

Cat refused. She needed to get to the point. "You and Reenie did an important service, Sheila. I hope you weren't fond of Mr. Cole because you won't see him again."

"Will you tell me what happened?"

Cat shook her head. "No, I'm afraid I can't do that."

Both stood silent for a moment while Cat gathered courage. "Mr. Dailey sent you a message. He said a number of married people who were having affairs while working at BP have been sent away. He suggests you be careful."

"The nerve . . ." Sheila started, but managed to control herself. After all, Davis didn't know about Roger. Perhaps he *was* trying to be helpful. "Well, you tell Mr. Dailey that I am a divorced woman. The final papers have been signed, so I can do whatever I want. But I have not been having affairs. I work hard, I just wanted some fun."

This was too much. "No, Sheila, I am not going to play dispatch between you and Mr. Dailey. If you have something to say to him, you'll need to do it yourself. Goodnight."

Sheila headed for the kettle. Cat might not need tea, but she did now. Perhaps Davis had done her a favor after all. Perhaps it would be wise to let people know she was divorced and could see anyone she wished. She thought about Peter. She had enjoyed his company until he became so pushy. It was time to think about what Mum always said. "Why don't kind men interest you, Sheila? Why do they always have to be wicked?"

"I don't know, Mum," she whispered.

Entry from Maureen Bradshaw's Diary
7 March 1941

Tonight will be spectacular. I'm sure of it. Gram made me the most beautiful dress for opening night. I don't know how she does it. Like magic, she created it out of old curtains, a tablecloth, and something she called just a remnant. The dress is all the colors of the rainbow—cotton, maybe a bit flimsy for the weather, but I don't care. I can't wait for Lee to see me in it! I told him we would meet at "the theatre," the ballroom where the play will be performed, but he said he would escort me, even if it meant he'd need to go back to work and return later.

I must arrive early because I am an usher. It's a responsible job; my name is even in the program. Maureen Bradshaw. Some people—especially Mum—are starting to call me that. Gram and Lee still call me Reenie, but that's all right. They are my two favorite people in the world. Pippa and Gemma aren't my favorites, but they keep forgetting.

Mum is bringing both girls. The play is too sophisticated for them, but I think they will enjoy seeing Gram and other people they know, as well as hearing the sounds of audience laughter. Only a few months ago, we wouldn't have been able to take Pippa anywhere, but she has improved so much— thanks to Lee and Lady Katherine.

Lady Katherine will sit in a front row seat with her husband Admiral Sir Hugh Sinclair. She plans to introduce him to all of us. Recently, I overheard something terribly secret about him. I probably shouldn't even write it here, but I am always careful to hide my diary. Sir Hugh is not just an Admiral; he is the head of the British Secret Intelligence Service. Back in London, I would never have known people like that. I wasn't happy last July about coming here, but I must say it was the best thing that ever happened to me.

Gram is at the theatre now, having greasepaint smeared on her face. It's rather nasty, but the actors think it's necessary. "At least I don't need to be aged," she said. That's when they put lines on you and add highlights to make it seem like you have wrinkles. Gram has plenty of her own wrinkles. She is so nervous, saying her lines over and over, making us take turns reading the other parts. Lady Katherine claims that both Gemma's and Pippa's oral reading have improved, thanks to Gram.

I must go downstairs and wait for Lee. We're hoping that this day, turning sunny after all the rain, is a good omen. Our forces have entered Greece at last. I don't understand what's happening, but many people here are worried. They don't say much but go around with very gloomy expressions. I hear them saying, "God be with them." I think they must mean soldiers like my father, so I'll say it, too. God be with them!

CHAPTER FIFTEEN

SHEILA AND MILLIE NEARLY BUMPED into each other as they left their respective huts after a late-night shift lasting later than expected. They were weary—barely able to walk—but neither could recall ever being happier. They exchanged glances and, although they didn't know each other, embraced. No words were necessary—or allowed.

"Let's have a cuppa and a bite in the canteen," Sheila suggested. "I need to sleep but don't think I can."

"Good idea," Millie said. "There won't be much to eat, but I'd appreciate the company."

Millie was correct about the food situation, Sheila thought, placing her hands on her too-slim hips. She was down to eight stone and doubted that her weight loss had ended. Mum tried hard to feed them properly, both at home and in the canteen, but the long queues in shops often produced little or nothing in the way of nutrition. Mum had grown alarmed by the rude pushing and cutting ahead in queues, not proper British behavior at all. Ah, well, a cup of tea with Millie, even if it were tepid would be lovely. Not even an empty stomach would take away from the glory of the occasion.

Others from the huts had also taken refuge, but Sheila and Millie found places across from each other at a not-too-crowded table in Hut 2. Briefly, Sheila put her hand on Millie's, and the two smiled at each other.

It had been such a night! Sheila, working on the Typex Machine in Hut 8, spotted a word she recognized—Italian rather than German this time. She held up her hand and Dilly, who was on duty and had learned to recognize excitement in his normally placid workers, rushed to her side. "Wake up Turing! Get him the hell outa bed!" Dilly's assistant left immediately for Alan Turing's room.

From the Enigma Machine in Hut 8 to the Bombe Machine in Hut 11, where Millie was on duty, and finally, right before midnight, success! The cheers, the hugs, the utter relief remained with everyone present for the rest of their lives. Sheila had the honor of the Professor shaking her hand. Dilly, who rather fancied the ladies, gave her the eye.

It wasn't the first time Enigma had been foiled, of course—the Poles had done it themselves back in the thirties—and it wasn't the final breakthrough that still needed to come. But that night was a first for most of the people in Huts 8 and 11. The best part of all was that this particular coded message was critical, although they were not given details. Innumerable lives at sea would be saved because of their successful decryption. Sheila had never doubted her work was important, but Millie realized it fully for the first time that night.

The two women tried to engage in small talk but soon gave it up as meaningless. Sheila invited Millie to return to the cottage, where she could sleep on the sofa. Millie nodded. The last bus had left, and she doubted she could endure even the short walk to the flat in Bletchley. Both women recognized that although scarcely a word had been spoken, a lasting friendship had begun.

She almost liked the Bombe Machine now, Millie thought, as she cuddled under one of Janet Hill's comforters and drifted off to sleep. She dreamed about rolling drums and rotors and wires that would confuse even a seasoned telephone operator accustomed to numerous party lines. She also dreamed of a *bombe surprise*, flaming at her table in the finest restaurant in Cardiff, where she was seated with Robert and her parents. She and Robert were announcing their wedding date when the dessert arrived—a true Polish bomba, sponge and meringue and a layer of chocolate, topped off with an enormous, delicious scoop of vanilla ice cream!

Just as sweet, Sheila's dreams were full of dancing and handsome men, all longing to be with her. But the dreams didn't end well. In one corner of the great ballroom sat Davis, looking with stern disapproval at her. She approached him. "But I helped crack a vital code today," she said. "You have no right to judge me."

"Loose lips sink ships, even in dreams," he replied. Then he walked away.

12 March 1941 was turning out to be a fine day for Davis, too. The results of last night's triumph in Huts 8 and 11 were now locked inside the special buff-colored box, on its way to Prime Minister Churchill. Ultra, their code name for Enigma decrypts, had won this round. Davis wanted to shout the good news from the rooftops, but he must always pretend to know nothing. And such welcome news of another possible breakthrough—the German trawler Krebs had been captured off Norway, with two Enigma Machines on board, now on their way to BP experts, anxious to ferret out its treasures.

Davis's high spirits also arose from the latest wire received from the U.S. Only yesterday, President Roosevelt had signed the Lend-Lease Act. While the news wasn't quite as welcome as having his country enter the war, the new act, which would enable Congress to appropriate money for arms and other defense supplies to the Allies, was most welcome. It was a positive first step.

When Cat arrived, ready to spend another day tirelessly plowing through files, Davis handed her the message. "Eventually, this will also mean more food from America. Most of it dried or tinned—maybe hard cheese and bacon—but food none-the-less." Cat smiled, nodding, but she seemed distracted. "Anything wrong, Cat?"

"I'm not sure. I hope not. My bunkmate didn't come home last night. She's never done that before, and I'm a wee bit worried."

"That's one problem I can solve. I saw Millie and Sheila Bradshaw leaving the canteen together early this morning. They were heading for the Bradshaw cottage. My guess is they pulled a late shift and Millie was going to catch some sleep there before heading home."

"That's funny," Cat said. "I didn't think they even knew each other."

"They looked like good friends to me."

Cat shrugged, sat at her desk, and examined her notebook. J was next on the list. Who in the world was J?

At the stables, Maureen waited for Lee to complete his inspection of Oscar before strapping the pigeons to the special carrier in back. This would be her first delivery so far away, and she was nervous. These small, feathered warriors were more important to the war effort than she was, and while she could do nothing to ensure their safety after they reached their destination, she must be certain the first leg of their journey went well. She also needed to give Pippa a glowing report as soon as she returned. Pippa had become devoted to her charges, who appeared to grow fond of her, too, as the days wore on.

The responsibility of turning the pigeons over to the waiting agent in Bedford, as well as facing the continuing foul weather, kept her from concentrating on Lee's mood, also foul and stormy. This happened often lately, but Maureen was wise enough to realize she couldn't nag him into telling her what was wrong. He would tell her in his own time—or not.

Lee double-checked Maureen's motorcycle, just serviced, before sending her off with many warnings about the pigeons. He was relieved Reenie hadn't seemed to take offense at his grumpiness or even remark on it. She just allowed him his moods, whatever they might be. He was more than grumpy, though. He was worried—and frightened. He had made an appointment for lunch with his mother, as odd as that sounded. He had come to the conclusion that he must talk to her about her behavior and the ramifications it could have for both of them if it continued.

"Well, this is an unexpected surprise," Judith Jessup said, admiring the onion and potato soup with soda biscuits Lee had prepared. "But was it necessary to make an appointment in order to see me?" Lee just stared at her. "Well, I guess it was. I haven't been around much lately."

"No you haven't. I have no idea where you go."

"Here and there, out and about," Judith said airily. "But Leon, I do appreciate your taking over some of my chores when I'm away."

Some? All of your chores. This conversation was not going to be easy. "Mum . . ."

"I thought I asked you to call me Judith."

"Very well, Judith. Do you want us to stay at BP? Do you want to keep on living here?"

She frowned, looking offended. "Of course I do. It's our home. Besides, I own this cottage."

"Then you need to be more careful of what you say."

"What?"

"You are too vocal in your disapproval of the war."

"Indeed I am. It is a great folly, although Britain has been guilty of many."

"You are entitled to your opinion, to be a pacifist or whatever is driving you. But if you're not careful, we're not going to be allowed to live here. Perhaps you'll even be thrown into prison." Guilt by association? It could happen to him, too.

She would not bend. "Nonsense. I don't need to listen to this."

"Please, M . . . Judith. Everyone here, even you, signed the Official Secrets Act. It's serious. People who talk too much disappear suddenly. Haven't you noticed?"

"That's not right!"

"Perhaps not, but we don't have a say."

"Let them try to make me leave."

"I will be eighteen next month. If you don't stop spreading your opinions, I will enlist in the Royal Navy on my birthday. I don't want to be here when you're arrested."

"No, Leon, it is far too dangerous. If you were captured and the Nazis found out your grandfather was Jewish, you would be killed."

"That's ridiculous. It would be no more dangerous for me than for any other sailor. Grandfather Leon never practiced his religion."

"Do you think that would matter to them? I forbid you to enlist, Leon."

"You won't be able to stop me once I'm old enough."

"But you don't have to go. You'll have a deferment because of your work here."

"That is true, and I don't want to leave. But what I do next is up to you."

"I'll think about it," Judith said.

And then his mother disappeared for a week, so once again Lee added her duties to his own.

What a diff'rence a day makes—just 24 little hours. Davis sang softly and sadly, as if the popular song were a dirge. The wire had just come in, and he'd sent for Cat immediately. Fortunately, she was still on the grounds.

"Davis?" She looked at his face and quickly sat. "What's wrong? What happened?"

There was no easy way to tell her. "A wire came, Cat. For some foolish reason, they want to keep it a secret, but you should know. Heavy bombing has been reported in Scotland."

"Inverness," she said in a dead voice.

"Glasgow. Although the wire doesn't say Glasgow, it says Clydebank. Same thing, right?"

Cat shook her head. "No, Clydebank is one of Glasgow's western suburbs. I have some friends there. A crowded little town, so densely populated—well, it can't be all right."

"It's not, Cat. The report said there were 235 bombers. The town is gone—thousands killed. I thought it was Glasgow and didn't understand why the wire said injured survivors were pouring into Glasgow."

"Survivors. Maybe my friends are . . ." Cat shook her head. Too soon. No way of knowing anything for certain. "But Dave, you said it was a secret. Why?"

"Who knows?" Dave said in disgust. "A decree from the Department of Information." Such irony. The Department of Information in charge of censorship.

"The Department of Information!" Cat began to laugh. And she laughed and laughed until all laughter turned to tears. Then she cried as if her heart would break. Dave placed a hand on her shoulder and waited.

Letter from Sheila Bradshaw to Davis Dailey
30 March 1941

Dear Mr. Dailey,

Ever since I received your message from Catriona MacLaren, I've been debating how to approach you. Perhaps the direct method is best. Recently, I was divorced from my husband, Roger. Maureen and my mother know, but I have not told others. Your message leads me to believe I should do so soon. I don't wish people to think I am engaging in extramarital affairs.

For the record, though, I have not had an affair with anyone since arriving at Bletchley Park. As you well know, I was seeing a man named Peter. When I became troubled that he was trying to make me divulge secret information, I talked with Maureen, who urged that I contact you or Miss MacLaren. You know more about what happened next than I do.

I am very sorry if I ever gave you the impression I had more than sincere friendship to offer you. You have been very kind to my girls and me. I believe you might have felt I was using you. I hope that is not the case and that we may comfortably resume our friendship someday.

Sincerely,
Sheila Bradshaw

CHAPTER SIXTEEN

J ANET CHECKED HERSELF CAREFULLY IN the hall mirror, proclaiming herself neat and well turned out in her old tan suit with its flattering, simple lines. Both practical and proper, she thought. Rumor had it that as soon as June came, clothing, like so many other items, would also be restricted, subject to precious coupons. Silk, needed for parachutes, had been banned since the beginning of the war. New dresses must not use more than two yards of fabric, and pleats, a waste of fabric, would be forbidden. Now, how would that work for her generous size? Fortunately, she was handy with a needle and too old to require the latest London fads. She had added a small green feather to her favorite brown felt hat and was pleased with her only purchased accessory in the last six months—a leather handbag embellished with her initials that had a special gas mask compartment. So pleasant not to carry around that unsightly box!

She was heading to Bletchley House, where she would meet Katherine, and then the two would do a bit of shopping in town, followed by a special treat at the teashop. They would walk together, holding onto each other in the event of a sudden gale. Mr. Dailey promised to bring them and their packages back in the staff car. Janet had her list, although it was doubtful she would be able to purchase all their needs. Everything was scarce and frightfully dear. She examined her list one more time, just to be certain she hadn't forgotten anything.

Janet's Shopping List

Using Janet's, Sheila's, and the children's Ration Books.
For one week, unless noted.

Meat—whatever available (or tinned) - 2 1/2 pounds each
Sausages—unlimited if available
Bacon or ham—100 grams (4 oz.)
Vegetables—whatever available (or tinned)
Jam—450 grams (1 pound) to last a month
Butter—50 grams (2 oz.) each
Cheese—50 grams
Milk —2 pints (or box dry milk)
Sugar—225 grams (8 oz.)
Sweets—350 grams (12 oz) to last a month
National loaf (bread)—total of three
Tea—50 grams
Ovaltine
Oatmeal
Potatoes—as many as available
Cod liver oil—bottle to last two months
Laundry soap—1 bar to last a month
Bar soap—3 if available, to last one month
Spool darning thread to last a month
Mending silk—if available (doubtful)
Pencils—whatever available (unlikely)

She shivered. Spring was late in appearing, but it would be here soon. At least that's what Janet and Katherine kept telling each other. And perhaps an end to the war, both added, although neither believed it. Pity Mr. Dailey couldn't drive them into town as well, but he had meetings scheduled, he explained, and Cat couldn't be spared either. No sense in complaining, the exercise would do them both good.

Janet was reasonably content. Reenie was becoming a fine young woman, Gemma and, Pippa were thriving, and Sheila's announcement that she and Roger had divorced was welcome news. Janet peeked in on Sheila and the girls, who were sitting quietly in the lounge, each absorbed in a book. For once, Sheila was spending a rare time off with her daughters. They made a living picture of harmony, Janet decided happily, before dashing off to meet her friend. If it weren't for the war, she would be perfectly satisfied with her present life.

Lady Katherine was anxiously waiting, full of news. She had received a long letter from her husband. Hugh would be visiting soon and was looking forward to seeing everyone again. "He loved the play. You especially, Janet."

Janet blushed. "So kind, but I had only a minor role. The others were just marvelous."

"What do you think the Dramatics Society will do next?" Katherine wondered. The two women speculated on possibilities all the way into town.

Davis felt in limbo, the first circle of Dante's Hell, he thought ruefully. From too much to do, he'd gone all the way down to nothing. The raids in London had been far too severe for any return meetings there or even to Wormwood Scrubs, outside of town. Not only was his morale low, but so was the entire country's. The Germans had isolated Allied forces in Tobruk, defeated Norway, and had landed four divisions in Libya. They seemed to be everywhere. The assumption here had always been that Britain would prevail. But would it? Too many people had lost confidence in Britain's power on the seas. Clearly, Britannia no longer ruled the waves.

Poor London, Davis thought, wishing to be there and, at the same time, relieved not to be. How much longer could people withstand the battering on their senses? Balloons resembling flying fish crowding the skies, preventing one from breathing properly. Dogfights. Spitfires. The steady barrage of lights, fires, whistles, crashes. The boarded-up shop windows, the thuds of walls collapsing. The rank smells of death. An old Oxford chum had been killed only last week, when a parachute mine exploded outside his flat on Jermyn Street. Had a wife and three small children, safely evacuated to the country, thank goodness.

There were moments of danger here at Bletchley Park, but most of the time he felt as if they were in a cocoon, and not one necessarily deserved. In towns all around them, there weren't enough public shelters. People were suffering, doing without, grieving for the loss of both lives and property. If only he could tackle that wretched Enigma Machine. Did he think he was better than the experts here? Not necessarily, but he sure as hell wanted to try.

Where was Cat? She could normally cheer him up with an amusing anecdote. He would wait a little longer before returning to his lonely room in Bedford.

Cat picked up the mail, late today. It included one telegram, always a cause for alarm. In this case, it was especially disturbing. Hopefully, Dave would still be at his desk. She'd ask his advice.

"Good, Dave, I'm glad you're here. Mail call. Thought you should see this. I'm not sure how to handle it."

"Mail this late? I wonder why." He noticed what she was holding. "Oh, dear, a telegram? Who is it for now?" Cat handed it to him. "Oh, my."

"It doesn't necessarily mean bad news." Dave just looked at her. Of course it meant bad news. "Shall I deliver it?"

"No, I'll do it." Without saying another word, he grabbed his coat and headed for Number Two Cottage Stable Yards. It was doubtful that the telegram sent to Mrs. Roger Bradshaw contained anything but the words "dead, or missing and presumed dead." How would the newly divorced Mrs. Roger Bradshaw react?

Cat had work to do. She would wait for him to return, however long it took.

Late that evening, long after the Dramatic Society's meeting ended, came a knock at the cottage door. A startled Janet responded. "Mr. Dailey, this is a surprise."

"I must apologize for the time, Mrs. Hill. No one was home earlier. May I come in? It is important that I see Sheila."

"Of course," Janet murmured, showing him in.

While waiting, Davis sat in a straight chair in the lounge. He was uncomfortable, but it didn't seem the right time for comfort.

"Mr. Dailey?"

Davis stood. "I'm still Davis, Sheila."

"I didn't know that." What was he doing here? He must have read her letter by now. It had been a long, tiring shift. All she wanted was to go to bed.

"Please sit down, Sheila." He led her to the sofa and sat next to her. There was no easy way to do this. He handed her the telegram.

"Oh."

"Do you want me to open it?"

"No, I'll do it." Sheila ripped open the lethal yellow envelope, read it quickly, and handed it to him.

Davis nodded. In a sense, it was good news; at least it was final. There was nothing to do but deal with it.

Tobruk. Lieutenant Roger Bradshaw died in action. 17 April 1941.

Ten days ago. That damned Rommel!

"Roger is gone," Sheila said flatly. "After everything, he's just gone. I suppose I should cry or faint."

"Shall I fetch your mother?" Davis thought she might be in shock. Surely, she should react more.

"No, I don't believe it yet. It's not real. Telling others will make it real."

Davis nodded. "I understand." He'd experienced death enough times to know that denial came first.

"I feel so many different things at once. Sorrow, relief . . . How many times have I wished him dead? I suppose I didn't really—I just wished him to be different or away from me. I loved him once, I guess, although it's hard to believe now."

Then tears came, and she went into his arms. Then he released her and went to find Janet.

Janet understood quickly what had happened and what the ramifications were for Sheila. Too early to go into them now, she decided. They needed to find out if Roger had changed his will. She doubted he'd had time. Heartless, perhaps, for her to even think of this, but his death would simplify matters greatly for Sheila. And being a widow would improve her position. No need now for Sheila to mention the divorce. Divorced women were not treated with respect; they must have done something wrong. Widows warranted compassion. In many ways, Roger had done Sheila a favor. Well, they would need to break it to the children. Gemma would be sad, and Pippa and Reenie might mind a little.

"What a failure you were, Roger, that you died, and so few will mourn."

Cat looked carefully at Dave when he walked back into the office. "It's late. You've put in enough time today," she said. He didn't answer. He didn't even hear her. Her heart dropped. It's Sheila, she thought. I thought he was over her, but it's starting all over again. Sir Galahad has returned. Without saying goodnight, she locked her files and picked up her coat. I miss Gramps, she thought, as she closed the door. I want to go home.

Writing assignment from Lady Katherine
Pippa Bradshaw
Final copy, spelling and grammar corrected.
Penmanship and punctuation much improved.
29 April 1941

My Father

I'm supposed to write about my father and how I feel about him dying. My sister Gemma is supposed to write about it, too, but she won't. Gemma cries a lot. Sometimes when I feel like being a big sister, I try to help. Other times I get mad at her for being such a baby.

It's wrong of me not to be sadder, but I can't help it. My father wasn't nice to me. He made fun and called me stupid. When Mum tried to stop him, he hit her. Sometimes he hit me, too. He left Reenie alone, but no one bothers Reenie very much. He only loved Gemma. She is young and little and cute. Maybe that is why he loved her and not me.

Sometimes I'm glad he's gone, but maybe he would have liked me better when I grew up. I don't think so, but I won't ever find out now. But I never want to go back to London. I want to stay here at Bletchley Park always.

CHAPTER SEVENTEEN

WORST LUCK—COLD AND RAINY again today, Lee thought, as he checked the next-to-last motorcycle in his fleet. He had been hoping the brief warm up, 59 degrees yesterday, would last. Normally, early May was pleasant in Bletchley Park. He shivered. At least Reenie had started her journey in good weather, but even if she had stayed overnight in Worcester, as he had recommended, she should have returned by now. Where was she? Lee would give her until after his lunch break, not that he could eat much. If she hadn't returned, he would contact his boss, Mr. Carroll, and maybe Reenie's Gram, Janet Hill.

Lee did not want to disturb Sheila, working in Hut 8. No one went there unless it was absolutely urgent. Besides, he was wary of Reenie's mum. He wasn't sure why, exactly. Maybe he was just off mums in general. Judith hadn't come home for five nights, and he didn't know where she was. He no longer had any trouble calling her by her given name. It wasn't the same thing at all, of course, but he almost understood how Reenie felt about her deceased father.

Reenie. His worry returned. He wasn't just concerned for her welfare, although that was the main thing. This assignment, the most important she had ever received, was also the farthest. Sixty miles away—probably three hours or more by motorbike—with pigeons to deliver and a packet, in addition to the usual pouch. Lee had no idea what either contained, but Worcester was critical in the war effort, and the news lately had been dreadful. Operation Marita in Greece and the April War in Yugoslavia, both lost. After the Allies had failed to hold them back, the Nazis forced Greece and Yugoslavia to surrender. If the unthinkable happened and there was a mass invasion here, Worcester instead of London would become the seat of government, and the War Cabinet would move to Hindlip Hall. Hard to imagine after the pounding the town had received last October. Lee shrugged. He and others had become hardened by news, especially news that wasn't recent. The most unlikely scenarios were happening daily. To concentrate on any one of them was futile.

He waited until fourteen-thirty before reporting to Mr. Carroll, who hadn't heard anything but said he would make some phone inquiries. Lee then searched for Janet Hill, finding her at last in Lady Katherine's library. The two friends were enjoying tea and a chat while Pippa and Gemma played with other children on the playground outside of Hut 4. Both women were worried about Gemma, who had behaved as one might expect to news of a father's death. Gemma was devastated. Lee's opinion was that Gemma's reaction was more normal than Pippa's and Reenie's, who were acting almost indifferent. Lee wondered if eventually that would become a greater problem than Gemma's sorrow.

Janet reacted immediately to Lee's news. "No, Reenie never came home, but I knew her mission would be longer than usual and that she might spend last night there. But this is far too late. We must tell Mr. Dailey at once!"

Mr. Dailey. Lee was afraid of that. He was hoping not to involve him. Janet and Reenie were thrilled that Mr. Dailey and Sheila were keeping company again. Lee hadn't decided how he felt, not that it was any of his concern. He liked Mr. Dailey but wasn't sure he and Sheila were a good match. They didn't seem like friends to him, at least not the way he and Reenie were—like partners. Sheila leaned on Mr. Dailey, and he took care of her, but maybe that's what Mr. Dailey needed—to be needed, and she was awfully pretty for an older woman. Oh, well, their relationship was none of Lee's business, but Reenie certainly was.

"Where are you, Reenie?" he whispered.

In faraway Worcestershire, in an improvised hall ward at Royal Hospital, Maureen recovered consciousness. First, she was aware of a pounding, piercing headache, and then, even more. Tentatively, she touched a large bump. "Ouch!" Where was she? She started to rise, but a sister rushed to her side, easing her back down, just as an attack of dizziness overtook her.

"Now, now, miss. You've had a nasty fall. You must try to be patient." The sister explained where she was. Worcestershire? At first Maureen couldn't remember anything about her mission or why she was in Worcestershire.

Then she did—some of it, anyway. "Oscar? The pigeons . . . my pouch . . . the packet . . . Where are they?"

"I'm sure I don't know, miss. You just rest now. I'm sure your Oscar will come soon. It will all be sorted out in time."

"But I must find out now . . ." but a stabbing pain near her right shoulder overtook her, and she fell back exhausted. The sister gave her an injection of morphine, and Maureen slept deeply—for many hours.

Maureen's day had started out well enough, although she had been hoping to leave BP earlier. At least it wasn't raining, and while the wind was brisk, the temperature was quite a bit warmer than it had been. But the trip soon became difficult when one mishap after another affected Oscar. Most of the repairs were easy—just time consuming.

A shard of glass stuck in a tire caused a necessary stop at Station VIII, where a new one could be put on. It was nearly nightfall by the time she arrived in Worcester, tired and hungry, but determined to accomplish her mission first.

Then, assured that she would find lodgings just off the High Street in the Shambles, Maureen followed directions past the medieval castle but missed the turn where High Street becomes The Cross. She needed to backtrack. It was too easy to lose one's way because of the blackouts and the missing, covered, or inaccurate signs. The intention was to confuse Nazi spies, but ordinary citizens were often bewildered, too. It was growing dark, but

Maureen still might have found her lodgings in time if she had not spotted a familiar figure on Friar Street, with its medieval, swaying Tudor buildings. Judith Jessup entering The Dragon Inn! Maureen brought her vehicle to a sudden stop. What reason could Lee's mother possibly have for being in Worcester—and in such an unsavory-looking place? Maureen wasn't sure why she didn't want Judith to spot her? It had been pure instinct that caused her to retreat. Waiting to see if Judith might come out again, though, proved her undoing. Darkness descended, and she was unable to see anything in the blacked-out twisting streets making up The Shambles. But she couldn't stay there. Cautiously, Maureen continued driving, thinking she might be going in the right direction, but she failed to see a log lying on the road. Oscar rode over it and toppled, trapping Maureen underneath. After one sharp jolt of pain, she lost consciousness.

After receiving a welcome phone call from the hospital in Worcester. Davis lost no time in requisitioning a staff car the next morning. Then, insisting there was room only for Sheila and himself, he began the stressful journey. For different reasons, Janet, Lee, and Cat misinterpreted Davis's action, but he was simply being practical. Maureen's mother would sit in front with him, and the back was reserved for Maureen, who might need to stretch out. In truth, Davis would have preferred having the others along. Sheila was certain to brood all the way to Worcester, although he couldn't blame her, but that's the way she often behaved with him. She smiled and laughed with friends, storing up her anxiousness for him. Not that he was complaining; he was glad she needed him. Still . . . if Cat were in the car, they would have found something to converse about, in spite of the circumstances.

"I must go, too," Lee insisted. "Oh, not just because of Reenie. I need to make certain she finished her assignment. It was important." While he didn't know the nature of the messages she was carrying, this time he did know her destination.

Thanks to Lady Katherine, another car was assigned. Cat would drive while Lee would try to read the map, in spite of the lack of signs. Janet insisted she would be quite comfortable in the back seat.

Cat's car was quieter than Davis's. Lee worried about Reenie's injuries, her assignment, and the possible condition of the motorcycle, an expensive item to replace. Janet fretted about Reenie and Gemma. At least Pippa and Sheila were doing well. Such a fine thing that Sheila was stepping out with Mr. Dailey again. Perhaps Sheila finally found kindness attractive. Cat thought only of Dave wanting to be with Sheila and no one else. No use pretending to herself that it didn't hurt. I wonder if I should ask for a transfer, she thought, knowing full well she wouldn't.

When Maureen awoke again, her family and Lee were at her bedside. "Lee," she said, "I don't remember what happened. I don't remember anything about yesterday. Did I . . ."

Lee patted her hand. "Yes, Reenie. You completed your mission before the accident. Pigeons, pouch, and packet safely delivered. You are what's important now."

On the other side of the bed, Sheila felt Reenie's forehead but stepped back when she winced. "You don't remember anything?"

A sister joined them. "A concussion—a fairly severe one at that. Doctor said her memory of the day might be restored, but it's unlikely."

"As long as I didn't ruin anything, it doesn't really matter," Maureen said. "Do I get to go home?"

"As a matter of fact you do," the sister said, "but only because we can't spare even this hall bed. Too many wounded men coming in non-stop, and there is a bad case of influenza going around. Also some reports of TB. You would be healthier away from here." The sister explained that Maureen had broken her collarbone and ankle. "She'll need to see a doctor closer to home. Will that be a problem?"

Davis assured the sister that Reenie would receive excellent care in Bletchley. The sister seemed puzzled. Excellent care in such a backwater community? But she wisely said nothing. She had become used to secrets. Besides, people with greater injuries were waiting for her. She called for a wheelchair.

"How did I end up on a street so far from my lodgings?" Maureen wondered.

"Lost your way in the blackout, probably," Lee said. "No harm done, Reenie."

"No harm done," Maureen echoed, trying to convince herself it was so.

Letter from Catriona MacLaren , Wren, HMS Pembroke V
To Douglas MacLaren
40 Ness Bank Inverness
8 May 1941

Dearest Gramps,

I have wonderful news for you and even better news for me. After such a long, long time, I've been granted liberty. And it's spring now, Gramps, although no one seems to have informed Mr. Weatherman. It is bitter cold here—more like early March. No doubt it's even nippier up north. But it doesn't matter. After all, it is only weather. Please tell my friends, if any remain in Inverness, that I'm coming home. If everyone is gone, tell Nessie I'm determined to find him this time.

What shall we do together, Gramps? On beautiful days, let's take long walks along Ness Bank and visit our favorite pubs. On rainy, cool days—and there will be many—let's sit by the fire and play cribbage or read or just dream. I shall watch you smoke your pipe and will scold you for smoking too much. Secretively, I'll enjoy the smell—my smell of home.

I leave on 12 May, and it's difficult to say whether this letter or I will arrive first. Fortunately, you enjoy surprises. Millie will not be with me. Her Robert has leave, and she will see him in Cardiff—for the first time in over a year.

As terrible as this war is, Gramps, would I appreciate going home as much if it had never happened?

Lovingly yours, Cat

CHAPTER EIGHTEEN

L ADY KATHERINE CLOSED THE DOOR to the small guest room, which had become a private infirmary, first taking off her protective coat and mask and washing her hands before joining her friend in the library. She shook her head when offered a cup of tea. "I don't believe I can handle another drop, Janet." She sank wearily on a sofa. "We'll just have to wait and see."

The two women sat in silence. There wasn't anything more to talk about. The doctor had left some medicine, muttering something about a new cure they might try as soon as he received clearance to use it, but implied that prayer could be the only answer. Almost as dangerous as the Blitz these days seemed to be hospitals.

But what choice had there been? An unconscious young woman with a broken collarbone and ankle? Of course she was taken to hospital, a place of contagious diseases and, no matter how hard the staff tried to prevent it, filth. Fortunately, if such a word were possible in this situation, Maureen had developed her symptoms on the automobile ride back to Bletchley Park. Only Sheila and Davis had been seriously exposed. By the time they arrived, Maureen had a high fever, chills, rash, delirium.

In order to protect Pippa and Gemma, Lady Katherine whisked Maureen away to a secluded guest room before calling a reputable and discreet physician in Oxford. Katherine was old enough to remember the last war and had her suspicions. She put Sheila into another room and told Davis to retreat to the small flat in Bedford he shared with no one. "You are both under quarantine until the doctor clears you," she ordered, making it clear she had taken charge. "If it's what I suspect, we must keep this very quiet. We cannot have all of Bletchley Park under quarantine. The work here must not stop."

Sheila and Davis were cleared in a few days, and the others—Janet, Cat, and Lee, who had not been exposed for very long— remained symptom free. The doctor confirmed what Katherine suspected. Maureen had the Irish Disease—Typhus.

In short order, everyone working at BP received a vaccination without knowing why. "Just a precaution," they were told. All might have wondered, but no one questioned it. Questioning was not good form.

Cat studied the poster hanging in her train carriage. This one, issued by the Railway Executive Committee, asked, *Is Your Journey Really Necessary?* Yes, she silently answered the soldier pictured with a rifle. Yes, it really is. I need to see Gramps, and I must have a break from Dave. She was fortunate, though, that he had been able to acquire this seat for her. So often, because of army and navy personnel requiring seats, there was standing room only. Strange that there was no one else in her compartment, she mused. Perhaps someone would join her at another station.

She turned to the Guardian, which seemed to be the only newspaper available on the train today. The headlines shrieked. *Westminster Abbey Hit, but Main Fabric Saved. Commons Chamber Wrecked.* The British Museum damaged, too. The raids had been dreadful the preceding weekend. Cat shuddered. Awful!

"Miss MacLaren, isn't it?"

Cat looked up, pleased for an excuse to abandon the newspaper. "Admiral Sinclair? This is a surprise!" She had first been introduced to him at a meeting she attended with Davis and had seen him several times since.

"May I join you?"

"Of course." Cat moved next to the window, allowing him the aisle seat in their second-class coach. She wondered why he wasn't traveling in first, but she could hardly ask.

"You're on liberty, I gather."

"Yes, I'm going home to Inverness."

"Then we'll be traveling together for some distance. I will connect with a local at the Thorntonhall station. A driver will meet me at my destination."

"I'll transfer from Glasgow Central. I won't reach home until late tonight."

"Blackout," Hugh Sinclair warned.

"Yes, but I have a small torch covered with a dark gel, which I'll turn on only if necessary. It's not a long walk from the station to Ness Bank. You might say I could do it in my sleep, and by the time I arrive, that may be what I'm facing."

"Blackouts are proving almost as dangerous as bombs," Sinclair said. "Well, not really, but they are dangerous."

"They certainly were for Maureen Bradshaw. But Lady Katherine says she seems to be improving."

"Yes, that new method the doctor is using may turn things around. DDT—nasty stuff, actually a poison . . ."

"But if it works . . ."

"Right." The Admiral offered Cat a cup of tea—he had an extra cup with his thermos—and she shared her biscuits, baked by Janet the day before. He was a good man, Cat thought, and every bit as nice as his wife. She wondered if he were aware she knew he was MI6. Evidently, he was . . .

"Miss MacLaren, they call you Cat, isn't that right?" Cat nodded. "Cat, perhaps you can help me on a special assignment. It would delay your arrival home somewhat."

"My grandfather doesn't know exactly when I'll arrive. Of course, if I may be of service, Admiral . . ."

"I would make sure you had continuing transport by a safer route and in daylight hours. The raids in Glasgow are becoming more severe. Even once you're in Inverness, I'm not comfortable with your torch and braille plan. Cat, I need your help translating."

"Translating? I studied French, but I'm not proficient, and I don't know any German except words we all know now."

"No, I need to understand Scotch."

Cat grinned. How typically English of him. "Scotch, sir? First, you pick the finest brand from a well-known brewery—I can recommend several—then pour it into a large chilled glass, and . . ."

Admiral Sinclair burst out laughing. "I should have known better. I meant to say Scottish."

"The Scots speak English."

"Do they? I sometimes wonder. You do. And if it weren't for a certain lilt in your voice and an occasional odd choice of words, I'd never suspect. I need to interview a farmer outside of Eaglesham, who had an unexpected houseguest. I'm fearful he may have quite a brogue, and it is vital that I understand him."

"Aye, ye'll hae a sair pech. Ken wit a mean?"

The Admiral sighed. "That's exactly what I mean."

"A onerstaun. Ane language is nivver eneuch." Cat stopped showing off, although she was having a fine time. "I would be glad to help."

Quietly, Admiral Sinclair explained their mission while Cat's mouth dropped in amazement. A farmer, David McLean, had rescued a German, whose airplane had crashed onto his field. He had helped him out of his parachute, brought him back to his house, where he offered tea before calling the police. The identity of the man? Rudolph Hess, Hitler's second in command.

"No! That doesn't make sense."

"Evidently Hess hoped to broker a peace deal."

"While treating us to the fiercest attacks we've had yet? Can he be sane?"

"How can any of them be considered sane? Perhaps that's our greatest advantage. The Nazis are crazy and are bound to do something stupid. Hess is in a heavily guarded prison cell in Glasgow—I'll interview him in time—but for now, I need to speak with McLean while his story is still fresh."

Hugh didn't have to ask Cat to keep this information private. Secrecy had become second nature. She wondered, though, if this were the reason no one else was seated in their carriage. Had this been planned ahead of time? It seemed likely. Eaglesham was a suburb of Glasgow. Surely, it would be easier for them to transfer from there. Perhaps the bombing was more severe than she realized, or perhaps there was another reason the Admiral didn't want to go to Glasgow. But she knew better than to ask questions.

Lee cut armfuls of late mayflowers—lilacs, wisteria, clematis—forming, with Janet Hill's help, a beautiful bouquet. Soon he would visit Reenie for the first time since the hospital in Worcester. Lee looked as if he should be in hospital himself—pale and thin, mainly because of a total lack of appetite. At times, the clouds of grief had been overwhelming, especially when it seemed certain Reenie would die.

Oscar the motorcycle had been repaired, which would please Reenie, but it was doubtful she'd ever drive again. He had trained a new dispatch rider, who was doing well. More experienced girls were taking over some of Reenie's duties.

Delivering the messages was critical. The war news was even more disturbing than usual, now that the German battleship Bismarck was becoming almost as feared as Hitler. The British Hood had been lost to it only a few days before. And close by in London? Lee shook his head. The House of Commons demolished—so difficult to fathom. The renewed bombing of London had unnerved everyone as mounting deaths were reported daily. Even Lee knew people who had lost friends and family members.

Family. Other than Reenie, his family had become Lady Katherine, Pippa, Gemma and, most important, Janet Hill, who seemed to mother them all. He would have included Sheila Bradshaw on this list, but she was so busy in Hut 8, he hardly saw her. When he did, she looked as ghost-like and unhappy as he. Sheila, too, would finally see Reenie. She had not been allowed to visit because of her work. Exposure to typhoid was an unacceptable risk.

Lee's mother, Judith, wasn't available for him, emotionally or physically. Days went by without Lee seeing her. Often, he no longer cared. A new groundskeeper had been hired, with Lee assisting when he could. If it weren't for Lee's job training dispatch riders and keeping the motorcycle fleet in good repair, he doubted they'd be allowed to remain—in spite of Judith owning the cottage. Ownership didn't seem to mean much these days.

Lee's greatest pleasure was working with Gemma and Pippa. With Janet's guidance and Lady Katherine's assignments, he had become one of their teachers. He had to admit that by teaching, he was learning more than his students. He was reading books he should have read years ago—stories he thought were just for girls, such as adventure books by Enid Blyton—and was improving his own writing by correcting theirs. They seemed like sisters to him, and Janet Hill, more of a mother than his own.

Intense, headache-producing concentration, as well as the day-after-day barrage of tragic telegrams and urgent wires, were taking their toll on Davis. He wasn't certain when he had felt more alone. He had been laboring tirelessly, even managing to catch a couple of German agents, who worked at stations other than BP, thank goodness. He thought they had been caught before doing any damage, but he couldn't be certain.

Conflicts at Wormwood Scrubs between people who should be working as a team had intensified to the point Davis doubted their assigned mission would succeed. Instead of concentrating first on destroying the present enemy and then planning the formation of an espionage group to carry on after the war, those in charge seemed more worried about Soviet Communists than Nazis. "You've got to watch those Bolshevists," they kept saying. One enemy at a time, please, Davis thought, but he didn't feel he had enough clout to speak his mind. Also, he wasn't totally certain he was right.

His personal life was at a standstill. Sheila was so involved in her work they seldom met. A rare breakfast or supper in the canteen, depending on her shift, with conversation filled with her worry about Reenie. He couldn't blame her, but he needed a reprieve from anxiety. They all did, of course.

Most of all, Davis missed Cat, although he was partly to blame for her being granted liberty. Not that he could really regret it. Cat had been useful in the dealings with David McLean, and Admiral Sinclair had thanked him for his recommendation. But she was needed here, too. She would have spotted some inconsistencies in the new staff folders before he did, and spies might have been captured sooner. There were still a few more initials to check out from Edith's infamous notebook. When would Cat return to tackle them? Not her fault, of course. A wretched bronchial condition had kept her in Inverness. Her missing laughter made the office seem empty. He felt the lack of the laughter, the jokes and stories, and the good humor and goodness that represented his friend Cat.

"Mail call, Mr. Dailey." His secretary entered, placing an unsorted stack on his desk before returning to the outer office. He frowned at the telegram and wire, knowing full well they should be dealt with first. Instead, he stalled, but felt self-righteous by at least perusing the BP news updates before the personal letters.

"So, the president declares an unlimited national emergency exists. Indeed, Mr. Roosevelt, you don't say . . . Yes, yes, I know. You're doing the best you can. And you, Prime Minister, remind us that earlier Ultra decrypts suggested Hitler would invade Britain either this month or next, but now the invasion is supposedly planned for 15 September at the earliest. You would like an update." He shrugged. "Beats me. They're certainly bombing the hell out of us now. Maybe they're waiting for better weather before getting serious?"

No longer finding any comfort in procrastinating, he opened the telegram, expecting death, of course. But this came as a complete surprise. "Oh, my, I wonder how Cat will react to this?" Edith Schmidt, still in her hospital/prison, had hanged herself. No note, but it was conclusive she had taken her own life; it was not murder. "Poor, lost, deluded Edith," he said. "Well, thank you, Edith, for the pointers you gave us that were correct." He stared at the wire. Perhaps whatever bad news it contained could wait.

A glossy envelope he thought might be business contained a wedding announcement from the states. "That's nice," he said, indifferently, to the news that his former fiancée, Barbara, had married his old friend, Brian. He would send them a note or card. But the next letter! That handwriting! To his amazement, his heart began thumping. A letter from Cat! Well, he would read it when he returned to his room. After all, he had work to do. He wouldn't admit even to himself that he wanted to save it—to savor it. Forcing himself to put the letter into his briefcase, he turned to the wire, opening what should have been read first.

"We did it!" he shouted. "By George, we did it! Hooray for the British Navy! We sank the Bismarck!" Was this the beginning of the end?

Sheila and Lee greeted each other briefly in the foyer of Bletchley House and admired each other's offerings. Lee's flowers were glorious, Sheila said, burying her nose in them. She had been inside the cold hut for more hours than she had been out, and spring was passing her by. For her, these flowers were the first sign. Lee exclaimed at the oversized box of chocolates Sheila carried, wondering how she had acquired them. Everyone had contributed ration stamps, she explained. Both hoped Reenie would be able to enjoy them. Because of their love for Reenie, a bond had developed. Nothing else mattered but their girl.

"You go first," both said to each other.

"Ladies, who are mothers, first," Lee insisted. Sheila acquiesced.

Finally, it was Lee's turn. And there she was—sitting up in bed—pale, less hair than he remembered, and probably less beautiful, too, but not in his eyes.

"Lee, how lovely. Did you pick them?"

"Of course," he said, handing them to her. "Soon you'll be able to gather your own."

"I will," she promised.

He sat next to her bed and held her hand. He would waste no more time. "I love you, Reenie," he said simply.

A letter from Catriona MacLaren to Davis Dailey
25 May 1941

Dear Dave,

I am terribly sorry to have let you down. Even though the major burden of work and responsibility belong to you, I suppose my wee bit lightened the load somewhat. My head cold has turned into pneumonia, and I will not be able to travel, much less resume my duties, until my doctor gives me the all-clear. An even harder clearance to obtain will be from Gramps, who is hovering like a mother hen.

At least Gramps understands now why I must return. No, I haven't divulged anything private, but he finally supports getting behind the war effort. In fact, he and his cronies have joined the Home Guard. They are all old men, the brunt sometimes of ridicule, but I am not laughing or making fun. They work hard, are terribly earnest, and have averted possible disasters close by, especially in their efforts to douse incendiary fires.

Because of the conditions in our local hospital, I was not admitted and have spent the entire time recuperating at home. Hearing from Janet of poor Maureen's situation, I must applaud both my doctor and Gramps for keeping me here.

I will have many thrilling adventures to relate to you when I return. I'm pleased there is someone I can tell.

Do give my best to all my friends stationed on HMS Pembroke V.

Sincerely,
Catriona MacLaren

Attempted replies to Catriona MacLaren from Davis Dailey—all abandoned.

Dear Cat,

You more than lighten the load, you bring happiness . . .

Dear Cat,

I can't tell you how lonely and bleak the office is. I would love to hear about all your recent activities . . .

Dear Cat,

Of course your health comes first, but . . .

Dear Cat,

If only I could share . . .

Dear Cat,

Wait until you hear about . . .

Dear Cat,

I truly miss . . .

Dear Cat,

Dear . . .

CHAPTER NINETEEN

F INALLY IT WAS JUNE—TRULY spring and sometimes summer. Davis had
read the letter from Cat so often it was beginning to tear. He searched it
for hidden meaning, something personal, but found nothing. He scolded
himself for being absurd, but he kept on looking. What was his problem? He
and Sheila were a couple now, and someday he would propose, wouldn't he?
When the war was over, he decided. He just missed Cat because she was his
partner, and he had far too much work to do alone. That was all that was
wrong.

His efforts to answer were either feeble or revealed too much for his
own comfort, so he finally gave up. Both Janet and Sheila reported hearing
from her and expected she'd return by mid or late month. Stop the
foolishness, he commanded. Get back to work. Code breakers were picking
up something called Operation Barbarossa. What might that be about?

In Inverness, Cat had almost recovered. She and Gramps took slow strolls
along Ness Bank and even enjoyed a few meals at the Station Hotel, although
they had become somewhat skimpy since the government had tightened
food rationing on the first of June. Still, she and Gramps were enjoying their

ventures out of the small house, away from each other's cooking. In addition to food, further restrictions were now placed on clothing. Other than shoes, she didn't expect it to be much of a problem for her. She had her Wren uniform to wear to meetings and when she left BP. On site, her old clothing, with proper care and mending, should serve her fine.

As much as Cat longed to resume her work at BP and, yes, to see Dave, she was worried about Gramps, who coughed much of the time and seemed to be fading right in front of her. She also worried about how he would manage his food ration stamps and eat properly without her supervision. He should eat more and smoke less and not go on so many night missions with the Guard. Fire fighting at his age was absurd. But he did not react well to nagging, and she learned, finally, to keep still.

One lovely June day, Maureen Bradshaw, aided by Lee, with her mother, sisters, grandmother, and Lady Katherine surrounding them, was allowed to go home to Number Two Cottage Stable Yards. A bedroom downstairs had been improvised in the small dining nook, and as far as Maureen could tell, all of her possessions were there—even the locked box containing her diary and other treasures. She still required rest—most likely for the remainder of the summer—but she was home!

Reluctantly, Sheila and Lee returned to work, both promising to return as soon as possible, and Lady Katherine and Gemma made their way to Bletchley House for Gemma's lessons. Janet, noticing Pippa's longing glances at her big sister, wisely muttered something about fixing tea and left them alone.

"Shall I help you into bed?" Pippa asked.

"No, I've spent too many hours in one. This chair will suit me fine for a while. Sit next to me, Pippa, and let's talk. You seem quite grown up."

"I'm almost fourteen. That's pretty grown up."

"It is indeed."

"I was scared you would die, Reenie. So was Gemma. Sometimes we cried ourselves to sleep."

"I was scared myself. But I was very lucky."

"You're awfully thin. None of your clothes will fit, and you can't just go buy new ones now."

Maureen smiled. "Good thing we've got Gram."

"I wonder what you'll do next. Lee says he will never let you ride that motorcycle again."

"We'll see about that!" Both girls laughed, but both also knew it would be a very long time—if it ever happened.

It was good to laugh at last, Pippa thought. And it was good to be happy. She would much rather be happy than sad. But sadness seemed to make people more grown up—more mature—than happiness. She wondered why that was. She wanted to be grown up, but she wanted to be happy, too.

Maureen gazed at the little sister who had been so impossible and needy only a year ago. Not for everyone, perhaps, but for the Bradshaw family at least, Bletchley Park was a wonderful place. She looked at the box containing her diary. It would be good to sort out her thoughts—to get caught up. I understand now why I was in Worcester, she thought, but not what took me to a street so far from my lodgings. No one else thought it important. But she knew she needed to remember.

Apparently, Davis wasn't the only one who missed Cat. Millie found the days bleak without her chum. Although they corresponded often, so much couldn't be said in letters. Not the secrets that couldn't be shared even in person with the best of friends but personal private things, like feelings. Millie longed to talk to Cat about Robert. During their recent reunion in London, he had ended their engagement, not because he didn't love her but because he did. He explained that he could be killed in battle and didn't want her tied down. She should be free to meet someone else. Someone else? Where? Who? And why should she, when she loved him? Millie understood Robert was hurting, too, and she didn't mean for it to happen, but they got into a heated argument resulting in his leaving her alone in a hotel lobby.

Millie thought about confiding in Sheila—the two had become rather good friends—but she couldn't when Sheila had more than her own share of problems. With a husband killed in action, a daughter who had been near death for weeks, and a demanding, heartless job in Hut 8, how could Millie consider burdening Sheila with additional woes? Millie's unhappiness paled in comparison. Not that Sheila seemed especially unhappy the few times they met for a cuppa or a meal. Then Sheila seemed determined to stay positive. The only times Millie saw Sheila looking miserable were when she was with Davis Dailey. She leaned on him, resembling, Millie thought, the wilted flowers removed recently from Maureen's room. And she thought the expression on Mr. Dailey's face was more one of tolerance—possibly even endurance—than it was of love. Of course, Millie might be engaging in wishful thinking because she knew how Cat felt about him.

New recruits continued to arrive, and if she had not received assurance Cat would return, Millie would have worried someone else might be assigned to her billet—that she would lose her bunkmate. Before she would permit that to happen, Millie would travel to Inverness herself and drag Cat back. She sighed. Fat chance! No liberty was possible now. Staff was limited, and progress in the Bombe Machine room was slow because of the number of girls who couldn't take the pressure and had to be assigned to other projects. Some had been impacted so strongly, they had to be sent home or to hospital with mental breakdowns. Millie refused to be one of them. She could tell from the brief shakes of Sheila's head that things were not going well in Hut 8, either. Both women had to work two shifts, with only a short break in between. The Allies couldn't possibly lose this war. Wishful thinking again, Millie scolded herself. Of course, it was possible. At this point, it was even probable.

"Unbelievable! Absolutely preposterous! Pure bosh!" So that was the meaning of Operation Barbarossa! Davis threw the wire down on his desk and then, for the fourth time, picked it up and read it again—just as Cat entered the office. Assuredly, he would have had a different reaction to seeing her if the message hadn't been so astounding. "Cat," he said, as if she had never left, "have you heard the news? Germany has attacked the Soviet Union!"

Cat put down her bag and sat wearily next to his desk. "But that's crazy!"

"Crazy, yes, but possibly good news for us. The last thing the Nazis need is another front, and it's doubtful now that Britain will be invaded. The Soviets have left the Axis side and have joined the Allies."

"And now people will consider them our friends," Cat reflected. "They'll soon forget everything that has come before."

"Seems to be human nature, doesn't it?" The room grew silent as neither knew what to say. Finally, "It's good to have you back, Cat."

"I can't stay long, but I'll resume work tomorrow. I bumped into Hugh Foss at the station. He ran me here in a staff car. Millie must be at our flat. I should go see her before doing anything else."

"Soviets be damned! I'll drive you," Davis said.

Well, that's that then, Sheila thought, as she took a quick break from the two shifts she had pulled, using the time to read her mail—a letter from her lawyer, settling Roger's legal matters. He had never drawn up a will. Thus, everything would go to her and the girls. There was more in the bank than she had anticipated. Evidently, Roger had been squirreling money away for years, certainly never intending for her to be the beneficiary. The lawyer also informed her that their flat in London had been completely destroyed by the recent bombing and that Roger had not taken out any insurance. No matter. Earlier, Davis had motored her back to London, and now everything Sheila valued was in the cottage or stored in the Bletchley House attic. While it was uncertain where she and the girls would live after the war, Roger's money alleviated some of the fear. She imagined Davis meant to marry her. He would take good care of her family. Of course there was no spark between them—no energy. Sheila shrugged. Perhaps friendship would be enough.

Better get back to work. After all the breakthroughs a few months ago, so little had happened this spring—few codes broken, the midnight failures commonplace. Although experts had assured them this would happen, even they had become frustrated by the dead spots. A different and even more dangerous kind of blackout had become their reality.

Lee wiped the oil off his hands. He would like a quick shower before going to see Reenie, but he suspected there would be no hot water. He'd clean up the best he could, hoping he would look good to her. Perhaps the two of them, and Pippa and Gemma, could play a card game. Janet would attend a rehearsal of *Pygmalion*, and Sheila had another shift at work. If Pippa and Gemma went to sleep early, he and Reenie might finally be alone.

Noises in the kitchen startled him. His mother? What was she doing here? It seemed almost as if she no longer lived in the cottage. "This is a surprise, Judith."

"Hello. Thought I would make us supper." She gave him a quick peck on the cheek, followed by a wide, ingratiating smile.

"I have plans," he said shortly.

"Oh." She seemed disappointed. "Well, I understand. I should have let you know I was coming. I'll be home for a while."

"I need to get myself cleaned up, Judith."

"Leon, it really would be all right for you to call me Mum again."

"That's okay. I've become used to Judith." He started to leave when she called him back.

"Leon . . . Lee, now that you're eighteen, I have no right to stand in your way if you care to enlist."

"I thought you didn't want me to have anything to do with this war."

"I've changed my mind. We must do all we can to stop the Nazis. After all, they're killing your people."

"My people? You mean because my grandfather, your father, was Jewish?"

"That's right."

"I have a deferment, and I'm needed here." He left the cottage without bothering to so much as wash his hands. Why the turnabout, dear Mum? It was too sudden and too drastic. A dark foreboding crept over him. His life was going to change, and not for the better, he feared.

Letter to Ensign Robert Evans
Somewhere in Africa
From Wren Millie Hanson, HMS Pembroke V
2 July 1941

Dearest Robert,

I want to apologize for becoming so emotional when we last met. Please understand that I was completely unprepared to have you break our engagement, especially after we had been so close. In my shock, I failed to appreciate how very difficult your life has been under such gruesome conditions.

However, I assure you there is no one else—nor will there ever be. I am waiting for you to return, and then we will determine together what is next. I will not give up on us or stop loving you, darling.

I am sorry you were troubled when I refused to relate what I am doing in this war. Certainly your work is more crucial than mine; I'm just doing my bit. But the nature of it requires me to stay silent. For me to divulge anything would be considered treason, as pompous as that may sound. But I never want to lie to you, and, thus, it is better to be quiet.

You are in my prayers, my thoughts, and in my arms when I dream. I will wait for you forever.

Lovingly,
Millie

CHAPTER TWENTY

9 JULY 1941—WOULD ANYONE at Bletchley Park ever forget that monumental date? From block to block, from hut to hut, the good news spread. Everyone knew to keep the secret, but sheer joy after so many months of drudgery could not be contained. Davis attended a small gathering of cryptologists late that night in Hugh Foss's quarters. Dilly gave the toast, as they all lifted their glasses of ale. "On this day, my friends, we conquered Enigma. The German Army's ground-to-air operations on the Eastern Front is a secret no longer."

"To Turing, our esteemed Professor! To wise old Foss! Cheers to sage and sexy Dilly! Let's hear it for highbrow Gordon!" There was even an unexpected cheer for Davis. "For deep, discerning Dailey." Well, it beat the old nickname, Dally, he thought. The cheers became deafening and the speeches slurred as bottles of spirits continued to lift human spirits, until the exhausted warriors dropped to sleep on chairs and floor, and snores were the only remaining sounds.

For the first time since the war began, Davis felt like a full participant— no longer on the outside looking in. In many ways, that's the way it had always been for him, even as a child. An observer, an onlooker—always watching others live. Perhaps now, he finally belonged.

While Davis didn't make it back to his billet, he did manage to reach the office, where he would spend the rest of the night in his comfortable chair. In many ways, he wished Sheila and Cat had been part of the celebration, but—he glanced at the bathroom mirror—perhaps it was just as well they didn't see him looking quite so unkempt.

What a night! Pity that all of Britain couldn't know what had transpired. If only the news could be shared, perhaps the morale that had sunk so low since the fall of Crete would be lifted. Davis knew there was much work ahead. Many keys still needed to be broken, each one requiring more secrecy than the last. The German Naval codes remained a major problem, but cracking them would be easier now. They had graduated from Enigma kindergarten, now able to efficiently turn the Nazi's weapons back on them. As much as he would like to have a greater part in this necessary and fulfilling revenge, his work ensuring security would be more vital than ever.

Lee had his mother back, and he felt like a different person. His premonition of disaster had been a mistake—only his imagination. Mum resumed many of her groundskeeper duties, seemingly with a good will. Lee called her Mum again and enjoyed their frequent meals together.

She did keep bringing up the topic of his enlisting, though. Finally, Lee told her an additional reason for holding back. It wasn't just his responsibilities at Bletchley Park, but also Reenie. He wasn't going anywhere until she was healthy again. Judith dropped the subject.

Oddly, when Lee wasn't around, Judith urged Maureen to return to work. "I heard you were one of our best dispatch riders."

Maureen shook her head. "I wasn't special—just a curiosity because of being the youngest. Like everyone else, I was doing the job I was assigned. If I ever return, it will be because my doctor, mother, and Lee say I may." She was pleased Lee was getting along better with his mother, but she couldn't forgive Judith yet for all those months of neglect. There was something about the woman Maureen didn't—she couldn't put her finger on it—didn't like or trust. But she cautioned herself to remember that Lee used to feel that way about *her* mother, and now he and Sheila were getting along fine. Keeping that in mind, Maureen determined to be more positive about Judith.

The days passed, one after another, and summer was almost over. Maureen was tired of being idle. She no longer expected to ever drive Oscar again, but she was anxious to be doing something. Lee grew tired, too, of her complaining, and came up with a solution both the doctor and Sheila approved. Maureen would help Lee train dispatch riders. Not by teaching them how to ride, but by explaining the parts of the bikes, showing how to make simple repairs, and how to take inventory before traveling. Most importantly, informing them of some of the pitfalls awaiting them if they did not follow procedure. She soon confided to her students that she had once stopped for a break before completing an assigned mission and that the repercussions could have been serious. "Never ever make my mistake," she said. She also warned them of the danger of blackouts. "You must complete your mission entirely and reach wherever you are spending the night before darkness falls. Let me be your example of what can happen." When she explained why she was no longer a dispatch rider, they looked at her in horror. "And don't be thinking you'll be fine if the moon is bright and the sky is cloudless. If there are no protective barrage balloons, you'll be sitting ducks for the Luftwaffe." Although her students were older than she, they nodded solemnly with respect. Maureen discovered she was a good teacher and was happy to be doing something positive again—and to be helping Lee.

Cat would have been astonished to learn that she and Dilly Knox had similar doubts, or at least some of the same questions, about Davis Dailey—not that either of them thought he was less than honorable. He just seemed to know too much for someone in his position. When Cat related her experience accompanying Admiral Sinclair to interview the farmer, David McLean, she could tell Dave already knew about it. He caught himself, pretending he was hearing of it for the first time, but she could tell he was . . . well, not lying exactly, but not telling the truth, either. Supposedly, Dave was just an American who had come independently to Bletchley Park, hoping to crack codes but didn't get his wish. Had he suddenly become an authority on British Intelligence? Surely, that was absurd, but she remembered it was Dave who had told her that Admiral Sinclair was MI6. Never mind that he shouldn't have told her, how did *he* know it?

Others, too, of seemingly higher rank—including Dilly Knox, Hugh Foss, and Alan Turing—seemed perplexed when receiving orders directly from Dailey. Sure, he'd been invited to meetings, and, yes, he was kept informed of Enigma decrypts. Gordon Welchman had told them Davis was an expert, who would have been more involved if he weren't an American. Must keep up appearances until the U.S. officially joined them, Welchman said. But what else was going on? So many things just didn't add up, such as Dailey being assigned a staff car. They didn't have one. Dailey had met Winston Churchill in London, while they only encountered the great man when he made a rare visit to BP. And why did he make so many trips to parts unknown? Who are you, really, Davis Dailey? Both Cat and others wondered.

However, those were suspicious times. Everyone at BP felt it. Sheila did, every time someone asked a question that could be construed as nosy. Any time someone was spotted in a place she didn't think they belonged, she had doubts, questions. It didn't help that the war news was dreadful. After that thrilling break-through in July, the majority of codes were cracked now, with the resulting secret information, code-named Ultra, making a huge difference in battles won and lives saved.

At the same time, the news leaking out about the Nazis' SS mass murder operations was horrifying. In spite of all attempts at secrecy, everyone seemed aware of the unbelievable atrocities. Even Gemma, in tears, asked Sheila, "They aren't killing babies, are they, Mummy? Surely they're not killing the babies."

Sheila held her close—"No, of course not, darling"—knowing she was most likely telling a lie. But, truly, the news must be false. How could anyone plan to murder millions of innocent people?

But secrecy was critical. If the Nazis were to discover their cyphers were broken now as a matter of routine, they would increase the settings again. Ultra decrypts must be disguised to look as if they had come from spies working abroad. To safeguard the work at BP, sometimes lives that could have been saved weren't. In spite of successes, this was disheartening, and a dark black cloud had descended on all of them at BP. No point dwelling on it, Sheila, she told herself. You are not in charge. Get back to work. As odd as it seemed to try to help the Soviets, they must find some hint of the Nazis' plans for Leningrad.

Millie dragged herself to the small flat on Wilton Avenue, where she would try for a small meal and a little sleep before forcing herself to return to that cursed Bombe Machine. Truly, she was starting to loathe it. Her hands stung from the deep welts caused by the cords and wires, and her brain ached in confusion from lack of sleep. She wondered if she would ever free her nostrils from the stench of oil or rid herself of the throbbing headaches due to the incessant din of the machines. Several workers were on medical liberty because of nasty, oozing boils near their eyes. They tried to keep clean and to avoid touching their faces, but the combination of oil, dust, mold, and fatigue was not a good one. They grew weary, forgot—and rubbed their eyes. A few of Millie's friends were so worn out, they were sent home for extended stays. She hoped the rumors of suicide weren't true but feared they could be. Such hellish times!

The small town of Bletchley should have been deserted that early in the morning, but because of the comings and goings of Bletchley Park workers, was not. What must the residents think of us? Millie wondered. They knew better than to ask questions, but occasionally someone would anyway. Millie always claimed to be a telephone operator. Well, in a way she was. Strangely, the tasks were similar. What with connecting all those wires and worrying about plugs and numbers, the bombe machine must be like the most difficult telephone board ever invented, with the goals of both—communication. Maybe that's what she'd do after the war, Millie thought. Work for the telephone company. She'd be quite good at it, actually. The idea didn't appeal to her, but if she and Robert were finished . . . The most common cover up for Bletchley Park, though, was to claim it was a radio station. Not a bad cover, although Millie doubted anyone believed it.

So much of the community had been commandeered for billets. The houses on Wilton Avenue, where Millie and Cat lived, could accommodate at least 244 women. Millie wasn't sure whether sheer luck or Mr. Dailey was responsible for the flat she shared with Cat. They had much more room than many boarders, who often complained of their hosts depriving them of good food, water, or heat. Millie and Cat even had their own tiny galley of a kitchen and didn't have to go far to find a loo. They also didn't have to rely on occasional shower privileges at Bletchley House. She must stop feeling sorry for herself.

"Cat said we'd each have a fresh egg today," Millie whispered as she fell into bed.

Entry from Maureen Bradshaw's Diary
25 August 1941

Something strange happened today, and I am not certain how to deal with it—or if I should. I have been taking regular walks around the lake and because the day wasn't terribly hot, I thought I would go a little farther. I wasn't quite ready, though, and needed to rest, so I went into Bletchley House, hoping to see Lady Katherine. In the entrance hall, I saw Lee's mother going into Mr. Dailey's office. There was nothing wrong with that, of course, but I had just seen Mr. Dailey and Cat down by the lake, so I decided to let Mrs. Jessup know where they were. When I opened the door, she turned around quickly, looking guilty. She seemed ready to open a file cabinet drawer. She made light of it, telling me she was just looking for Mr. Dailey. I told her where he was, and she took off. Then I tried to open the drawer. It was locked. I changed my mind about seeing Lady Katherine and went home instead.

Now what? Was that enough to warrant a report? It was probably innocent. Certainly Mrs. Jessup couldn't be a German spy, and surely I couldn't hurt Lee by suggesting such a thing. He is so happy that his mother is a mum again. But there was something strange about seeing her go through that door. It reminded me of something I can't quite grasp.

Lee thinks I'm pushing myself too hard with my walks. My foot isn't healing right, and I walk funny. The doctor says my ankle might have been set wrong—that someday it may be need to be re-broken and set again. I made it quite clear—and Mum and Gram backed me—I will not be going into a hospital for a long time. My stay at Royal Hospital in Worcester nearly killed me, not that anyone was at fault.

It's grand to work with Lee, though. He says I'm as good as he at training new recruits. That isn't true, but I am pleased he thinks so. Over a year has passed since we arrived at Bletchley Park—the greatest year of changes I've ever known. As far as my family goes, the changes have been for the better, other than my accident and father's dying, of course. But for the rest of the world, probably not. It is in a terrible mess right now. Everyone wishes the United States would join the fight. We need help!

Since this is turning out to be a war diary—who knows I may be famous someday—I should write an update on what is happening, other than just saying the world is a mess. But it's difficult because it is so dreadful. As much as England is suffering, we are lucky in comparison to people on the Continent. We've heard that the Nazis are making Jews wear yellow stars and that they're putting them into concentration camps, probably killing them in horrible ways. The cruelty can scarcely be believed. There are Jewish people working at BP. Here, they've always been just normal people—like everyone else. Now their faces are devoid of all expression. Do they wonder whom they can trust? "Me," I want to tell them. "Trust me!" But why should they, and how could I convince them? I couldn't. So, I will continue to smile and wish them a good day. And then pray a lot before I am finally able to fall asleep at night.

CHAPTER TWENTY-ONE

THE SMALL BUT VERY FINE Bletchley Park Orchestra had started to play the overture, "Robin Adair," a song Jane Austen herself used to play and sing. Backstage, Pippa sniffed the fragrances of so much expensive before-the-war perfume that they almost drowned out the unpleasant smell of the greasepaint smeared on her face. Her costume, a long gown the color of peaches, with an empire waist, made her look so much older than almost fourteen. She loved the dress and her ringlet hairstyle and wished she could wear her hair like that always. For the first time in her life, she was pleased by her height. Otherwise, she might not have been cast as Kitty in *Pride and Prejudice*. In truth, Pippa thought the director must have been desperate, but Gram told her it was an honor to be chosen and a tribute to her talent. "Me, talented?" Pippa had never thought she was good at anything before, except maybe taking care of pigeons.

Such a thrill, listening to the murmured voices and rustling of programs coming from the audience—until there was a different thrill, coming from her stomach, making her feel rather nasty. Then Gram made it worse by peeking into the dressing room Pippa shared with the other actresses. "We're sold out. SRO!" Gram whispered. Pippa knew that stood for Standing Room Only. It would be the first time the Bletchley Park Dramatic Society had experienced a full house. In some ways, the plays were even more popular than the pictures, although Pippa was pleased cinemas were no longer restricted as they were at the beginning of the war. Some of the movies were wonderful, especially from America, such as the one by Walt Disney called *Dumbo*, but most of them were about the war and terribly depressing. And before you saw them, you had to watch all those war newsreels that brought you down again. The plays had no newsreels; you could watch them and forget about your troubles. There. The audience was singing "God Save the King." Soon, the improvised curtain would open. Oh, dear, she felt like she was back in school and didn't know the answer. What was her first line? Pippa struggled to remember.

Gemma was well aware of how nice she looked and glanced slyly at her classmates to make sure they noticed, too. Pippa had fixed Gemma's hair in almost the same style as hers, although not so grand because her hair wasn't as long. Ever since becoming an actress, Pippa had become a much nicer big sister. Maybe Gemma would go on stage someday, too—until she fell in love, of course. A girl could never be certain of what she was going to do until she fell in love. She would be an even better actress than Pippa, the way she was always better at everything. Meanwhile, playing with her friends was more fun, and going back to school was lovely. She wasn't afraid of strangers anymore. And the teacher wasn't nearly as strict as Lady Katherine.

As soon as the anthem was over, Sheila sat back next to Gemma, who was proudly stroking the party dress Janet had created. It was a lovely red velvet Sheila suspected came from one of Bletchley House's old draperies, no longer needed because of the blackout curtains. It was quite amazing how resourceful they had become. And how fortunate they all were that Sheila's mother and Lady Katherine had become such fast friends.

Sheila watched the great lady welcoming the audience, calling them her honored visitors. Would their lives be so pleasant if it weren't for Lady Katherine's kindness? She reminded them that ticket proceeds would go to the poor orphans who had been evacuated from the coastal towns, now living in their vicinity. "And thanks to all of your ration point contributions, you'll be served a proper tea during intermission." For that, she received hearty applause. Then, before the curtain opened, she read the familiar words. *It is a truth, universally acknowledged, that a single man in possession of a good fortune, must be in want of a wife.*

Sheila supposed that must be true of Davis, although she didn't know if he had a good fortune. She was sure he wanted a good wife and certainly deserved one. A fine man indeed but not the one for her—and she wasn't the one for him. She owed him the courtesy of telling him soon.

Her mouth dropped when Pippa entered. How lovely she looked, tall and slim, with her dress and hair so elegant and make-up that emphasized her beautiful dark eyes. How could they ever have considered her homely? Sheila still couldn't understand how Pippa could act when she could barely read the script. But Janet assured her that with Katherine's help, Pippa was managing fine.

Then she spoke her first line. Why, the child was excellent! They had missed what must have been inside her all along. Much of that had been Roger's doing—as well as her own ineptness at standing up for her children. From talking with Lady Katherine, she was fairly certain Pippa had some kind of retardation. She shuddered, thinking of the horrible time Roger had flung Pippa to the floor when she was only an infant having a tantrum. She had never told anyone about that and probably never would. Nothing good would come of it now. It was too late.

A refreshing change from tragedy, Davis thought, settling back in his seat in the ballroom, the perfect setting for this period piece play. He would try to permit himself a brief escape from the horrors of the last ten days. On September 19, the German army had captured Kiev, and while the BP code breakers had received and passed on some information, there was little anyone could do to stop what happened next—the Babi Yar Massacre. Nearly 34,000 Jewish men, women, and children had been executed, machine gunned into a ravine just north of the city, before receiving the final degradation, being covered with dirt and rock. Impatiently, he rubbed away the tears of sorrow and weariness that had become habitual. He must pay attention to right here, right now.

Could there be any greater contrast between Kiev and this frivolous Jane Austen performance? No, he scolded himself, he shouldn't think like that. After all, the Napoleonic Wars were going on when Austen was writing. Perhaps it hadn't been all that different back then. Perhaps Jane Austen, too, realized that without light, happy events to distract them, they would surely go mad.

Davis grinned when he thought of Churchill's recent statement about the workers at BP. He called them the geese that laid the golden eggs but never cackled. Early days, Prime Minister, he thought, but the cackling will certainly be kept to a minimum with a Cat on the prowl. And may we continue to lay those eggs, he thought, although so few people here truly knew what was at stake. Every person in this room had an assignment, which they did without question, assured by superiors that they made a difference.

Seated alone at the rear of the house, Davis was able to watch two women as well as the play. Sheila and Cat. Did he love Sheila? He was becoming more and more unsure. Yes, he admired her for all the difficult, careful work she was doing in Hut 8, and he certainly found her desirable. Something was missing, though—something that mattered. Perhaps he loved her entire family but was not in love with the head of that family. He could see Cat seated with Millie in the third row. Occasionally, he noticed her looking back at him, as if wondering how he was enjoying the performance— perhaps even worrying that he might be dwelling on the sinking of HMS Ark Royal, sunk at Gibraltar on the 13th, but not Babi Yar. He had tried to keep the details of the massacre from her.

He smiled, and she gave him a slight wave, looking relieved. That was the thing about Cat. She cared about how he reacted. They were interested in the same things and had such jolly times together. When she was away, especially that one time, he had felt rather empty. But that wasn't love, was it? She was a bonny lass from Scotland, eleven years his junior, who would go home to her grandfather after the war. Where will home be for you then, Dave? He couldn't help wondering.

Then the crowd roared with laughter, and Davis returned to the play. Janet Hill was magnificent portraying Lady Catherine de Bourgh. If the rest of the players didn't rise to the occasion, she would surely steal the show.

In the distance, Davis heard the *ack-ack* sounds of anti-aircraft—so common now he and others scarcely noticed and just kept on keeping on with their business. Right now, their business was applauding this fine effort. Davis joined the rest of the audience in a standing ovation.

Letter from Ensign Robert Evans to Wren Millie Hanson, HMS Pembroke V
Sent from Cardiff General Hospital
30 November 1941

Dearest Millie,

As you can see from the return, I have been sent home and am now at Cardiff General receiving proper care. Nasty case of malaria picked up in Africa. Worst luck. A bit touch-and-go for a while. It's hard to tell now whether or not I shall return to action. I haven't decided yet what I wish.

I do not want to worry you excessively, but if you could manage to swing liberty, it would do my heart good to see you, not that I would blame you in the least if you no longer wanted to see me. I thought I was acting for your own good when I released you from our engagement, but I realize now I succeeded only in being cruel—as well as a stupid fool.

All my love,
Robert

CHAPTER TWENTY-TWO

CAT HELPED MILLIE PACK BEFORE walking with her to the Bletchley Railway Station. She might have found a ride, but there was plenty of time, and they needed to talk, even if it was mostly small talk.

"I'll miss you, Millie."

"And I you, Cat. It's hard to say how long I will be gone. The terms of my compassionate leave were generous. It seems Robert was a hero before contracting malaria—fancied himself as a latter-day Scarlet Pimpernel."

In spite of her worries, Cat could tell how proud Millie was. "Both of your families went to America. Where will Robert go?"

"Once he's released from hospital and accepts that he will not be going back to the front? I'm not sure. He has an elderly cousin living in Flintshire; he might go there. He has a long recovery ahead of him. If he is well enough to travel, perhaps he will join his parents in America, and I can follow once the war is over."

The women sighed. When the war started, everyone had assumed it would end in a few months. Now it was such a part of their lives, they felt it would be with them always. At the station, Cat bought a platform ticket for a penny, so that she would be able to remain with Millie for as long as possible.

After embracing, promising they would be friends forever, Millie boarded the steam train for the long journey to Cardiff. Cat watched until it was out of sight, and wondered. When would she see Millie again?

Remembering that she had forgotten to pick up a current train schedule, Cat re-entered the station, where she saw Judith Jessup, Lee's mother, standing at the ticket booth. Cat could hear the thumping sound of the date stamp and saw the agent handing her the thick, green cardboard ticket, indicating that Mrs. Jessup had purchased a return in third class. Might as well be friendly, Cat thought, starting toward her.

"There you are, luv. One out and back to Worcester."

Cat stopped at the agent's words. Worcester? So far away and where Maureen Bradshaw had had her accident. Those tickets were expensive and not always easy to obtain, especially if one weren't in uniform. How extremely odd!

Quickly, she left the station, taking care not to be seen. Unbidden came a startling, disturbing thought—the letter J. Edith had said that was the only initial they needed. Every person, whose first or last name began with J, had been re-vetted, but Cat had never thought of Judith Jessup—the daughter of Lord and Lady Leon, who wasn't actually involved in war work. Certainly she couldn't be the elusive J. Impossible! But Cat was learning there was no such thing as impossible. She wasn't sure what to make of the situation but decided to act upon a hunch. What would Maureen's reaction be when she learned Judith was heading to Worcester?

All was in a dither at the stable yards garage, where Maureen was trying to comfort Lee. "We'll find it. It must be here somewhere. Let's look harder. You left for only a second."

"That's all it takes, Reenie. Just a second. I can't believe I was so careless!"

Cat walked in on this. "What's the problem?"

Lee groaned. "A missing pouch for a dispatch rider. I've been looking for close to an hour. I walked away for less than five minutes because I mistakenly thought I heard my mother, but when I returned it was gone."

"Why don't you retrace your steps to see if you took it with you by mistake," Cat suggested.

It was a good idea, so Lee rushed out immediately.

"You weren't around, Maureen?"

"Unfortunately, no, I just got here. Did you want to talk to Lee?"

"No. I wanted your impressions about something." Cat described seeing Judith Jessup purchase the ticket to Worcester. "Any idea why she'd go there?"

"Worcester? Oh!" Maureen sat quickly, trying to abate an attack of vertigo—perhaps even a faint.

"Maureen? What's wrong?"

"Dizzy. I don't know. Lightheaded."

"Shall I fetch Lee?"

"Just a minute. Let me think." Maureen breathed deeply, closed her eyes, and watched images begin to appear. Standing in a doorway . . . going through a doorway . . . going into a building . . . It all came back. No wonder she had been unsettled by the sight of Lee's mother going into Mr. Dailey's office. Still shaking, she told Cat everything she could remember about both incidents.

"The pouch!" Cat exclaimed. "We must tell Mr. Dailey at once!"

When Lee returned, the stable yards were empty, and he was left with worry, not only about the missing pouch, but also about why Reenie hadn't waited for him.

After the staff car arrived, Cat insisted Maureen sit up front with Dave. "You must give directions," she said.

Maureen followed orders but shook her head. "I'll do my best, even though it was too dark to see much. This is crazy. Mrs. Jessup couldn't have taken the pouch."

"I agree that it's improbable." Davis started the car. "But crazy things seem to go with the territory these days. Cat's hunches are often right on target, though. Let's pray that this time she's wrong."

In spite of taking several wrong turns and needing to backtrack on the narrow, twisted roads of Worcester's Shambles, Maureen finally recognized the Dragon Inn. Because delayed trains had become the norm, they arrived well before Judith did. Davis showed the desk clerk his credentials and gave Judith's description. After hearing the clerk say Judith was a frequent visitor to a room on the second floor, Davis, Cat, and Maureen took the stairs and found a place to hide around a nearby corner where they could observe the room without being noticed.

An uncomfortable three quarters of an hour passed. Just as they were about to give up, they heard the creaky elevator stop, followed by quick footsteps coming down the hall, and soon there was Judith, knocking on the door. Maureen watched in horror as a man opened it, held out his hand, and Judith pulled an unmistakable pouch from her satchel. Maureen just managed to control a gasp. She had been hoping against hope she was wrong.

Once Judith handed over the pouch, Davis drew out a gun and with very little fuss arrested both of them. Judith stared at Maureen as Davis led them away. "Please take care of my son," she whispered.

Maureen followed the group out. How do I tell Lee his mother is a spy for the Germans?

Not a Nazi spy, Davis explained later. "She was working for the Soviets. Not in an important capacity, up until the attempted delivery, but had she been successful, she would have earned much acclaim."

"The Soviets? Aren't they our friends now? They've joined the Allies."

"Having a common enemy doesn't make us friends, Maureen," Cat said, her first words in some time. She hadn't quite overcome her shock at realizing Dave carried a gun.

Lee's face was ashen. "It makes a sick kind of sense. She was so against the war until Germany attacked Russia. Then she insisted we had to go out there and win. I guess that's why she wanted me to enlist. Suddenly, I wasn't so important . . ."

Davis didn't know when he had felt so sorry for anyone, and he thought again of Dante. The Nine Circles of Hell, and the ninth, the worst sin of all, was betrayal. He put his hand on Lee's shoulder. "You had no idea, Lee?"

"No, Mr. Dailey, but in retrospect, she was so bitter about not inheriting the property after living in BP her entire life. She felt it was unfair. It was, of course, but that it should have led to this . . ."

Maureen wanted to hold him and would have had they been alone. "What do you think will happen to her?"

His eyes filled. "It was treason, Reenie. She'll be tried, convicted, and then punished as a traitor, and there's nothing I can do about it."

The next day, Leon Herbert Jessup, grandson of Lord Herbert Samuel Leon, enlisted in the Royal Navy.

"Why?" Maureen sobbed. "You have valuable work to do here. You have reserved occupation status. We all need you. I need you."

"You must carry on for me, Reenie. I've taught you all I know, and you're every bit as capable as I am."

"But I'm not, Lee. I can't do it without you."

"Going out there and fighting for England is my only way to make amends for what my mother has done."

"No!"

Lee held her tight. "Yes, I must. You see, darling, I can never live here again. I'll return, Reenie. Then we'll be married, and I'll find the right place for us. I promise."

They embraced, no longer able to look at each other or to share their hopeless, wounded thoughts. And soon Lee was gone, taking her heart with him.

Letter from Lady Katherine Sinclair to Admiral Sir Hugh Sinclair
Delivered by secret dispatch
2 December 1941

Darling Hugh,

I imagine you have heard our latest dreadful news. Since you are hit by the unspeakable more than once on a daily basis, I should be more specific. Judith Jessup, mother of my student, Lee Jessup, has been arrested for attempting to pass secrets to a Soviet agent. Hugh, she is the daughter of Lady Fanny and Sir Herbert Leon! It truly must be a mistake. If possible, and I know I may be asking too much, would you try to launch an investigation? Lee is devastated and has enlisted in the Royal Navy. He is such a sensitive young man I worry about what military action will do to him, and he already has an important position at BP. We all wish for him to stay, but he swears he will never live here again. The young lady who cares for him, my student Maureen, is heartbroken, especially since she is the one who reported Judith. Maureen's family and I are having a difficult time convincing her she is not responsible. Even Lee does not blame her. But she persists in wrapping herself in guilt. If there is anything to be done, please try.

Keep well, my dearest, and come see me soon.
Your Katherine

Letter from Admiral Sir Hugh Sinclair to Hon. Lady Katherine Sinclair
Delivered by secret dispatch
4 December 1941

My dear Katherine,

An investigation is taking place, but don't get your hopes up, dearest. While the situation is not as serious as it would have been had Mrs. Jessup delivered classified information to a German agent, she still, in all likelihood, will be found guilty of treason. The pouch, had it fallen into wrong hands, could have cost many lives. The agent she met was someone we have been watching for a long time, well before the Soviets switched sides, and he might not be what he seemed. You may tell young Maureen that Mrs. Jessup would have been captured eventually, although probably not before she had done a great deal of damage. Maureen acted as a good British citizen, and I hope Lee will not hold it against her. As hard as it is, I do understand the choice he made, and we must respect him for it.

The situation in North Africa is quite grave at the moment, but after Monty's performance at Dunkirk and successes at El Alamein, we have high hopes for him (no matter what Churchill may think). It may be some time, my dear, before I am able to return to BP. But know that I think of you always with love.

Be brave, my darling,
Hugh

CHAPTER TWENTY-THREE

7 DECEMBER 1941. CAT WONDERED if Dave had heard the news and, more, how he would take it. She found him seated at his desk, head down.

"Dave?"

Davis stood quickly. Then, without either saying another word, they were in each other's arms, where they stayed for several long minutes. When he released her, both were shaking, and tears were streaming down Dave's face.

"I ... I wanted to be sure you'd heard," Cat said.

"I prayed that something would happen to awaken my country. But ..." He pulled a handkerchief from his pocket, trying to control his emotions. "The U.S. is certain to declare war now."

"That part at least may be good news," Cat agreed. Truly, there was no need for Dave to blame himself. His prayers hadn't caused this. "Perhaps, we shall see things happening now."

"But at such a cost. Pearl Harbor bombed ... So unexpected ... So many lives ... I never dreamed or wanted it to be this way. I ... I know some people stationed there. I ...." He held the handkerchief to his mouth, waiting for his lower lip to stop trembling. Should he really be surprised— so caught off guard? Why didn't anyone see this coming? He'd always known it would take something catastrophic to spur Washington into action. Now if only they would take up the battle against Hitler, as well as retaliating for Japan's disastrous move.

They sat together on the sofa, their heads close together. Neither saw Sheila, who had taken a break to see how Davis had reacted to the news. She watched them carefully and gave a soft whistle. So that's the way the wind is blowing, she thought, before leaving quietly.

8 December, the United States and Britain declared war on Japan. 11 December, Hitler declared war on the United States. It was time for Davis to return to Wormwood Scrubs to consult with Gene Bifford, who now had an important position in MI5, the branch in charge of in-country espionage. Who would have dreamed back when they were college chums that someday they would be reunited like this? Biff wasn't the only person Davis needed to see. More important was a meeting with Wild Bill Donovan, concerning their work with OSS, the Office of Strategic Services, and the non-military intelligence service they were forming. "There are still many skeptics," Donovan had warned the last time they met, "but such a unit is necessary, and the sooner the war in Europe is brought to an end, the sooner it will be up and running." The time may be coming soon, the committee had all agreed.

"With the stars and stripes finally on board, that time is now!" Davis grabbed a briefcase and headed to the staff car. He would park it at Bletchley Railway Station, though. His petrol allowance was more limited than ever, so he would take the train to London.

January that year was all about the Americans, Pippa decided. On New Year's Day, the bells rang with renewed optimism for 1942—everyone was pleased to say goodbye to awful 1941—and also for a declaration signed by the Allied nations, agreeing to form a United Nations as soon as the war ended. Nations would finally work together to bring peace to the world. Pippa supposed it wouldn't be that simple, but it sounded splendid, and she and others were filled with hope. Some said the war would be over in a few months, now that the Americans were involved. Others shook their heads and said it could last years more because no one should underestimate the Japanese. Pippa didn't know any Japanese people and decided not to estimate them at all— under or over.

The Americans arrived in Britain toward the middle of January, and suddenly they were all over the place—even at Bletchley Park. They brought smiles, good spirits, and candy, all of which had been in short supply. One soldier gave Pippa a box of Chicklets Chewing Gum. "Here's some gum, chum," he said. She didn't really like the feel or the flavor, but the yellow box was so pretty she planned to keep it forever as a grand souvenir.

Rations were better once the Americans came. Pippa was glad because she was getting sick of baked beans on toast, sometimes even for breakfast. And the Americans were so funny. They ate everything, even rice pudding, with a fork. Sometimes they tried to copy the English way of eating, but they could never figure out how to handle knives and sometimes dropped them onto the floor. All laughter stopped, though, when they showed up at the lake. They were ice skating experts—even better than Mr. Dailey! But mostly they didn't show off and were happy to give pointers and lessons to the children.

Pippa was the youngest worker at BP, a fact that made her proud. When she wasn't doing schoolwork, she was helping Maureen with the motorcycles. Maureen didn't talk much; she was deeply upset about Lee being gone. Pippa missed him, too. Taking care of pigeons with Lee was more fun than with Mr. Carroll, although he was ever so nice letting her have a proper funeral for Mary of Exeter.

Pippa continued studying with Lady Katherine, even though she could have gone back to the Bletchley Village School, now that evacuees were included in the regular classrooms. Gemma, newly turned eleven and able to walk back and forth by herself, had returned and was happy with her many new friends.

Pippa didn't make friends easily, especially if they taunted her backwardness, calling her stupid, but she also considered Lady Katherine's feelings in her decision to stay. Her teacher couldn't be enjoying working with glum, unhappy Maureen anymore and was certain to miss Pippa if she were to leave. Once Pippa overheard Lady Katherine telling Reenie she must stop blaming herself for Lee's mother. Pippa didn't understand. Reenie didn't turn Lee's mum into a dreadful spy. She asked Lady Katherine to explain but didn't get a satisfactory answer.

She hardly ever saw her Mum but realized it was not her fault. Sheila worked long hours without complaining. All she said was, "We're starting to have success again." Once Pippa heard her mutter, "That's one U boat that won't do any damage." Mum looked around to see if anyone was listening, but Pippa pretended she hadn't heard a word.

Sometimes Pippa wondered where they would live after the war, but she didn't dwell on it. She, Mum, Maureen, and Gemma couldn't go back to their old flat off Tavistock Square because it wasn't there anymore. She was certain Gram would stay with them wherever they lived. Surely she wouldn't want to return to Nottingham and live alone. Perhaps Maureen and Lee would be old enough to get married, but Lee said he'd never live in Bletchley Park again. What would happen to everyone else? Lady Katherine would move back to her husband in London, and Cat to her Gramps in Scotland. They might never see her again. Would Mr. Dailey go back to America? Pippa used to think he'd marry Mum, but now she didn't think so. Almost everything was perfect in Bletchley Park, but Pippa was old enough now to know that nothing lasts forever.

Telegram from Inverness County Hospital to
Wren Catriona MacLaren, HMS Pembroke V
20 January 1942

Bruce MacLaren admitted Inverness County Hospital—Stop—heart
attack—Stop—Come at once.

CHAPTER TWENTY-FOUR

D AVIS PLACED CAT'S BAG INTO the boot of the staff car. Without speaking a word, he drove her to Bletchley Railway Station, just in time to meet the train leaving for Glasgow Central. There, he handed her a package containing magazines, sandwiches, and a small bag of boiled sweets, wondering if she would even open it.

They made brief eye contact. Although Davis longed for it, the magic moment of being in each other's arms did not occur again.

Cat turned as she entered her compartment. "I'll be back," was all she said.

Davis gazed at the endless line of tracks—long after the train was out of sight.

PART TWO

Nothing Lasts Forever

Letter from Wren Millie Hanson
To Wren Catriona MacLaren, HMS Pembroke V
29 April 1942

Dear Old Cat,

Such a long while it seems since you cheered me off at the railway station. I bring you news, whether good or not time will surely tell. Robert has improved enough to be moved. His doctors feel he should go to America, where there is an excellent hospital for the treatment of malaria near where my parents are living. I am not allowed to say when, where, or how this will take place, but I may tell you that I am going with him and will be employed. Now that the Americans are fighting along with us, I am permitted to do service there. It seems that what I learned while stationed with you on HMS Pembroke V will be useful. I will become an instructor of a rather unusual subject.

Cat, you must know how sorry I was to learn of your grandfather's health problems and that he is no longer living at home. Such a dear man, I count myself fortunate to have met him and pray I will see him again someday. How wonderful that you were able to assist him in the move. I'm sure the two of you managed to have a jolly good brawl before he went into the convalescent hospital. Too bad it became necessary for your home to be turned over for billets. I am wondering where you will stay when you make the trip north again.

You must feel very much alone, and I wish I were able to offer more comfort. You are not alone, though, in that many people are finding themselves displaced and uncertain where home will be once this is over. Might I venture just a "wee" bit of advice? Don't give up on a certain gentleman with the initials D.D. Keep hope alive! Perhaps if you show a tad more interest than you have in the past? Men can be awfully dense about some things. Our paths will cross again, Cat. We're true friends, through and through, no matter the time and distance between us. For now, let's keep faith and write whenever we're able.

Affectionately,
Millie

CHAPTER TWENTY-FIVE

▬▬▬▬▬▬▬▬▬▬▬▬▬▬▬▬▬▬▬▬▬▬▬▬▬▬▬▬▬▬▬▬▬▬▬▬

A T LONG LAST THE BANGING stopped. Davis hoped he would finally rid himself of a chronic headache present for almost a year. The cement blocks, which were to take the places of many of the huts, were complete. They were somewhat more comfortable and definitely more secure, but he now had the troublesome job of deciding which huts would re-locate into what block. Hut 8 had already made it known that they would keep the name Hut 8, even though their work would take place at Block D. And they were not pleased that Huts 3 and 6 would join them, even if there was plenty of space, and their interactions would become more efficient. Alan Turing refused to move his office; not so much as his teddy bear would go into Block D. Well, if anyone had the right to be childish, it was Turing, Davis thought.

He paused to gaze worriedly at Cat, stone-faced, diligently going through files. Her task was becoming more difficult, as was his. So, he supposed, was everyone's. Starting with fewer than a hundred recruits and volunteers, there were now thousands of people to vet and, at times, to fear. He used to know everyone working at Bletchley Park. This was no longer the case.

Cat must have noticed him watching, for she looked up and managed to give him a slight smile of understanding. "I'm okay, Dave. I just need more time."

Time to grieve. Davis understood. Time to mourn the loss of her home, her friend Millie, and most of all, her grandfather as she knew him. It had not been quite four months since she returned from Inverness, although it seemed much longer. Winter had passed, the chilly spring was almost over, and occasionally summer made an appearance. How long had it taken him to get over the loss of his family and home? He couldn't remember—certainly a long while. Barbara hadn't understood; that had been part of their problem. Now he understood Barbara better. He realized finally how hard it was to see someone you . . . cared about . . . suffering. Of course, Cat's beloved Gramps was still alive, but Cat was no fool. She knew he would never be the same, especially since he couldn't remain in his Ness Bank home, where he had more control of his own destiny. Davis nodded to her and turned to the news updates.

It was, as usual, terrible—especially, it seemed, for England. And he had thought it would ease off with the Nazis engaged in defeating that great land mass called Russia. Well, it wasn't quite as bad as 1941, but still . . . Bombing the great cathedral cities, Norwich, Exeter, Canterbury, York. The Nazis were calling them Baedeker Raids, after their tourist guidebooks. The German air force, *Luftwaffe*, planned to bomb every building that had received "three stars." What else other than demoralizing people would that accomplish? No doubt that was exactly what Hitler and his henchmen intended. And to retaliate, the British forces were bombing Cologne. A pity, that. He remembered his college visit to the city's great cathedral. Madness, he thought. What will we have left?

And the worst part, for Davis anyway, was the knowledge that the Allies might have saved some of the cathedrals as well as many lives—but at what some considered too great a price. All intelligence derived from Enigma, called Ultra, was to be used sparingly so that the Germans would not know their ciphers had been broken. Davis was grateful he wasn't in charge of determining the worth of a human being. And back home, American citizens, who happened to be Japanese, were being herded into re-location camps. He hoped that didn't mean what he thought it might. "Madness," he whispered, just under his breath.

Cat looked up, closing the file cabinet. "Got a tough one here, Dave. Afraid I'll need to take a trip to Oxford."

"You want company?" Dave offered, and then shook his head regretfully. "No, I have a meeting. Sorry. Shall I ring for a staff car?"

"I'll take the train, but thanks, anyway. No need to waste the petrol. Now I'm off to see if a certain woman is who she claims to be."

"Perhaps I'll see you later?"

"Perhaps."

Actually, Cat was anxious to get away from Dave and his concerned, soulful glances. She wished she *could* lean on him, she thought, as she walked quickly from the Bletchley House office. Certainly, he had been friendly since she returned, sometimes acting as if he wanted more than friendship. But she must not take a chance. There was always Sheila to consider—Sheila, who was keeping company with a different man now. But once that was over, Dave would go rushing back, true to form. No, Cat had been hurt enough.

She stopped first at the stables to let Maureen know she might not return in time to join her for dinner in the canteen. The younger girl was her best friend these days. Without speaking, they understood each other. Maureen was hurting, too, and while Cat didn't believe misery loved company, it certainly craved compassion—and that they had in abundance. Maureen knew how much Cat missed and worried about Gramps, and Cat knew how much Maureen missed and worried about Lee. No words were necessary.

Because of a request from Lee, backed by Admiral Sinclair, Maureen had moved into Judith's small cottage, inviting Cat, who had lost her billet mate, Millie, to join her. Pippa pleaded to be allowed to come, too, and the three girls were getting the place ready to offer living quarters to a few more young women. Pippa, doing the lion's share of preparation, was excited enough for both Cat and Maureen. "It will be fun," she assured them. "Just like a girls' boarding school but without lessons." In time, Cat thought she and Maureen might be able to share Pippa's enthusiasm.

Pippa moving next door made room for a new resident at Number Two Cottage Stable Yards. Helen Price, who had recently lost her husband, would help her dear friend Janet, still recovering from a spinal injury caused by a bad fall during a dangerous ice storm early February. Helen cooked, nursed Janet, watched the girls, and even sewed costumes Janet had designed. She discovered strength and a certain amount of healing by focusing on people who needed her, rather than on her own losses.

Cat found Maureen, assisted by Pippa, working with a new crop of dispatch riders. A quick whispering of plans to Pippa, and Cat was on her way again.

Pippa signaled to Maureen, who had almost completed the day's training, that she was taking a break to check on Gram. Gram loved visits, especially when she had the opportunity to help Pippa memorize her audition monologue. Ever active, the Bletchley Park Dramatics Society planned on producing Lillian Hellman's *The Children's Hour*, even though (or because) it had been banned in Boston. They didn't believe the play would pose problems at BP and felt quite daring and modern attempting it. The main reason Pippa hoped for a part was to please Gram. Not being able to participate was hard on her, especially since in all likelihood she would have been cast as the grandmother, Amelia Tilford.

"Now, don't get your hopes up about me," Pippa cautioned. "I may be too tall."

"Nonsense," Gram had replied. "Who else could they find as talented as you?"

Silently, Pippa conceded the point. She probably was the best of the young people. The director wasn't going to have an easy time casting the boarding school girls. She also wondered if the audience would be happy with such a gloomy story. Everyone she knew wanted to be perked up a bit.

But Gram would have been a wonderful Mrs. Tilford. Pippa could tell Gram knew that, too. If only . . . Then she had a brilliant idea. Why couldn't Gram do it? Couldn't the Tilfords have a servant push her around in a wheelchair? The servant wouldn't even have to speak; Mrs. Tilford could just snap her fingers or ring a bell. Performances wouldn't be for a few months—everyone was so busy with the war effort—and Gram was getting stronger every day. A part like that would do her worlds of good. Pippa vowed to be brave enough to talk to the director about it. She would make it clear it didn't have anything to do with her being cast. She wasn't terribly keen on having a part at all. Actually, she thought doing this play was a very bad idea. It was all about rumors—not very nice ones—and they certainly had to guard against rumors at Bletchley Park.

Helen Price took a quick peek at her patient. Good. Janet was busy, happily coaching Pippa. Sheila was not yet home from work and even if she were, she would not stay long. Helen was not quite sure when Sheila slept. No matter. Sheila's lack of concern in family matters was Helen's good fortune. While coming here hadn't literally saved her life, it had come bloody close. No more husband, thanks to emphysema, and no more flat in Chelsea, thanks to the Blitz. BP was her new home—for as long as the war lasted, anyway. That day might not be too far away. Helen had read the horoscopes and had seen an especially bleak aspect for Hitler. Good news, that. And her own horoscope said it was a fine day for her to go out and about.

Scratching out a quick note for Janet saying she wouldn't be long, Helen headed for Bletchley Thursday Market. She'd received a tip that sultanas were to be had and with the ration points she had collected, it would mean rice pudding with sultanas and maybe a few raisins. Milk was a bit more plentiful now and more enjoyable than the tinned stuff, not that she was complaining. What else might she serve for supper? Probably just some Bovril meat drink. They were all sick of it, of course, but the pudding would make up for it. Everything was so costly, even if it were available. She felt quite wealthy with seven shillings in her purse but knew it wouldn't stretch far.

All was well at home, Sheila thought, as she met Helen on her way to market and learned that Pippa was with Mum, and Gemma playing with a friend in town. Helen would bring her back after shopping.

"Have a date, dear?" Helen asked, kindly enough.

At least Sheila thought she meant to be kind. Common nosiness, perhaps; she couldn't detect any hidden barbs. "Yes," she said, "and I should freshen up." It was easier to go along with people's assessment of the situation than to explain what was really going on. She wasn't quite sure of that, herself.

Date was the wrong word to describe these meetings with Hamish Fergusson. He was her teacher, also her boss—the latest in a string of supervisors in Hut 8. He worked closely with Dilly Knox and Alan Turing and, like Turing, seemed interested only in her mind. The same couldn't be said for Dilly; "Dilly's Fillies" had become a BP legend. Sheila sighed. She only wished Dilly were still adding to his stable. Lately, he was losing more and more time due to illness, and Mr. Fergusson finally confirmed what she had suspected: Dilly Knox was dying of cancer.

Her relationship with Mr. Fergusson, if it could be called that, had started about a month ago when he called her into his office. She had entered as nervously as Mum heading for a callback. But Mr. Fergusson was smiling, so perhaps it wasn't bad news. "Sit down, Mrs. Bradshaw," he said. They had since graduated to "Sheila and Gus."

After complimenting her abilities to the point of a full-face blush, Gus asked her what she planned to do after the war. "I'll be a typist in a secretary pool, most likely," she said.

"Perhaps you should aim higher."

Sheila was taken back to the time Davis promoted her out of the kitchen, but this turned out to be a different matter altogether. To her astonishment, Gus suggested moving her away from Typex machines to actually interpreting codes and perhaps even helping to determine Ultra's destinations. "Mrs. Bradshaw, you are always among the first to identify the key words. Many of our deciphers have come from your discoveries. I understand that you deserve much credit for our success during the battle of Cape Matapan. You have a gift for determining what's important and what's not, but not, alas, the education required for much of an advancement."

That would be, Sheila knew, her main drawback in ever moving beyond the role of ordinary secretary. She had never attended university. "It might be too late for me to do anything about that now, Mr. Fergusson," she had said, somewhat hurt and disappointed. What was the point of complimenting her if it ended in an insult?

"Wait," he said. "Dinnae get yersel' into a flap. That's where I come in. I'd like to offer myself as a tutor. All we need to do is make sure your science and math skills are up to date and prepare you to take a series of tests. If you pass them—and I think you will—doors will open."

Gus explained the great need for increasing knowledgeable staff at BP. Dilly would become more and more incapacitated as his illness progressed, and Turing was making arrangements to go to the United States to instruct the Allies on the use of the Bombe Machine he and Gordon Welchman had invented. True, new scientists and mathematicians, such as Gus himself, would arrive, but stronger assistants were needed. After giving the matter much thought and some time, Sheila agreed to be tutored. Her incentive— greater chances of employment after the war.

Where to meet Gus was a problem at first, but Sheila confided in Lady Katherine, who offered the Bletchley House library for their studies. They now met the only two evenings a week they didn't have late shifts. Lady Katherine, perhaps seeing herself as a chaperone, usually had a book demanding her attention. This was not necessary—Gus had no personal interest in Sheila—but she found Lady Katherine's presence both amusing and endearing.

Sheila supposed she might have seen Gus as a romantic possibility if the situation were different. He was certainly a fine looking man—red-headed, rustic, and indestructible, he looked as if he'd be more at home trekking through gorse hunting grouse than fussing over the damned Enigma Machine. She did discover the grouse part was correct. Gus owned a large estate south of Oban in the Argyle region of Scotland. He was also a mathematical genius as well as the first man, other than the Professor, who fancied men, to seem more interested in her mind than in her figure and blue eyes. He was offering a future much more promising than that of a mere typist. For now, her studies and his impossible assignments were all she had left after difficult days, and often nights, in Hut 8, as she, too, continued to refer to Block D.

It seemed odd not to be discussing her classes with Davis, but as they often concerned secret operations, Sheila must adhere to the BP rules that forbade any confidences with outsiders. Davis, like everyone else, must think Gus was Sheila's latest conquest. Happily, she and Davis were friends now— good friends—and both of them wanted to keep it that way. The truth of the matter was Davis seemed to care deeply about her entire family. Because he didn't have one of his own? Sheila had no idea.

Lady Katherine had tea waiting for them. They would sit and visit—for just a bit, Gus insisted, and Sheila said a break from brainwork would be most welcome.

"Is Pippa's audition tonight?" Lady Katherine wondered.

"Yes, and Mum is more excited about it than she is."

"I heard they're doing *The Children's Hour*," Gus said. "Excellent play, but not really any good parts for men."

"And would you be interested if there were?" Sheila asked.

"I might, if I had any spare time. Always liked a good Shakespeare at university."

Katherine poured him another cup of tea. "Any you would recommend in particular?"

"*The Taming of the Shrew* would be a good one, as long as I could play Petruchio."

Katherine burst out laughing, and Gus gave her a wink. Sheila didn't know or like Shakespeare much, other than reading *Romeo and Juliet* when she was a fourth form student. She wondered what all the foolishness was about. Lady Katherine and Gus seemed to be taking delight in a private joke.

Excerpt from Maureen Bradshaw's diary
20 September 1942

It's been a long time since I've been able to write anything. While war news is simply dreadful—we're all concerned about the horrid fighting in Stalingrad—personal news has improved, and I feel I can try again, although I am very rusty and may make many grammatical and spelling mistakes. Thank goodness Lady Katherine is not privy to this diary!

The best news is I finally heard from Lee. I feared he was wounded or worse—or so discouraged he no longer cared about me, or anyone here. That was not the case. He hadn't heard from me, either, until ten letters were delivered all at once. He said this made him the brunt of many envious jokes. He also said he'd written often to me, so perhaps I'll be drowned in a deluge as well. No one here will be envious—just terribly, terribly relieved. As soon as I read the precious few pages, I raced around to everyone and read the letter out loud, except for the parts that were just for me. Lady Katherine would be pleased if she could see those secret passages; Lee writes a very satisfactory love letter. If it hasn't been worn away to nothing from all my frequent readings, I will enclose it in this diary where it will stay forever.

That word "deluge." I shudder that I even wrote it—twice. I used to love the sea, especially during our many holidays at Brighton and thereabouts. I even loved storms—so dramatic, the dark, fierce mountains of turbulent rising water. Now I just think of men, floundering, helpless, waiting for death by drowning—and am frightened Lee is one of them.

Enough gloomy thoughts. Back to Lee's letter. He reports that he is fine, although the conditions he is facing are deplorable, and he has witnessed things he will never forget. He is not able to tell me where he is, of course, but I wouldn't expect him to. Nothing in the letter was censored. One thing we've learned well at BP is how to be discreet. Lee was even able to say a little about his mother—that he had heard from Judith and hopes to see her again someday. He didn't say where she was imprisoned, of course, but under the circumstances, mentioning her at all was somewhat risky. I don't know what I hope for Judith—

whatever is best for Lee, I suppose. I don't want her put to death, but I can't forgive her for what she did. Fortunately, my forgiveness or lack of it isn't required.

It's been over two years since we came to Bletchley Park, and I am almost seventeen. I wonder if I would have grown up this quickly if there had been no war and we were still in London. I doubt it. Before the war, seventeen was young, full of parties, pretty dresses, and flirtations. Those days will never happen for me, but that's all right. Now that I know Lee is unharmed and Gram will recover, I am almost happy. No one could or should be truly happy right now.

All of us are horrified by the news we've heard about the treatment of the Jews. At first they were just rumors but now that we've seen a few photographs, no one is pretending any longer. Cruelty beyond anything we've ever known is taking place, and it could happen in England, too. I've never seen Mum or anyone who works in the huts and blocks look more serious or exhausted. And no one looks more drained than the many Jews working here at BP. Our best dispatch rider, Miriam, is scared to death for her family in France. I can't help wishing Lee's grandfather hadn't been Jewish. I worry that because of this, it would be even worse for him if he were captured.

And now for some happy news. My very best friends have become Cat and my own sister, Pippa! We are enjoying creating our own little home in Lee's cottage. Soon we will take in more girls. Cat will smile more, in time, and so will I. We are anticipating some lighter days ahead.

Pippa has done an amazingly kind thing for Gram. She talked with the director of *The Children's Hour*, and Gram is going to play the grandmother—performing in a wheelchair! Gram is thrilled! Pippa was cast as Mary, and thus will be Gram's granddaughter on stage as well as off. Performances won't be for another month. People have so little time now for amusement, including rehearsals. Everyone is busy. I rarely ever see Mum.

I've made an important decision. A lot depends on whether or not I'm able to walk properly again, but I've decided to become a nurse. Davis says there is a hospital in America that might be able to fix my foot, but in the meantime, we're going to find me an additional tutor. Lady Katherine is wonderful with literature, of course, but I am going to need more instruction in science and maths. I am not telling many people about this yet. I don't want to be told I'm foolish.

CHAPTER TWENTY-SIX

"G RAM," GEMMA BEGAN CAUTIOUSLY, "YOU know how some of the people here at BP are ginger beer? How will they feel about the play?"

"What did you say?"

"You know, Gram, the men who like each other instead of girls. Ginger beer."

Janet Hill gasped. "Gemma! Where did you ever hear such an expression?"

"Maybe on the playground. The children talk about some of the men."

"And they use rhyming Cockney slang? Ginger beer?"

"Yes. Those from Southwark and Lambeth do. I don't know what the right word is."

"The right word is . . ." Janet paused, wondering if the word "homosexual" would only create more problems on the playground, where Gemma was certain to share it. Any word with "sex" in it was bound to cause a stir. "Queer" might be better, but not much. She remembered her reaction when Pippa said "fruit." Somehow she didn't think washing Gemma's mouth out would have the desired effect, and they really couldn't spare the precious soap this time. Not with one small bar having to last a whole month now. What should she say to the child? She sighed and gave it a feeble effort. "Well,

Gemma, never you mind what word to use. It's not nice to gossip about people. It would be far better for you to say nothing at all."

"All right, Gram, I won't, but I can't stop the other girls. They just talk and talk. I won't say it anymore if it makes you mad. But why did the Dramatic Society pick the play if it's about something we're not supposed to talk about?"

Janet sighed. She was tired of answering this question. "Because it's a fine play about something that concerns us all—rumors. It's about how two people's lives were ruined because of idle tongues. Think about all the harm rumors can do. We're certainly aware of that at Bletchley Park, aren't we?"

"Yes, Gram. I remember. 'Loose lips sink ships.'"

"Now, do you have any schoolwork?"

"No, Gram. I finished everything at school. It's so easy."

"Well, off you go until supper then."

Janet sighed. She hadn't handled that very well. If only her daughter were a better parent. Gemma's mother should be the one answering the tough questions. But Sheila was either slaving away on secrets in Hut 8, seeing the new beau, Mr. Fergusson, or sound asleep. She seemed to have forgotten her main role—Mother. In Janet's opinion, Gemma was on her own entirely too much, but then she had always been a good child. She gave a brief thought to Gemma not being challenged by her schoolwork—top marks with scarcely any effort. Ah well, everything would be all right, although Janet had been happier when all of the girls were studying with Katherine. Life was more peaceful then.

She returned to her script, although she knew all of her lines—as well as everyone else's. So nice of the director to give her a new script after she had lost her assigned one. Very unusual for her to lose anything, especially something that important. What could have happened to it?

Cat surveyed her cozy new quarters in the cottage and was well satisfied. Claiming what had once been the box room, with space for only one cot, had been a wise decision. Unlike the others, she had no use for doodads. Her few treasures were now stored in Gramps's small attic, since the rest of the house in Inverness was providing billets for the war effort. Here, Maureen and Pippa were bunking together in Lee's old room, and three new girls would share Judith's large suite. Soon they could anticipate good times. How strange it would be, though, to vet people who could become her housemates and possible chums. Wendy Dean, Karen Holmes, Abigail Brooks. Without their suspecting, she must learn everything about them. It didn't seem proper, somehow, and she wished she could ask Dave to do it. But he seemed so troubled lately about his own responsibilities. He had stopped sharing what they were, and she sensed it would not be wise to inquire.

Cat was beginning to relax, though. The ordinary, day-to-day problems weren't hard to handle, and the news from up north was better. Letters from Inverness, both from doctors and even one from Gramps, indicated he was making steady improvement and was no longer confined to a hospital ward. Soon, he hoped to join some of his friends at a retirement home. But the days of just the two of them at the little house on Ness Bank were over. Perhaps she would talk to Dave about taking liberty in a few months, maybe at Christmas time. She needed to see for herself how Gramps was doing. By then, it would be close to a year.

Sheila hurried to meet Gus for their appointment in the Bletchley House library. She was late, she knew, and Gus would not be pleased. She couldn't blame him; he had important work, too. But there were times she wished he were more understanding. It had been a difficult day—and dirty, she mused, staring down at her filthy hands. She hadn't taken the time to wash in her haste to get to Bletchley House. One of the Bombe instructors had come down with a bad cold—that they were all hoping wasn't the flu—and Sheila had to take over instructing new recruits how to fiddle with wire, avoid breathing oil or touching their faces, and all the other nasty chores involved in working with Bombe machines. And she had to pretend it was all so pleasant, although she was fairly certain the women saw right through her. The Bombe Machines were still located in Huts and 11 and 11A, rather than in a more secure Block. Sheila wondered why but didn't voice her concerns. It would do no good.

My, it was cold—even for October. She shivered, hoping she wasn't becoming ill, too. She glanced at her watch. A quarter hour late? Gus would be furious. But, no, she found him standing next to a glowing fireplace, wearing an excited smile. "Sheila!" he cried, giving her a hearty bear hug. "You did it!"

She removed herself from this unexpected embrace. "I did what?"

"Your test results came! Bob's your uncle now, m'dear. You're certain to get a peach of a promotion."

And the tutoring will stop, Sheila thought, suddenly wondering if this were really good news.

"What's wrong, Sheila? You don't look pleased at all."

"Oh, but I am, Gus. Just let me catch my breath. It's been quite a day."

"Right. I heard about the Bombe instructor. It was good of you to help out. Nasty job. Soon, you'll never have to do it again."

Sheila insisted on washing up before another word was said. Until that moment, she hadn't realized how much she had looked forward to these study sessions with Gus, in spite of his being a harsh taskmaster and of her often being the brunt of his wit. That would end now, of course, and she might even have spare time again—in which she would be expected to spend more of it with her children and taking care of her home. Odd how little the idea appealed to her.

When she returned, Lady Katherine had joined Gus and seemed as elated as he. "Sheila, my dear. Well done! Well done, indeed!"

"Thank you," Sheila said. "Thanks to both of you, my prospects are looking brighter. I will miss our library gatherings, though."

"Oh." The smile disappeared from Gus's face. "I hadn't thought of that. You won't need me anymore to keep you swotting away."

He's sad it's over, too, Sheila thought, somewhat in triumph. She sipped her tea, wondering what new twists and turns lay ahead.

"Mail Call! Letters for Bryce, Armstrong, Jessup . . ."

The voice droned on, but Lee dashed forward when he heard his name. Three glorious letters from someplace that was not Hell—also known as

Gibraltar. Taking time to light a rare cigarette, Lee leaned against a rail and opened the envelope that looked the least interesting.

An official envelope, it seemed, from London. Lee stared at the contents and then carefully extinguished his cigarette, the rest to be enjoyed later. It was about Judith. She was dying and wanted to see him. Because of the complexity of the situation, the matter had been turned over to Admiral Sinclair, and Lee had been granted compassionate leave. He needed to speak with his commanding officer about making arrangements to go to a prison hospital in York. York—so far away. "Reenie," Lee whispered. "I need to reach Reenie." Could she possibly go to York, too? Perhaps he could send her a wire once he reached the mainland. A mistake to rely on the undependable, sluggish mail service.

Judith was dying. Why was he thinking only of Reenie? Surely he should be feeling something—certainly sorrow—about his mother. But strangely, he didn't. At least, not yet. For him, it almost seemed as if Judith had already died—at the Dragon Inn. He had no one now except Reenie and her family. He wanted to see all of them, but not at Bletchley Park—not yet, and maybe not ever.

Break was over. Time to go onshore for surveillance duty. Back to the filth and mud. Back to where Kelly had taken a bullet only the day before. And back to numbing boredom—except for times when it wasn't boring, and boredom became something to be longed for.

Letter to Lady Katherine Sinclair, Chairman of the Bletchley Park Recreational Club, from a concerned parent.
10 October 1942

Dear Lady Sinclair,

I hope you will forgive my bothering you, but the following requires your urgent attention. On behalf of the Bletchley Village School Parents' Association, I want to express my concern about the Bletchley Park Dramatic Society's (under the auspices of the Recreational Club) proposed production of that vile play by Lillian Hellman, *The Children's Hour.* While I am unfamiliar with the script, I do not like the shocking accounts I am hearing from my daughter and her friends, who somehow managed to obtain a copy. The parents have met with our headmaster and are unanimous in insisting that this production be removed from your current, or any other, season. We look forward to your return to programs the whole family will enjoy, such as drawing room comedies and light-hearted musical revues.

Kind regards,
Mrs. Henry Cunningham
President of the Bletchley Village School Parents' Association

CHAPTER TWENTY-SEVEN

L ADY KATHERINE SAT WEARILY ON her settee, first taking a sip of tea before responding to their anxious faces. "Well, I did my best," she told Janet and Davis while Pippa, on the other side of the study, tried to blend in. "I asserted over and over that the play is more about rumors and how they spread and destroy people's lives than it is about homosexuality."

"And you succeeded?"

Katherine smiled at Janet, who seemed to have more to lose than anyone. She knew Pippa never expected that the show would be allowed to continue. "No, I'm sorry. Because I'm the chairman of the Bletchley Park Recreational Club, they did listen respectfully, but my vote holds no more weight than anyone else's. I explained how much labor has gone into this production and how demoralizing it would be for our hard BP workers, who were either involved or looking forward to seeing it."

Janet grabbed a handkerchief from her knitting bag.

Pippa joined the group, hoping she wouldn't be sent away. "It's all right, Gram. There will be other plays."

Disappointed, Janet wiped her eyes but patted Pippa's hand. Pippa had become such a comfort. "Why a recreational club should have any say over a dramatic society is beyond me," she said, even though she knew it was a meaningless name chosen for all the extracurricular activities at BP. "Couldn't you have asked the Admiral to interfere on our behalf?"

Katherine shuddered, knowing just a little about Hugh's present activities. "No, it wouldn't be fair to him. He has far more vital concerns right now."

Davis, who knew even more than Katherine, nodded soberly in agreement. Both espionage agents abroad and Ultra decrypts had reported mass murder by the SS, and that Hitler had ordered the execution of all captured British commandos. On top of that, Davis knew the Admiral was dealing with his own failing health. But here and now, the women were worried about a play. Well, perhaps they were right; freedom, in all its forms, was what they were fighting for.

"Couldn't you have mentioned that we have queer people working right here at Bletchley?" Janet asked, continuing to argue.

Davis put war worries to one side. That kind of talk was dangerous and needed to be stopped. "Rather like telling the Nazis that Jews were in their midst," he said. "Well, maybe not that bad, but bad enough. There would be an investigation and probable arrests. And we would lose several people's valuable contributions. No, we must find ways to protect them and to squash all speculation."

"Did the board mention how the school even heard about the play?"

"I'm afraid they did." Katherine told her horrified listeners that the chatter was started by a group of schoolgirls, who managed to spread their tittle-tattle around the community. A group of irate town parents then contacted the Dramatic Society, saying they were appalled we would even consider producing a play, which advocated the illegal and sinful practice of homosexuality.

"Life imitating art, following the theme of the play," Davis said. "A bit ironic, don't you think?"

"Gemma," Pippa said. "Gemma might have been a part of it."

Janet, recalling a recent conversation, said, "I'm sure she was." And all of a sudden she knew what had happened to her missing script. "I need to talk with Sheila—and Gemma." Although she hardly knew how she might approach the child.

"Did the board say anything else, Lady Katherine?" Davis asked.

"Yes, they wish us to submit scripts for their approval from here on out."

Janet sighed. "Back to silly comedies."

That was hardly the case, but the rest knew better than to argue until her disappointment had passed. Gemma! Katherine shook her head. Gemma, overly praised as the perfect child, wasn't that different from other children after all.

Deja vu, Davis thought, as he saw a familiar figure trudging along the road. He remembered the first time he'd offered Sheila a lift into town. Cat had been in the car then. It had been the beginning of their getting to know each other. Davis wished he could go back and start that particular relationship over again. He pulled the staff car next to her, reached over, and opened the passenger door. "Sheila, would you like a ride?"

Gratefully, Sheila sank into the seat. "Thanks, Davis. I would have waited for a bus, but I was able to take a break now."

"Always glad to help, Sheila. You know that. What's the destination?"

"The school again—a message from the principal saying both she and Gemma's teacher wanted to talk to me. I can't imagine why. Her reports have been exemplary."

Davis could give a good guess but decided to let the school authorities handle it. "I've got nothing pressing at the moment," he lied. "Just need to make a quick phone call in the village. I'll wait and run you back, unless you have time for a cup of tea."

"That sounds lovely." Sheila sighed. "I'll make time for it."

"You don't think Mr. Fergusson would mind?"

"Why should he?" She paused. They had reached the school. "Davis, I'll try to explain about Gus over tea."

Davis intended to let her go—to hear the probable complaints that were coming—but decided against it. Better that she be somewhat prepared. "Sheila," he called her back, "before you go inside, there's something I need to tell you."

Sheila sipped her tea and tried to come up with the right words. "You were correct, Davis. The teacher wanted to complain about a group of gossiping girls, of which Gemma was one. There appeared to have been an epidemic. All of the parents are being called to account. The consensus is that it's our fault—that we are not supervising our children well enough. In my case, that's certainly true." Sheila smiled at Davis's expression. "Go on, say what you're thinking. I know you quite agree with them."

"Actually, I was thinking how much you've changed. You're just facing facts and are not being driven by emotion. A different Sheila from the one I knew in the past."

"Although you think I should spend more time with my children."

Davis shook his head. "Everyone who works at BP and has children needs to spend more time with them but can't. I wouldn't presume to judge. You're in an impossible situation. Any idea what you're going to do?"

"Not yet. First, I need to talk with Gemma and see what she has to say for herself." Sheila sighed. "Concerning the other matter, I think I should make something clear, Davis. My seeing Gus had nothing to do with romance or anything social. He was tutoring me."

Davis stared. "Tutoring, Sheila?"

"Yes, he and several other supervisors wanted me to pass some science and math tests. They seem to think I'm capable of more than I'm doing." She grinned. "Well, I did pass—with flying colors. I don't know what that will mean yet in the short term, but it will mean more opportunities once the war is over."

"Sheila, that's wonderful news. Congratulations!"

"Thank you."

"And so you and Hamish Fergusson are . . ."

"Student and teacher or employee and employer—presumably, friends as well. But that doesn't mean . . ."

Davis nodded. "I know, Sheila. You and I are just friends. Good friends, and that is more than enough."

They smiled, both feeling that they finally understood each other.

"We both need to get back to work," Davis said.

"Yes. It won't be easy, but I must take another break today to talk with Gemma. I am no longer comfortable with her attending Bletchley Village School, but I don't think private instruction with Lady Sinclair is the answer either. She is the brightest of my flock and needs greater challenges. And more discipline, I'm afraid, than any of us can provide."

"You may have options, Sheila. Let me think about it. Oh, and don't be surprised if you start seeing me frequently in Hut 8 and in other Blocks and Huts—at least until December." Sheila stared at him. "With Turing leaving for America and Dilly Knox's health worsening, it appears I'll be brushing up on my cryptanalysis skills." And pretending I know nothing about what's been discovered so far, he thought ruefully.

Cat left her cottage to go next door to the Make Do and Mend party. Her shoes were in deplorable shape—soles worn straight through, not enough coupons for new ones. Much more wear on these, and she would be walking barefoot. But Helen had come up with an ingenious way to create new soles. She stopped, though, at the site of a staff car parked outside of Number Two Cottage Stable Yards. The driver gave his passenger a hug before she opened the door and stepped out. Sheila, and the driver was—Dave. Here we go again, she thought. Well, never mind. She had other prospects. Hamish Fergusson had invited her for a drink to share memories of Scotland. She had planned to turn him down but now . . . Repairing her shoes could wait. Instead, she'd leave a message for Gus, accepting his invitation. Why, oh why, were she and Sheila always involved with the same men?

Cat was relieved to see Gus already there, although the Eight Bells had changed since the time she'd waited for Dave. The majority of new workers and people billeted in Bletchley and Fenny Stratford were now women, who were not going to put up with a Men-Only pub, even though the men in town were not especially pleased. But a gentleman was still a gentleman, Cat thought, as Gus pulled out a seat for her. "Glad you could come," he said.

They soon found they had little in common, other than Scotland. For the moment, that seemed enough to Cat. She had never been to Oban, but Gus had made several visits to Inverness, and they reminisced about their favorite shops and pubs.

"Will ye be going home for Christmas?" Gus asked.

She shook her head. "No, I can't get liberty. My boss will be away, and I'm needed here. Perhaps in the springtime . . ."

"Aye. Well, Christmas isn't much of an event in our parts."

"True, but I wanted to see my grandfather. He's not been well."

Both sipped their scotch in silence. Dave's refusal to grant Cat liberty bothered her greatly, although she understood. "I will be away for most of December," he'd said. "I must return to America for meetings in D.C. I wouldn't be comfortable if you were away from the office as well."

Cat agreed, of course, knowing she didn't really have any choice. Gus was correct that Christmas was fairly low key in Scotland. In fact, celebrating it had been legal for only a few years, the Scots Presbyterians leery of anything that might be construed as Popish. After church on Christmas Day, she and Gramps always walked along the river, no matter the weather, and then had a fine dinner at the Caledonian, a fancier splurge than their normal going-out meals at the Station Hotel. While none of those things could have happened this year, and Cat wasn't entirely certain where she would be able to stay, at least she and Gramps would have spent time together.

Not going home until spring was a definite hardship, but Dave insisted that she remain at BP. "Foul weather, crowded trains filled with sick people—really too risky, Cat." He reminded her of the time she'd been gone for weeks.

"What about you?" she asked Gus. "Will you journey home for Christmas?"

"No, but it doesn't matter. There is no one in Oban for me right now."

They returned to their drinks and their thoughts. "But I have a wee thought, lassie." Gus's eyes sparkled with excitement.

"It must be a bit more than a wee one," Cat said.

"Aye, it is that. What if we celebrate our own Scottish New Year's Eve right here at Bletchley Park, and invite everyone who is still around?"

"Hogmanay," Cat breathed. "But is it possible? Where would we hold it?"

"Bletchley House's ballroom, of course. I'm certain Lady Katherine will agree, and since she is not going to London . . ."

"I didn't know. That's too bad. I know she misses Admiral Sinclair."

"Yes, but the party will be a welcome distraction. So we have much to plan, but we have a few months. Will you help me, Cat?"

"I would be happy to, but I'm surprised you aren't asking Sheila."

Gus shook his head. "She's too busy, and besides, she's not from our parts. I only hope she will be able to come."

"New Year's Eve? Oh, but I'm sure . . ." But Cat stopped. These days, how could anyone be sure of anything?"

Wire from Able Seaman Leon Jessup to Maureen Bradshaw
20 October 1942

Mum dying. Leaving for York.
Too far for you to come.
Instead meet in London 23 October, noon, Langley Hotel.
Lee.

CHAPTER TWENTY-EIGHT

LEE WALKED ALONG YORK'S GREAT Micklegate Bar Wall. The Romans were lucky, he thought, believing a wall would offer protection from the Danes. And it did, for a while. If only life were as simple today, and a wall could protect them from the Nazis. And him from having to face what lay ahead. From his vantage point, he surveyed the damage from last April's Baedeker raid. "The night of terror," they'd called it. Close to one hundred people were killed in the span of two hours. What remained was curious. York Minster was spared, but St. Martin's Church was decimated. He would like to see more of the city, but soon it would be time for his appointment at the prison hospital. Why York, he wondered? So far away from London, and surely not a place where his mother belonged. "My mother is dying," he whispered. Then he made himself say it over and over, louder each time. "Mum is dying. Judith Jessup will be dead soon!" No one was around to hear. He was almost sorry he couldn't tell someone, especially a stranger, who would listen without feeling. Alone, he must make himself believe it—to make it real. But nothing seemed real now—not even Reenie, many miles away. He wondered if she had received his wire and would be able to make the trip to London.

"Off you go then." Janet gave Maureen a fierce hug and sent her off to pack.

Janet was trying hard to hide her depression. Certainly a part in a play couldn't compare in importance to what others were going through, but the role had meant everything to her. Pippa didn't seem disappointed, in spite of all the time she, too, had devoted. At least Katherine was supportive. The dear had convinced the director to use the set for a short comedy one of their members had written. Janet, Pippa, and the other *Children's Hour* cast members would surely be included.

Lady Katherine was such a comfort. Thanks to her, they had secured a place for Gemma in a girls' boarding school in Oxford. There was no reasoning with the child, of course. Gemma was certain she was being sent away as punishment for her part in rumor spreading. "I didn't mean to wreck Gram's play," she'd said, "but I wasn't the only one. Why do the others get to stay at school?"

Without re-hashing the theft of her script, Janet used another reason to explain. "You weren't making enough progress in school, dear," she'd said. "Even you say it's too easy and that the only reason you like it there is because of your friends." Gemma needed her mother, but Sheila was rarely around. Whatever her new assignment was, it was wearing her down and making her desperately unhappy.

"Oh, you look very nice, dear." Janet put down her knitting to gaze admiringly at Maureen in the smart tweed traveling suit she and Helen had managed to put together. Reenie's hat had lost its shape and her shoes were in deplorable condition in spite of the refurbished soles, but the rest of her looked grand. "I do wish you didn't have to travel alone."

"I know, but I'll be careful. Try not to worry about me, Gram. I know you're sad about your play. Perhaps when I return, you and Pippa will perform a few scenes just for me."

Janet forced a smile. "We'll do that. Don't worry about me, either. Lady Katherine and I are planning a fine evening together. Now, how are you getting to the station?"

"Cat is running errands for Mr. Dailey today and has a staff car. She'll drop me off first." Maureen lifted the light suitcase. "I'm off then."

The front door opened and banged shut. "Janet?"

"In here, Katherine."

A more frantic Lady Katherine than they had ever seen rushed into the room. "Janet, it's Hugh. He's very ill. I must go to London immediately! Maureen, I will travel with you. Come! Cat is waiting for us."

And then they were gone. "That will teach you to wish, Janet," she whispered. Reenie would not be traveling alone now, but *she* would be alone—with her thoughts. Helen was here, of course, but she didn't really understand that Janet's involvement and success in the theatre had been one of the few things giving her life purpose. Their friendship, although strong, was based on long-ago memories and the day-to-day necessities of the present. Not that she wasn't grateful for Helen, but . . . Oh, don't be so selfish, she scolded herself. What's more important—your silly play or Lee's poor mother and Katherine's husband?

"Mum?"

A voice. Not a doctor, not a guard, but a voice recalling happier times. Using what little strength she had left, Judith rolled to her other side. The light was dim, and her vision was poor, but she could just make out a young man in uniform.

"Mum?"

"My boy," she breathed with great effort. "You came. I wasn't sure . . ."

Lee pulled a chair next to the thin hospital cot and held her hand. "I'm here, Mum. Don't you worry."

"Leon . . . I'm . . . sorry . . ." Judith struggled to say more but began to gag. Quickly, Lee poured a glass of water, although neither the glass nor the water looked clean, and helped her manage a few sips.

"Don't talk, Mum. You don't have to. I came as quickly as I could. It wasn't easy."

"Leon, please for . . . for . . ."

"I forgive you, Mum, and I understand."

"Box in attic. My treasures."

"I'll find it, Mum, I promise. Now hush and rest. Concentrate on good times."

Judith gave a slight smile and closed her eyes while Lee held her hand and let the past flow from his lips. Holidays, birthdays, the geese on the lake, Mum teaching him to ice skate, Grandmama, Grandfather Leon. He recited happy memories of her beloved home until finally she could hear no more. Lee kept his hand in hers even after he heard the rattling sound the war had made familiar. He stayed until a sister found him there and led him, numbly as in a fog, out of the room.

His mother would not be buried in York, he decided. The place had no meaning for either of them. Robot-like but determinedly, he made arrangements that might not have been thinkable in another situation. Cremation was not a common practice, but he chose it for Judith. Her ashes would be sent to Bletchley Park. The authorities balked—too much trouble for a prisoner found guilty of treason—but Lee's uniform and demeanor, combined with names of well-known people who would vouch for him, finally made them agree. The ashes would be delivered to Lady Katherine Sinclair, the wife of Admiral Sir Hugh Sinclair, and someday, after the war, a memorial service would be held in the only possible place. This was not the worst ending for Judith; incarceration for the rest of her life would have been. It was not a happy ending, but it was one Lee could bear.

Before boarding the train for London, Lee walked aimlessly again along the wall, seeing nothing, deep in thought. He had told his mother he'd forgiven her, and he had. He also said he understood. But I don't, Mum, not really. Who were you? Did I ever know you at all? Do children ever know their parents, or do they just see them as extensions of themselves? All of the pleasant memories he'd related were true, of course, and those were the ones to focus on as much as possible. "I love you, Mum," he said. But he vowed never to let a property—a mere place—be more important than the people he loved. Reenie. It was time to go to Reenie.

Davis, who had a business meeting in Oxford early evening with Eugene Bifford, volunteered to escort a sorrowful Gemma to her new school. "Try to cheer up," he urged. "You'll make new friends, and you know quite well you're far too intelligent for the village school."

Gemma stared out the window, singing under her breath, *Nine green bottles hanging on the wall, nine green bottles hanging on the wall, and if one green bottle should accidentally fall, there'll be eight green bottles hanging on the wall.*

"Gemma."

Eight green bottles hanging on the wall, eight green bottles hanging on the wall, and if one green bottle should accidentally fall, there'll be seven green bottles hanging on the wall.

Davis pulled to the side of the road. "Gemma," he pleaded, "talk to me."

"You'll make me lose count."

He grinned. It wasn't as if she were singing *Ninety-nine bottles of beer on the wall.* "You're on seven. I'll remind you. And before you start singing again, let me tell you that I won't start the car again until you talk to me."

Finally, Gemma turned toward him, her eyes brimming. "All right," she said. "I know the school will be better, and I am good at making friends. It's just hard having everyone angry with me because Gram's play was cancelled."

"I doubt that they really blame you, Gemma. They know you weren't the only student gossiping, but there's nothing they can do about the others— only you. But it's time to put it in the past. You apologized nicely to your grandmother and Pippa, who both love you and will forgive, especially if you work hard on your studies and try to be a little kinder."

"Oh, I will, Mr. Dailey. I promise."

Davis patted Gemma on the shoulder and pulled out onto the road again. "Now you sit back and enjoy the ride. I imagine that when you come home for a visit, all will be well again."

Time to forgive and forget, he mused, giving a great sigh before turning his thoughts back to his own concerns. "Nothing wrong," he assured her, "just thinking." Keeping one hand on the steering wheel, Davis managed to reach into his pocket for a wrapped piece of chocolate for Gemma and an American cigarette for himself.

Gemma nodded, unwrapping the chocolate. Abandoning the green bottles, she returned to her window gazing, giving no more thought to Mr. Dailey's worries. She wondered what her new school friends would be like.

Davis's sighs were both personal and work related. From too little responsibility, Davis suddenly felt an overload of too much. For health reasons, Admiral Sinclair had stepped down as Commander. Alistair

Denniston now had that official title, with Davis as his assistant—an assistant doing most of the work. Denniston planned to resign before the year was over. What would happen once he left, Davis could only speculate. He would continue helping in the huts and blocks, of course, and vetting new recruits with Cat, and oh yes—his secret work for Wild Bill Donovan. He could remind people that he was only one person but doubted anyone would listen. Everyone was overworked and exhausted.

As far as personal concerns, Davis had received some tragic news from home. His old high school and college friend, Buffer, who had married Barbara, was dead. Killed several weeks ago off Guadalcanal when two Japanese submarines attacked the aircraft carrier USS Wasp. Two hundred men, including Lieutenant Commander Brian Prince, had either burned to death or drowned. Buffer and Barbara had an infant son.

Davis couldn't put it off any longer. After he dropped Gemma at her school, he would go to Oxford's Bodleian Library and write two letters: one to Barbara and the other to Buffer's parents.

Letter to Barbara Prince from Davis Dailey
Wilmette, Illinois

Dear Barbara,

Please accept my sincere condolences at this sorrowful time. We have both lost a dear long-time friend. That Brian became even dearer to you is cause for even more sorrow, but also joy. I am grateful that he was able to both give and receive love during his short time on this earth.

While I'm certain there will be many struggles ahead, you will undoubtedly find comfort in your little Brian. Please tell him what a fine person, as well as a hero, his father was. He died trying to save the goodness of the world.

My prayers are with you and him always.

Sincerely,
Davis

Letter to Mr. and Mrs. Charles Prince from Davis Dailey
Lake Forest, Illinois

Dear Mr. and Mrs. Prince,

I am in Oxford today, walking the streets and campuses, remembering happy times with Brian when we attended Balliol College together. I never had a dearer friend, and I'm sorry we lost touch the last few years. For this, I blame the death of my parents, our mutual attachment to Barbara, and, of course, the war. I am very grateful he and Barbara found each other and knew some happiness. And I'm certain you and little Brian will find comfort in each other. I know he will appreciate your loving home, as I did each time I was your welcomed guest.

Oxford has managed to change little since the days Brian, whom we called Buffer, and I pulled pranks, studied hard, and tried to solve the problems of the world with our deep, deep discussions, often lasting all night long, aided by ale at the Eagle and Child. We were such earnest, innocent intellectuals. It is quite amazing that I ended up with a degree in mathematics and he a career in the U.S. Navy. Life never seems to stop handing out surprises.

Sometimes Brian and I tried to out-quote each other with our knowledge of Goethe. This was one of his favorites: "Death is a commingling of eternity with time; in the death of a good man, eternity is seen looking through time." Brian was a very good man, and although it should have been much longer, he had a good life. I shall miss him for the rest of mine.

I am writing this letter in the immense and awe-inspiring Bodleian Library. While sitting here, I remembered a poem Brian was fond of. A librarian helped me to find it. I shall copy it on a separate page for you.

Mr. and Mrs. Prince, you, Barbara, and little Brian will stay in my prayers, and I truly hope we shall meet again.

Sincerely,
Davis Dailey

The Spires of Oxford
by Winifred Letts

I saw the spires of Oxford
As I was passing by,
The gray spires of Oxford
Against a pearl-gray sky;
My heart was with the Oxford men
Who went abroad to die.

The years go fast in Oxford,
The golden years and gay;
The hoary colleges look down
On careless boys at play,
But when the bugles sounded—War!
They put their games away.

They left the peaceful river,
The cricket field, the quad,
The shaven lawns of Oxford
To seek a bloody sod.
They gave their merry youth away
For country and for God.

God rest you, happy gentlemen,
Who laid your good lives down,
Who took the khaki and the gun
Instead of cap and gown.
God bring you to a fairer place
Than even Oxford town.

In memory of Lieutenant Brian Prince,
August 12, 1906 - September 15, 1942

CHAPTER TWENTY-NINE

TRAVELING WITH LADY KATHERINE WAS a godsend, Maureen discovered. The train to London was packed—soldiers crammed in the aisles and between cars, no space available. But Lady Sinclair was able to acquire seats in First Class for both of them. Maureen hadn't been to London since they left their home over two years ago and was not prepared to see the landscape so drastically transformed—pits where houses and stores used to be. A few signs remained and were accurate, but practically everything on the streets unrecognizable. Half-houses with contents spewing out, dust, grime . . . She shuddered. "It's horrible! Simply horrible!"

"I know," Katherine said. "Hearing about it is a very different thing, isn't it? Even though I've been back a few times, I'm never quite prepared."

"I wonder if I'll be able to find a taxi to take me to the Langley."

"Henry will help." At Euston Station, the Admiral's driver was to meet Lady Katherine and drive her to Millbank, the informal name for St. Alexander's Military Hospital. "I would feel better knowing you arrived safely."

Maureen, no longer certain she was mature and grown-up, decided she would feel better, too. Seventeen wasn't such a great age after all. "Thank you, Lady Katherine."

"Street's closed. No getting through this mess. Sorry, sailor, you'll have to turn back."

Lee knew better than to argue with police, but he tried pleading his case. "I'm on leave, and I told my girlfriend to meet me at the Langley. She's very young; I'm worried about her."

"That's a shame, and I am sorry, but the Langley was bombed last night. Rescuers are fishing through debris now looking for people. No one will be allowed in, including your lady-love." The policeman stopped talking as shouts and a commotion came from the building. "There now, they're bringing someone out. Ah, poor blighter. Won't be any help for him in this world."

Lee turned away, surprised at how upset he was by the sight of the dead man. Surely, he should be used to death by now. But that was death in the water and in foreign lands—not here in London. Uncertain, he considered what to do next. A telegram to Bletchley Park wouldn't accomplish anything. If she were coming, she would have left by now. If he could find a taxi, he supposed he could go to Euston Station, just on the off chance of finding her there.

He tried for an hour. It was well past noon. Nothing to do but make his way, walking, to Victoria Station, where he would take the late afternoon train back to Brighton. Then what? Before he left Gibraltar, his commander had hinted at a new assignment. But where, Lee didn't know or care.

"Oh, there's Henry. Over here, Henry!" At last, Katherine spotted the driver in the maze of cars and people.

"I don't see any taxis, though," Maureen said.

"Don't you worry, dear. I'm certain Henry will drive you to the Langley."

"Is it close, Lady Katherine?"

"I'm sure I don't know, but Henry will. Near or far, Henry will take you there."

Once in the car, Katherine informed Henry of the alternate route but got no response from the normally garrulous, accommodating driver, who had attended Sir Hugh for years. "Henry? Is something wrong?"

"Very much so, my Lady. I won't be taking your young friend to the Langley, I fear. There is no more Langley Hotel and no more Arnold Street, either."

"What?"

Katherine put her hand on Maureen's arm. "Hush. What happened, Henry?"

"Air raid last night. They're searching for survivors, but it doesn't look good."

"Last night. At least we know Lee wasn't there. Take us to the hospital, Henry. Hugh will advise us."

Fortunately, Admiral Sinclair, who seemed older and tired but in better shape than Maureen had expected, managed a few phone calls and discovered that Able Seaman Leon Jessup would return to his regiment from Victoria Station. The train for Brighton would leave at sixteen hours that afternoon. "Not much time, when you consider the snarled traffic and so many streets closed, but there's a chance she'll make it," the Admiral said.

"I'll leave at once," Maureen said.

Katherine protested. "Hugh, I'm not comfortable letting Maureen travel alone. I'm not certain she'll even find a taxi. I hate to leave you, but . . ."

"No! No, Lady Katherine, you came to London to see the Admiral. He needs you. I'll be all right. Really, I . . ."

"Ladies, I have a solution that will work for both of you." Admiral Sinclair turned to his driver. "Henry, please take Miss Maureen to Victoria Station and help find her sailor. They won't have time for a lengthy reunion, but it would be sadder if they didn't see each other at all. Whether or not you locate Seaman Jessup, you are to bring Maureen back here as soon as soon as the train leaves. She and Lady Sinclair will then return to Bletchley from Euston Station."

"Very good, Sir," Henry said. "Come, Miss."

Maureen's eyes filled. She couldn't find the words to express her gratitude. "Thank you," she whispered, following Henry from the room.

Hugh patted the bed, as Katherine sat next to him. "Does that satisfy you, my love?"

"Indeed it does. Now, my dear, let's talk about you. What do the doctors say?"

Maureen faced a city she no longer knew, not just because of the bombed out, smoldering wrecks and unfamiliar foul odors. London was now filled with frightened, bewildered, exhausted people. Without Henry by her side, she knew she would be one of them. And without him, she never would find Lee. "They all look alike," she exclaimed. "All of the men look the same in their uniforms. I thought I'd know Lee anywhere, but I was wrong. What shall I do?"

"Let's just go to the platform, Miss, and then be very patient."

"Could we ask someone to announce his name on a loud speaker?"

Henry shook his head. "Do you think anyone would hear?"

No they wouldn't. Maureen could hardly hear Henry, who was standing right next to her. She thought she knew Victoria Station because of her childhood trips to the seaside, but this swarm of humanity was part of a different world. For the first time, she realized what her mother had done for her and her sisters by getting them away from London, even if it meant taking a job as a menial cook. Without Sheila's efforts, she could be homeless or just another casualty, one of the thousands, perhaps even forgotten by now.

"The train is due to board at 15:30," Henry said, bringing her back to the present situation. "We'll stand here and watch as each man approaches the steps. Shall I fetch you a cup of tea while we're waiting?"

"Oh, no, please. I don't want to chance losing you. Tea doesn't matter now."

Henry gave her his first real smile. "Very good, Miss. It should be only a half hour more."

Later, Maureen claimed it was the longest half hour she had ever spent. When the line started to move, she examined each man's face as soldier after soldier, sailor after sailor passed by.

Finally, close enough for her to reach out and touch was a young sailor, bleak, pale, lost. "Lee," she whispered.

He jumped. "Reenie!" He leaped out of the line. Their embrace would last almost until all had boarded. Discreetly, Henry turned his back, clearing his throat when he saw that time was running out. Reenie and Lee broke from each other, tears streaming down both their faces.

"How did you ever find me?" Lee asked. "I had no way of reaching you after I learned about the hotel."

"Admiral Sinclair and Henry, his man, were able to locate you." Maureen wiped away his tears. "But oh, Lee, I couldn't find you. You looked like all of the others. I couldn't tell you apart."

Lee smiled. "I believe that is the intention. Same clothes, haircut, and grim expressions, creating an all-for-one and one-for-all appearance. Do tell Lady Katherine I remember my Dumas." Again, he held her close. "Reenie, thank God you're here."

"What about your mother?" She was almost afraid to ask.

"I was able to say goodbye," Lee said softly. "She died with me holding her hand. It's all right, Reenie. It was the best ending for both of us."

"I'm sorry," Maureen whispered.

"When you get home, do me a favor. Mum said she left a box of her treasures in our attic. See if you can find it, and keep it safe until I return. Unless it contains things that need to be censored, let me know what's there. It seemed very important to her."

"All aboard, sailor. Kiss your lady one more time. The train is about to leave."

"I love you, Reenie," Lee said, his voice shaking. "Write to me."

Then he was gone.

Henry tactfully cleared his throat again. "We best fetch Lady Katherine at Millbank, so as to arrive at Euston Station before blackout."

"We'll be fine now, Henry," Lady Katherine said, as they approached Euston Station. "It would be wise for you, too, to hurry off the street. Go home to your wife and have your supper."

"Very good, m'Lady."

"I can't thank you enough," Maureen added. "I would have been lost without you."

"It was my pleasure, Miss. I'm glad it worked out for you."

Just as Lady Katherine and Maureen started into the station, sirens began to wail, and the two women found themselves swept up and carried along to a shelter deep under the Euston Road. They clung to each other, doing their best to avoid tripping on the stairs.

Once Katherine found a prized empty space against a wall, she and Maureen slid wearily to the floor—to wait for the all-clear siren. Some people had blankets and even chairs. For many, coming nightly had become routine. "Now tell me about Lee," she insisted. "Is he well?"

"He seems to be. We didn't do much talking," Maureen admitted, blushing.

Katherine smiled. "That is how it should be. I remember when Hugh and I didn't do much talking either. How did Lee find his mother?"

"She died while he was with her, but Lee seems to be at peace with it now. I believe he'll be able to return to Bletchley Park, although perhaps not to live there again. What about the Admiral, Lady Katherine? I thought he looked very healthy indeed."

"You are being kind," Katherine said, her voice shaking. "He's tired and his heart is very weak. But he is improving, and the doctors say he can continue to work in a limited way." But not doing what he loves best, she thought. He would be confined to an office in an underground war room, either in London or Dover. "He won't be managing BP any longer. That job will fall to Major Denniston and Davis Dailey."

"Mr. Dailey? Quite a promotion!"

Katherine didn't reveal that Davis had far more power than most people realized. She wasn't certain of the extent herself. "Let's try to rest now," she said, "and be grateful that this filth and discomfort are not our norms. These poor, poor souls. However do they endure?"

Maureen stood and stretched, feeling achy, cramped in this dank, heartless shelter. She shivered, from both cold and anxiety. What did people do who suffered from claustrophobia? If the all-clear didn't come soon, she was uncertain they'd reach home that night. Lady Katherine was asleep, even snoring slightly. It had been quite a day for both of them.

They weren't totally without light. Some of the people sharing their space had torches, even food baskets, and were busily consuming early suppers as if enjoying a late fall picnic. Maureen hadn't eaten since breakfast. At first, she hadn't minded not having any food. Certainly, she had thought, eating would be impossible surrounded by the stench of urine and feces. Toilet facilities must be few and far between. Now it seemed that hunger would win every time. Her stomach growled at the sight of others eating.

Then she noticed a little boy approaching a family and, judging from his held-out hand, asking for food. They ignored him except for the mother who shook her head. The boy returned to his corner to rest his head on his knees, but not before Maureen had seen tears on his grubby face. He was alone. Where was his family? Clearly, he needed help. Cautiously, she approached him, placing her hand gently on his shoulder. He jumped in fright.

"I'm sorry. I didn't mean to startle you, but you look like you might need assistance." She kneeled down next to him.

"Just food, Miss. Do you have any? Or a bit of lolly to buy some. Cor, I ain't 'alf starving."

"Sorry. I'm hungry, too, and money won't do much good until we're out of here. But as soon as we hear the all-clear, I'll make sure both of us get something."

"Could be all night, Miss, but thankee kindly."

He was a friendly fellow with good manners, even though he was filthy from head to toe. Maureen sat next to him. "My name is Maureen," she said. "What's yours?"

"Danny, Miss. Danny Prendergast." He gave his scalp an almost absent minded scratch, as if he were used to dealing with its tiny dwellers.

"Well, Danny Prendergast, you seem rather young to be on your own. Where is your family? Where do you live?"

"I reckon I live right here for now." Danny gave a feeble grin. "Of course, it's not fancy, but it keeps the rain out." Then he barely whispered, "Mam was hit in the Blitz and my da was already dead. They was my family. No one else."

Maureen pinched back tears. This brave little boy, whom no one was helping—what if it were Gemma? While it might be risky to interfere when she knew nothing about him, how could she turn her back on the child?

"Danny, I don't know how yet, but I will make sure you're all right. Will you trust me?"

"You do seem like the right sort, Miss."

"Maureen? Maureen, what in the world?"

Maureen stood to face Lady Katherine. "Oh, good, you're awake. Lady Katherine, this is Danny Prendergast."

Danny also stood and gave a short polite bow. At least his poor mother had taught him manners. Maureen gazed into Katherine's eyes, pleading with her to be helpful and kind, as always.

Lady Katherine extended her hand. "How do you do, Danny Prendergast?"

Danny's lower lip quivered. "Not very well, ma'am."

"Danny has a sad story, Lady Katherine. Both of his parents are dead, and he has no family left. He's been living alone down here, and he's very hungry."

Lady Katherine put a tentative arm around Danny's filthy, ragged jacket. "My goodness, I'm hungry, too. As soon as we're allowed to leave, let's get ourselves a meal. And then I think you had better come home with us, and we'll sort this out. What would you say to that, Danny?"

"That would be very pleasing, ma'am," Danny said.

Lady Katherine looked into Maureen's eyes, communicating volumes. Maureen nodded. Of course they didn't know if one word out of Danny's mouth was true, and taking him back to Bletchley Park was a huge risk. But no Shelter Marshall was about, and no one else seemed inclined to help. As Lady Katherine said, they'd have to sort it all out.

Letter from Gemma Bradshaw to Pippa Bradshaw
11 November 1942

Dear Pippa and Everyone,

Are you surprised to receive a letter from me? I'm sure you weren't expecting one. But you may as well start. I'll send it to someone different each time, but it is for all of you to share. We are required to write once a week, and the Head Girl makes sure we do. No, she doesn't read the letters, but she collects the addressed envelopes and sees that they're stamped and mailed. She started to make fun of me having a post office box, but I told her our house was bombed. That shut her up fast, and the rest of the girls gave her dirty looks. Well, I didn't really lie; our flat in London was bombed.

The Head Girl is M-E-A-N! If you do anything wrong, like breathe, you get an order mark. Too many of those and you lose your privileges. I'm so behind in my classes, I don't have privileges. It will be awhile before I'm able to come home—probably not until Christmas. But I'm trying my best not to get into trouble and to stay out of the Head Girl's sight so I'll be allowed to attend Mr. Fergusson's and Cat's Hogmanay celebration. I must try to forget all the rhymed Cockney I learned at school—and the Yankee slang I learned you-know-where. It's not even okay to say "okay." Automatic order mark.

I shouldn't complain. This is a fine place. I've made friends and like most of the girls in my wing enormously. We have great times; even the classes are interesting. Thanks to Lady Katherine, I'm doing "swell" (order mark) in writing, penmanship, and literature. And I know more than almost anyone about the war. I keep most things to myself, though. We children couldn't help knowing a lot. Adults never seemed to think what we overheard mattered. I am behind in maths and science but am determined to catch up. Perhaps I'll be Head Girl someday. If I am, I will run a tight ship but will try to be kind at the same time.

I am writing Pippa first because I'm sorry for what I did to the play, and I will write to Gram next week. I will try never to be mean like that again. Pippa, sometimes I watched you and Gram rehearsing. I didn't like the play much, but I think you are a very good actress. Maybe you could be a real one in London after the war. It wouldn't matter so much that you aren't good in school subjects. At least I don't think it would.

The warning bell just sounded. I need to seal this quickly and get ready for sports. I miss all of you.

Lovingly,
Gemma

CHAPTER THIRTY

"GRAM, DO YOU THINK GEMMA is right? Do you think I could be a real actress someday?"

Janet put her ironing aside. Finally, she was able to stand and do some of the housework. "It isn't an easy life, dear. You would need to want it more than anything else. Do you?" She handed Pippa the dress she would wear to the Hogmanay festival that night.

"I don't know. Maybe, since I'm not good at school subjects."

"That would not be a good enough reason, Pippa, but you have time to think about it. The war would need to be over first, and you should be at least seventeen."

"I will think about it. Thanks, Gram. Oh, this dress is perfectly splendid. Pink is my new favorite color."

"It's more of a dusty rose, but yes, Helen did a fine job, and you will look quite presentable. Time to get dressed now."

Pippa gave Janet a quick hug. "I will, Gram. I'll take Gemma her dress, too. She will look almost as brilliant as me."

Janet sighed. Oh, to be young again and excited about dresses. It was lovely to have Gemma home for the holidays and, for the most part, happy with her school experiences. Janet poured a cup of tea and opened her newspaper. Secretary Eden reported mass executions of the Jews. Admiral

Darlan, Vichy leader who had switched to the Allies' side, had been assassinated. Petrol rationing had begun in the United States. She snorted. About time. She skimmed through the paper, searching for any good news.

At least Prime Minister Churchill and President Roosevelt were meeting right now in Washington D.C. They were calling it the Arcadia Conference. It seemed that everything nowadays required a fancy name. Roosevelt seemed determined to ignore his critics and continue a Defeat Germany First strategy. Well, he had to—that's all. If the U.S. were to ignore Germany and go traipsing off to Japan, all of Europe was doomed. Then she put the paper aside, swallowed the last sip, and then closed her eyes. Please God, make 1943 a better year, she pleaded, knowing she had prayed the same thing about 1942.

No trace of any of Danny Prendergast's relatives, or even friends of the family, could be found in London. The boy settled himself into life at Bletchley Park as if he'd lived there always. And to Maureen's amazement, Hamish Fergusson had taken Danny under his wing, once the boy revealed that Da had once mentioned a brother in Scotland. "A Prendergast in Scotland," Gus had mused. "Would be more inclined to find one in Wales or Ireland. Tell you what, lad, as soon as this war is over and they give me my walking papers, the two of us will go searching for this lost uncle. In the meantime, your home is here."

That suited Danny fine. After the painful and bloody embarrassing experience of having Miss Maureen and Mrs. Hill, armed with "Keating's Powder to Remove Parasites," declare war on the nits and lice in his scalp and, in his opinion, leaving him practically bald, Danny quite enjoyed being clean. He had what he considered a grand room in Bletchley House, although Pippa told him it had once been a broom closet. Everyone, especially Lady Katherine, kept a close eye on him. He confided to Maureen that he would rather be with his mam back in Camden Town, but since that couldn't happen, he would prefer that the war not end. He was warm, the food came at regular times, and his pal Gus was like a da.

When not studying with Lady Katherine or hiking with Gus, Danny's favorite activity was assisting Miss Maureen and Pippa with the motorcycles. Well, he couldn't do much yet, but he could hand them parts when needed. "Someday, when I'm as old as Pippa, I will take over the motorcycle repairs," he bragged.

Pippa shook her head. "Surely the war will be over by then, Danny."

"Will it? I don't know. I don't remember anything else." Danny was nine, so it was unlikely he recalled the days of peace.

"I know what you mean," Pippa said. "Sometimes I feel the same way."

"That's okay," Danny said. "I like it here just fine, don't you?"

"Oh, yes. I could stay here forever."

Maureen recalled when she felt that way—when Lee was there. But not now. "I can't wait until the war ends." She sighed. "I want Lee back again, safe."

"Then I do, too, Miss Maureen."

"Oh, Danny, what are we going to do with you? You must stop calling me Miss. Just Maureen would be fine."

"I don't know if I can do that, Miss. Doesn't seem right."

"Her nickname is Reenie. Would you mind that, Maureen?"

Maureen smiled. "That would be fine."

"And I will call you Pippy," Danny announced.

"You will not, you little imp." Pippa took off after a giggling Danny, who gave her a merry chase around the grounds.

Maureen watched with some envy—a little longing for childish days long gone. Danny had brought new energy to BP, and Pippa was having more fun with him than she ever did with Gemma. While Pippa would never be a scholar, she had developed self-confidence and an appreciation for what she was able to do. She no longer had to compete with her younger sister.

At first Maureen worried about Danny. What would happen to him if Mr. Fergusson were unable to find Danny's uncle or if he did and found him not the right sort. She no longer worried. Mr. Fergusson adored the boy and would make sure he ended up with a good home. They looked somewhat alike, she thought, with their russet hair and silvery-gray eyes. Danny was one of the few children invited to attend the Hogmanay celebration.

Katherine, Helen, and Janet examined the ballroom decorations, well satisfied with their efforts, although quite certain BP had never been decked out for New Year's Eve like this before. "Extraordinary! What would Lord Leon have thought of this?" Katherine mused. The other women shook their heads and smiled.

Probably no one living, unless Leon's son, George, were still alive, could answer that. The decorations were Viking-inspired, with a Scottish flare, including different tartan drapes covering the blackout curtains. How Gus had managed to accumulate these trappings was something the women weren't sure they wanted to know. Gus had promised a solo bagpipe concert, and there were enough workers at BP who played instruments to provide more traditional music for dancing.

"Lovely to look at," Helen lamented. "A feast for the eyes but not for the stomach."

"Never mind," Janet soothed her friend. "We did the best we could. We warned people to have their supper before they arrived. And those biscuits you baked look a treat."

"An almost sugarless, butterless treat."

Lady Katherine laughed, happy for the first time in many months. Her husband was with her for the holidays, so much improved, but still promising to cut back greatly. She would make certain he kept that promise. "Now, Helen, don't you worry about what people eat. Hugh and Gus have provided so much scotch and wine, people will scarcely notice the lack of food."

Officially, Gus and Cat were host and hostess, so unofficially they were each other's date. Without Lee, Maureen was reluctant to attend until Cat assured her she would be at her side often.

Cat and Gus demonstrated a few Scottish country dances, such as the Gay Gordon, Mairi's Wedding, and the Dashing White Sargeant, and then began teaching circle dances to those willing to try. Maureen found herself dancing with the few men without dates and with many women, who greatly outnumbered the men. During a break, Cat and Gus demonstrated the Highland Fling, to the amazement of the crowd.

Cat hadn't considered that others might think she and Gus were a couple until she noticed the looks Sheila was giving Gus. Was Sheila jealous? She must not be aware of the furtive glances Gus was giving her back. So that's what's going on, Cat thought. The Laird of Cockpen is playing hard to get. She grinned, remembering the old Scottish folk song. *The Laird O' Cockpen is proud and he's great; his mind's ta'en up wi affairs o' the state.* There was something cocky about Gus, especially dressed in full-clan garb— self-assured, but perhaps too arrogant? At least for Cat. Well, Sheila could have him; Gus was not Dave, and Cat was not interested. Gus was an extremely kind man. He would be good for Sheila and her family. He was certainly nothing like Roger. Maureen had confided about what their life had been like with her father. And Gus, this Laird O' Cockpen, definitely wanted a wife his *braw hoose tae keep.*

"May I have the next dance?" Cat turned to answer a Wren she didn't recognize.

"Certainly. But it's a reel. Are you up to it?"

"I'll try. I love your outfit!"

Cat was pleased with her appearance. She wore her blue and green Clan MacLaren long tartan with matching sash—her sandy curls as active and bouncy as her feet, her cheeks flushed pink by the exercise. How unfortunate that the one person who should see her looking so fine was not here.

"Phew . . ." was the collective sound in the room as soon as the reel was completed. The orchestra, picking up on their cue, switched to a waltz. Cat took a seat next to Maureen, who was too young to understand that dancing close to a man would not make her disloyal to Lee. "Oh, good," Cat whispered. "Gus finally asked Sheila to dance."

It was exciting being in Gus's arms, Sheila thought, although she was not in the least bit interested in him, of course. Not a bit. She was only pleased to be dancing with someone who knew how—that's all. But she must be very careful what she said. She had consumed far too much scotch and was becoming rather giddy. She must stick to small talk. "I haven't seen you lately. Of course, you're not tutoring me anymore, and we're both very busy."

"That must be the reason," Gus replied. He never liked talking while dancing. He wanted to enjoy the sensation of holding a woman close as well as the beat of the music.

"I want to thank you for helping Maureen with her maths and science," Sheila said.

"It is my pleasure. Hush now, Sheila. Let's dance."

Not understanding, Sheila was left wondering what she'd done wrong.

By midnight, almost everyone was fairly pissed, Cat noticed. Little food, too many glasses of spirits—and a desperate wish to escape the war, for just a while. Cat decided early on that one whisky was enough, although she would have indulged in rather a lot at a typical Hogmanay back home. Some of the people still to be vetted were there, and she should watch and listen—in case she might learn something or if there were any loose drunk lips that could sink ships. She sighed inwardly. She was never far away from her job.

Then it was midnight, and everyone cheered, many grabbing the closest person for a hearty kiss. The kiss Gus gave Sheila was more than hearty, Cat observed. She wondered if either would remember it the next morning.

"This year will be better for you, Maureen," she said, giving Maureen a warm hug.

Then it was time for the song, beloved to all Scots, wherever they might be in the world.

> *Should auld acquaintance be forgot and never brought to mind?*
> *Should auld acquaintance be forgot and auld lang syne.*
> *For auld lang syne, my dear, for auld lang syne.*
> *We'll take a cup o kindness yet, for auld lang syne.*

Drunk or sober, many were moved to tears. For old time's sake. For days long gone. Would those days ever come again?

"Thank ye all for coming. A braw New Year tae ane an a'," Gus bellowed, in a slurred, joyful voice. "May 1943 be the blessing that brings the return of our friends and loved ones. Only one thing is missing to insure our good luck: a dark complexioned mon to tak the first foot into the house. And here he comes now. Not especially dark, but not a big blonde Viking with an ax, either."

Who could it be? All eyes were on the doorway.

"A Happy New Year, everyone!" Carrying symbolic pieces of coal and shortbread and a dram of whisky, a grinning Davis Dailey gave the celebration all that was needed to make it perfect—a "First Footing" into the new year.

Dave and Gus must have worked it out together, Cat thought, crossing quickly to welcome Dave home. But she would have preferred it if he'd arrived a few minutes earlier. Then she might have received a New Year's kiss.

Letter from Maureen Bradshaw
To Able Seaman Leon Jessup
12 January 1943

Dear Lee,

Not a word from you since our brief meeting in London. I do hope you are well and safe, wherever you might be. I have written a few letters and am wondering if you received them.

We are well enough here, continuing to do our best for the war effort. My mother, especially, seems to be working extra hard and is greatly troubled. I wish she were able to discuss her concerns with me. I am enjoying living in your cottage with Pippa, Cat, and some jolly new recruits.

I finally had the opportunity to search through your attic for the Treasure Box. It is indeed a treasure, and I have given it a new home on the top shelf of my closet, next to my treasures.

While I don't understand all of the contents, it's clear they are all about— You! Perhaps some day very soon you will be able to explain them to me.

1. A dried flower arrangement, possibly a corsage.
2. Your secondary school diploma.
3. Wonderful childish drawings—of geese, ducks, and horses.
4. Hand-made greeting cards from you to Mum.
5. A collection of poetry written by You.
6. Letters from you to Mum and Grandmama from a time you attended Scout camp.
7. A sparkly rhinestone bracelet.
8. A baby book, recording all of your "firsts."
9. Photos of you and people I don't know.

All of these things make it obvious, darling Lee, that your mother loved you dearly. Keep that in mind. No matter what happened to make her so bitter, she loved you. And so do I.

Your Reenie

CHAPTER THIRTY-ONE

M AUREEN HAD LEFT ONE ITEM off of the list. There was a number ten, but she decided to exclude it, for now. It was too much for Lee to concern himself with when, assuredly, he had much to bear already. Judith had included a yellowed-with-age newspaper clipping, telling of Gerald Stratton Jessup dying in a factory fire at the time Lee must have been about three-years-old. Lee always assumed his father had left them. Well, in a way he had. There had been strong evidence pointing to arson, and the police believed that Mr. Jessup had started it himself, although they were uncertain if the motive were suicide or if Jessup had simply wanted to get back at his employers and was trapped inside. A horrible story—not yet one for Lee to face. Poor Judith, Maureen thought. This was the probable reason for her great fear of fire. She refolded the article, returning it to the box of treasures.

Davis left Hut 8 for a quick trip to his office when Cat entered, unusually solemn. Oh, dear, he thought. Trouble. Cat had taken charge of meeting the mail delivery, and each day brought the telegrams directly to him. Even though the Allies were advancing, it seemed that casualties were becoming greater—telegrams, now addressed to the recipient in care of Deputy

Commander Davis Dailey, arrived several times a day. Cat's expression warned him that this one was going to hit home.

"Cat?" She handed it to him. He read it quickly. "Oh, no! Oh, dear God, no!" He held it out to Cat.

Her eyes filled. "What should we do, Dave? Who should deliver it?"

"Well, not you or me. The best person to tell Maureen is Janet Hill. Do you know where she is?"

"At home or with Lady Katherine, I imagine."

"I'll check the library. Things have come to a standstill here. Was that the only telegram?"

Cat nodded. For now it was. She remained on the sofa with her head down while Dave left on his grim errand.

He found Lady Katherine in the library, giving Pippa and Danny a reading lesson. Both appeared to be using the same textbook and greatly enjoying each other's company.

"Davis?" Katherine asked, surprised by the unusual time of his visit. And then reading his somber expression rose quickly. "Children," she said, "please read to each other while I see how I can help Mr. Dailey."

"What is it, Davis?" Katherine asked, as soon as they were out of the room. He held up the telegram and then watched in alarm while Katherine grew pale and started to sway. "Hugh?"

Davis grabbed her before she fell and led her to a hall loveseat. He cursed himself for being every kind of stupid. "No, Lady Katherine, forgive me. I was looking for Janet. The news is for Maureen."

"Lee? Something has happened to Lee?"

Davis agreed to wait with the children while Lady Katherine took the telegram to Janet. It was a good idea. Janet, too, would be affected by the news.

Pippa scrutinized him. "Something is wrong."

"Yes," Davis admitted, "but it's not my place to say anything."

Pippa nodded. That's the way it often was in Bletchley Park when news arrived in a yellow envelope.

Janet and Helen were in the lounge building costumes for the upcoming spring program. Other than the silly little one-act, there had been nothing but song and dance reviews since the disastrous *Children's Hour* venture. But hope was on the horizon.

"It's true," Janet said. "I heard it from the director herself. This will be the last review for a while. The Dramatic Society plans to perform *Little Women.*"

Helen laughed. "Quite a change from *Children's Hour.* But doesn't it have a war?"

"The American Civil War, long over, and they're leaving out the bloody bits."

"As long as it isn't a bloody performance."

The two old friends smiled at each other. This living arrangement was working out splendidly, and it was likely they would stay together once the war was over. Perhaps in Janet's former home in Nottingham, if it were still standing, or somewhere else.

An urgent rapping on the door caused looks of alarm. Neither could rise with the mounds of material on their laps. Helen now had pins in her mouth and couldn't speak. "Come in, please!" Janet shouted. "Oh, Katherine, it's you. Have you come to help?" Then as she looked at her more carefully, "What is it, dear?"

"Something has happened," Katherine said. "Let me help you put that lovely gown away."

Helen took the pins out of her mouth. "Shall I . . ."

"No, please stay, Helen. You may be needed."

Katherine helped them clear their laps, and then took the envelope out of her handbag. Both women gasped.

"Who is it for?" Helen asked, trembling.

"For all of us, but mainly Maureen," Katherine said. "It was addressed to Mr. Dailey, and he came to the library looking for Janet. I thought perhaps I should be the one to bring it here. It's dated over a month ago, the tenth of April."

Janet stared at the feared object, gathering her strength before reading.

We regret to inform you that Able Seaman Leon Jessup reported
missing in action. Tunisia, 7 April 1943. Presumed dead.

"Oh, Lee. How is this to be borne?"

"Tunisia?" Helen said. "But we've taken Tunisia. The Allies have won there."

Janet shook her head. "But not a month ago."

"Where is Maureen now, Janet?" Katherine asked. "At the stables?" Janet nodded. "I'll have Pippa relieve her there. I won't say what has happened, just that you need to see Maureen." Janet had begun to sob while Helen ineffectually patted her hand. "Remain strong, Janet," Katherine said, barely able to hold back her own tears.

"Gram?"

"In here, Reenie. Come, sit next to me."

"Gram, you're scaring me."

"Reenie, dearest, there's no gentle way of telling you this. Something terrible has happened. We've received bad news—a telegram."

"Just show me."

Maureen read the telegram while Janet watched her for signs of . . . well, she wasn't sure what. Hysterics? Perhaps a fainting spell? But Reenie stayed still.

Finally she spoke. "It will be all right, Gram. Don't worry. Lee is alive, you'll see. He'll contact me once he's able."

"But it says . . ."

"It says what it always says if someone doesn't die outright. Don't you see, Gram? If Lee were dead, I would know in my heart. No, we'll go on and wait patiently."

"Of course, dear," Janet said, although she knew it was just young love talking. *I would have known,* young love always says, but Janet knew that was not true. Perhaps sometimes it happened, but it was most unlikely, and it had certainly never happened to her. But if it gave Maureen comfort, they must all act accordingly. They must all pretend that nothing really horrible had happened to Lee.

"If you don't mind, Gram, I think I'll spend a little time in my room now."

Lady Katherine had pleaded a headache after sending Pippa to the stables. The lessons were officially over for the day. Davis encouraged her to lie down. He welcomed the opportunity to become better acquainted with Danny—and to have a distraction from the new sorrow they were facing. The boy loved to chatter and was a fountain of information. "Gus will be my new da," he informed Davis.

"Oh? Does Gus know this?"

Danny thought it over. "I think he probably does. He might look for my uncle, but maybe not too hard. If my uncle cared about me, why did I never meet him? I don't think my da liked him much."

"No way of knowing," Davis said. "But would you like Gus to be your father?"

"Oh, yes. And Pippa's mam will be mine, too."

"Whoa, young fellow! That's a big assumption."

"Nah, he's dead gone on her. Anyone can tell that."

Well, Davis hadn't been able to tell—not that he had been looking. If Danny were correct, he wondered if Sheila returned the feelings. And how do you feel, Davis? Just fine, he answered himself. It seemed that at long last, he was completely cured. He must have been silent for too long for Danny seemed troubled.

"Cor, I should have kept my great gap closed. I forgot that someone told me Mrs. Bradshaw was your lady."

Davis smiled. "No, that was long ago, Danny. We're good friends now, that's all. I hope everything you wish for comes true."

"Sure to," Danny said.

And the days dragged by, slowly, sorrowfully. Dilly Knox finally lost his battle against cancer—at a time both his skills and positive spirit were needed desperately. Turing was still in America, and Foss, Dailey, and others worked tirelessly during a code blackout so severe they wondered if the Nazis were aware they'd been discovered and had abandoned Enigma entirely. Ships and planes and lives were lost while Churchill's geese at Bletchley Park carried on, without a word of complaint ever uttered outside the huts and blocks.

Sheila lost weight and what little color she had left as her indoor mission for countless hours at a time became more and more heartbreaking. "Nothing is wrong," she said, whenever her family inquired about her. Gus and Davis just looked at each other and shook their heads. They knew Sheila's task and worried.

They waited for further information about Lee. Admiral Sinclair, at Lady Katherine's insistence, had put forth an investigation, but there was no record of Able Seaman Jessup ever being stationed in Tobruk. The Navy reported he had been assigned to Gibraltar but after that no one seemed to know. All of Lee's friends at BP, except Maureen, now eighteen, had given up hope. "He will write once he's able," she said to all doubters. Finally, the doubters kept their peace, but those who loved her quietly began to consider her future.

"Perhaps Maureen doesn't have to wait until the war is over to go to America," Davis said to Cat and Janet. "She wants to train to be a nurse but will need an operation on that unfortunate foot of hers. If she were to have something to think about besides Lee . . ."

Cat agreed. "She's acting as if she's not thinking about him at all, but surely that's not possible. Do you have any ideas where she might go—both for surgery and training?"

Janet shook her head. "I don't know. She is very young to be alone, and how could we possibly afford to send her?"

Davis had given the matter much thought. "I will talk with Sheila. She has some money, and perhaps Lady Katherine would know how such a thing might be funded. Johns Hopkins Hospital for the surgery might be the best place. And then her doctors would determine how well she recovers before nursing school could be considered. Of course, that doesn't solve the problem of her being alone. But wait . . . Johns Hopkins is in the state of Maryland. Isn't that where your friend Millie is stationed?"

"Yes, in Baltimore."

"An unlikely but welcome coincidence," Davis said. "Janet and I will talk with Sheila and Lady Katherine. And, Cat, will you write to Millie?"

"Of course," Cat said. Her heart and spirits dropped. What was best for Maureen came first, of course, but she had become her dearest friend at BP. It appeared Cat was about to sustain another loss.

Letter from Millie Hanson, Wren, Bainbridge Naval Center, Maryland USA
To Catriona MacLaren, Wren, HMS Pembroke V
23 September 1943

Darling Cat,

Such a pleasure receiving another letter from you so soon after the last one, which I have not yet had the opportunity to answer. Indeed, this will not be a reply to that lovely note, since the matter in hand, young Maureen, is more urgent.

Actually, Bainbridge is not in Baltimore, although not terribly far away. As luck would have it, both my parents and Robert's live in Baltimore. Either would be willing to do whatever they're able to make Maureen's stay successful. Robert had additional surgery at Johns Hopkins and goes there still for physical therapy. His father is now a professor at the university and may be of assistance at determining a good nursing school for Maureen.

Do send us a wire to let us know if or when she might make the journey. I agree that this would be a positive move, but I also detect some sadness from you, dear friend, in losing her.

Cat, don't give up hope about anything—not Lee, Gramps, or even D.D. Believe in miracles, Cat. I see my Robert progressing daily and know they happen.

Affectionately,
Millie

CHAPTER THIRTY-TWO

IT HADN'T BEEN EASY, BUT at last they talked Maureen into leaving for America. It was probably the thought of being able to nurse Lee and others someday that finally swayed her. Did she really believe Lee was still alive? Davis doubted it, but apparently she still needed to pretend. Nursing was a fine profession, and surely Maureen couldn't continue to explain motorcycle parts forever. A new trainee had been successfully vetted, and Pippa and Danny would help him, at least for a while.

Davis looked over his notes for the day. He and Lady Katherine would bid goodbye to Maureen at Croydon Airport in South London before he escorted Lady Katherine to her husband's underground office in the War Rooms. Davis would then proceed to Wormwood Scrubs, where plans for the new intelligence operation were going slowly but were becoming more critical. On October 13, in a radical move, Italy had declared war on Germany. Not bad news at all, but the logic still escaped him. After all, the Jerries had rescued Mussolini only the month before. Better intelligence was essential for this crazy, mind-boggling war. At least the Enigma blackout was over and Turing had returned safely. Progress seemed to be possible once again.

He opened another envelope. Cat's liberty request had been approved. There wasn't a lot of work for her at the moment, and she did need to see her grandfather. He tried not to dwell on how much he would miss her. She would be in Scotland for Remembrance Day. How sad and ironic. All of the reports coming from Douglas MacLaren's convalescent home warned of his increasingly failing memory.

"Gramps?" Cat peeked into the room before entering, startled by the sounds of raucous laughter. "Is this the right room?" she asked the sister accompanying her.

The nurse nodded. "Go ahead, Miss."

And there was Gramps, seated around a table playing whist with four other gentlemen, although they didn't seem to be behaving with gentlemen-like manners.

"Gramps?"

He looked up and smiled at her, but his smile seemed different. It lacked . . . something. Recognition?

"Welcome! Grab a chair and join us. We aren't used tae such fetching company." He proceeded to introduce the men—Harry, Malcolm, Lester, Rowan—"And you are . . ."

"Cat, Gramps."

"Cat? What kind of name is that?"

"Well, Catriona, actually. You know . . ."

"Catriona! Fine name. Let's play a few rounds. Speaking of rounds, a round of ale for my guests, Sister."

The nurse shook her head. "Tea and biscuits coming shortly, Mr. MacLaren." She winked at Cat. "I'll be back."

Stunned, Cat watched the men play. What was happening? The game stopped when the sister returned with the tray of refreshments.

Suddenly, Gramps turned and stared at her, and an entirely different expression appeared. "Cat? You're here? Fine, fine. Be a good lass and fetch my pipe."

The sister put her hand on his shoulder. "No pipe smoking allowed here, Mr. MacLaren. You know that. Perhaps a cigarette?"

"Confounded woman! Well, bring me my mac, Cat, and off we'll go." When she hesitated—"Come on! What are ye waiting for, lassie? Let's go home."

Her eyes welling, Cat turned away slightly. "We can't, Gramps." She didn't want to tell him he was no longer well enough. "Our house is being used for billeting soldiers. There won't be a place for us there until the war is over."

Gramps set down his cup. Then he stared at her, alert, seeming to understand, until his eyes grew vacant. Finally, he picked up the cards and turned back to the men. "Ah, yes, the war . . . There's a war on, you know," he said, just making idle conversation.

They returned to their game, ignoring Cat, who quietly left the room, the sister following.

The tears fell. "Is he always like that?"

The nurse shrugged. "Some days he remembers some things—other days, nothing. He's happier when he doesn't remember. When he does, he becomes quite belligerent, demanding to see his wife and son, wanting his pipe and home. You'll need to keep that in mind when you come."

Cat nodded, not bothering to explain how difficult it had been for her to get liberty, and left the nursing home, grandly called The Inverness Residence for Retired Gentlemen.

Before heading to the railway station, she took a long walk along Ness Bank. She wound her scarf another time around her neck, wishing she had dressed with the weather in mind. While England was cold, she had forgotten what cold really meant, when it entailed not only low temperatures but also bitter North Sea winds. And she shouldn't forget that back in England, she worked in Bletchley House, where there was at least a modicum of heat.

As for their house, it appeared that no attempt was being made to keep it in good condition. How many people occupied it? Couldn't they all pitch in? Shutters askew, paint peeling, bannister rail broken. But she shouldn't judge them. Their needs were more important now. They certainly didn't have time or funds for home repair.

Not a fancy house. Just a two-storied brownstone, squeezed between two ancient churches, but her home since the death of her parents in the influenza epidemic of 1919. From age two on, Gramps had been her mother, father, grandparents, cousins, everything and everyone, and he might not remember her again. She stood in the frigid air, staring at her home before closing her eyes—to let the scene embed itself into her memory. "Happy Remembrance Day, Cat," she whispered.

Time for the long, exhausting trip back to . . . home, she realized suddenly—she had no home now other than Bletchley Park.

Sheila sat at her desk, staring at the photos from their London contact and reading the compiled reports gathered from successful decryptions: Auschwitz, Buchenwald, Bergen-Belsen. She had been reading horrifying words for so long, and now these photos gave the final proof. The horrors were real. The whole thing was bloody awful real. She couldn't do this any more. She wouldn't. She started to laugh, loudly, hysterically—before the laughter turned to tears, followed by great, overwhelming sobs. "Sheila, what's wrong?" A woman rushed to her side. Sheila stood and tried to walk away from the desk. She wanted to talk, to say she was all right, even though she knew she wasn't. But the minutes, hours, and years crashed down on her like dead weights. She saw nothing but blackness and fell in a heap onto the floor.

And she knew nothing until she awoke with Gus by her side. Where was she? The photos, the reports—her hysteria—surely she was in a regular hospital and not a . . . "Gus, where am I?"

"Oxford General, my dear. Don't worry. I've talked them out of their nervous breakdown diagnosis. Convinced them you were overworked and likely coming down with a case of influenza."

"I . . . I . . . Gus, I can't do it anymore. It's too horrible. I can't look at their eyes, the faces, those bodies starved to nothing."

"Rest, dear heart. Sleep. Trust me to make it right for you again."

Sheila closed her eyes. "If that were only possible, Gus."

Great Scot—he'd make it possible! Gus drove back to BP and headed straight for the office, where Davis had been waiting.

"Gus, sit down. You look worn out. How is Sheila?"

"Exhausted. On the verge of a complete breakdown. But I managed to convince the staff it was nothing rest wouldn't cure."

"A little rest? I suppose we can manage a short liberty for her."

"Dave, she requires more than a short liberty. She must have a long rest, starting right now, and she needs to be taken off this assignment. It's more my fault than yours—I was the one who encouraged her. 'Get more education,' I said. 'Study hard; take some tests.' But you're in charge now and the one to sign the release papers. She's been working here for how long—four years—without ever taking so much as a holiday?"

Davis went on the defensive. "She used to socialize a great deal. Parties and such things."

"But not lately, and never away from here. I have some liberty coming, and soon Gemma will be on term break. Here's what I'm going to do. I'm going to pack the two of them and Danny, of course, into my automobile and take them to my home outside of Oban. We will take a holiday from war and see if we can bring Sheila back to sanity."

"Can it be that serious?"

"Aye, that it can. Without my intervention, they would have locked her away into an institution."

"Surely not. And the war . . ."

". . . will not be won by Sheila Bradshaw. She's done her bit, and bloody well, too. Now the Allies, thanks to your countrymen and the Soviets, are turning the tide. Our work at BP may be over soon."

"How can you say that?" Davis protested. "Because of Ultra, we sank the Scharnhorst. Our code breakers are succeeding every day now, not just sometimes."

"And Sheila has been doing her part for almost the whole time. You must let her go."

Davis smiled. "You really care about her, don't you, Gus?"

Gus nodded. He could have told Davis that he was anticipating a short stop at Gretna Green either before or after the trip to Oban, but he supposed it might be wise to inform the lady first.

Davis couldn't help being jealous. Not because of Sheila, but of Gus's love and his absolute confidence in showing it. Little Danny was correct that Gus was "dead gone" on Sheila. Davis hoped Sheila felt the same way. He was well aware of her pattern concerning men.

Poor Sheila. And he had been reluctant to give her leave. Had he been working with machines so long he had become one? How would he have handled her assignment? To keep record of all Nazi atrocities discovered by Enigma and other sources, to be used as evidence at the war trials once the Allies had won. No wonder she had collapsed.

His work for the OSS was difficult enough. Being part of a U.S. team starting a brand new intelligence agency working abroad was a departure from anything his country had ever done. In addition, he was essentially Commander of Bletchley Park. The actual commander, now Webster Holmes, hadn't so much as visited in months, although he made sure his face was seen when the first Colossus computer arrived in February. Now the maintenance of the machine was Davis's responsibility, as it spewed out thousands of German messages a day, more than five times the amount they were accustomed to. Suddenly, their work on the Enigma and Bombe machines looked juvenile in comparison. Even the Lorenz cipher had been broken, and the Allies were finally practicing some of their own deceptions. At long last, Davis thought the end might finally be in sight. But the vetting of the new Colossus team as well as all the new BP personnel had added even more burdens to his impossible days.

In the middle of all this, he wondered where Cat was and what she was doing.

Letter from Gemma Bradshaw, Oban, Scotland
To Maureen Bradshaw, Baltimore, Maryland USA
10 May 1944

Dear Maureen,

Did you notice the stamp and return address on the envelope before you even opened this? I'll bet you are wondering what in the world Gemma is doing now. Yes, we're in Scotland at Gus's home—Mum, Danny, and me!

Why are we here? Well, it is my break before summer term, but the reason we came is serious. Mum became very ill because of her work. I don't know what was wrong exactly, but Gus said she badly needed to get away. Because she's not an enlisted volunteer—not a Wren or anything like that— she never had been granted an automatic liberty, not that she ever requested one. Gus put his foot down. I am glad he did!

Actually, Gus's home is a farm outside of Oban—way outside, or it would have certainly been requisitioned for billets. Gus says the government doesn't need it. Good thing because we love it! Scotland is so beautiful, even though spring has not come here as much as it has back home. Oban is magical, with its shining loch, ferries heading out to the Western Isles, and a folly at the top of the hill that looks like it belongs in ancient Rome. Gus says he will take us on a cruise through the Isles. Once the war is over, of course.

The farmhouse is a big old drafty place, not as large as Bletchley House, but we each have our own bedroom and lots of down comforters. Danny and I spend the days hiking and fishing or playing board games when the weather is too cold or rainy. It rains a lot here. Mum is relaxing and feeling much better. She is starting to look pretty again. Gus must go back soon, but we will stay until the end of my break. He will return for us. We could travel back by train, but he will not allow it.

I wish Pippa were here, too, but she and Gram are in another play, so they had to stay and rehearse—I don't remember the name of the new one. Besides, Pippa has to help with the motorcycles and pigeons, taking over for Danny, who now feeds them most of the time.

Gus wanted Danny to come so he'd have a quiet, private place to talk with him. He also wanted to be sure Danny liked it here. Investigators discovered that Danny's uncle died several years ago, so Danny has no kin at all. Gus asked Danny if he would mind being adopted by him. Not likely! That's what Danny was hoping for right along.

Mum told me that you will attend university in Boston. How exciting! I am glad you're becoming a nurse, Maureen. We should have one in our family. We'll have a nurse and an actress and a . . . well, I don't know yet, but I want to be someone smart and important. We all miss you, and we pray for you every night.

Love from your sister
Gemma

P.S. I didn't really forget this next bit of news. I just wanted to add a P.S., which means postscript. Danny's other wish will come true, too. Mum and Gus are engaged to be married. Danny will have a new "mam and da," and we'll have a stepbrother and a stepfather, who will love all of us.

CHAPTER THIRTY-THREE

"I BELIEVE THIS IS THE FIRST time we've quarreled, Cat." Davis grinned maddeningly, trying to turn the problem into a joke.

"Only because we've never disagreed about anything," Cat lashed back. At least, not about anything work-related, she amended silently.

"Look, I'll try to explain again. Perhaps I wasn't clear enough." Cat couldn't stand Dave's look of forbearance and his warm, too patient eyes. For the first time, she felt as if he were trying to put her in her place, trying to make her feel like she was an incompetent *woman*. "All of our vetting has come up empty for months now—not a spy or wannabe spy in the lot. You're wasting your time on this and should accept a different assignment. I would think you'd welcome a change."

Cat picked up a folder crammed with papers from her desk. "Dave, I would if I thought you were right, but I don't, not that you'll really give me a choice. I haven't forgotten you are my boss. Most respectfully, though, I believe you are wrong. With all the advances the Allies are making, the Huns will grow desperate. We can't afford to let up. But I really must go. I can't be late for my appointment."

"We'll talk about this later, Cat."

"Very well," Cat said calmly, but proved she was not in the least bit calm by storming out of the office and almost, but not quite, slamming the door.

Davis shrugged, pretending indifference, before turning again to his own work. Managing BP and helping to organize the new American intelligence network were taking their toll on him. He could use Cat's help with some of his tedious duties—not with the secrets at Wormwood Scrubs, of course, or with many of the doings in the huts and blocks. Bletchley Park's newest commander was only a figurehead with a title—rarely seen on the premises, and the man he'd chosen for routine maintenance had been transferred for unknown and questionable reasons. It all fell on Davis now—every mundane problem, even ordering new supplies for the canteen and requisitioning a handyman to check out a reported lack of heat in Hut 4. Certainly it was a chilly spring, but soon they would be complaining of the heat. At least Turing had returned, and Davis's cryptology skills weren't needed quite so often. From cracking codes to ordering toilet paper, Bletchley Park certainly kept a person humble. A soft rap on the door was a welcome relief from tedious chores. "Enter," he said eagerly.

The visitors were a jubilant Hugh Foss, followed by Gus, looking quietly pleased. Foss peered around the office. "Where's Catriona MacLaren?" he demanded. "We want to thank her."

"She had an appointment," Davis said. "Thank her for what?"

"For possibly saving one of the most important operations of the war!" Foss shouted. "Unbelievable discovery!"

Davis stood. "What?"

Gus explained. "She fingered a Nazi. Name of Porter, stationed in Hut 8. He had been vetted early in the game—by you, actually—but something was missed. If Porter had revealed a recent Ultra decryption, it's possible the Western Front would be lost."

"We're not able to tell you what's at stake here," Foss said, "but soon everyone will know. That Scottish lassie of yours helped prevent the operation from being a disaster."

Davis sat with a thud. He knew Porter—a quiet but brilliant, unassuming man. How could he have made such a serious mistake in vetting? He had been wrong. And possibly even worse, he admitted to himself, he had been wrong in thinking Cat's job had become meaningless. To think he had just told her vetting was no longer needed—no wonder she was angry. He couldn't blame her for not sharing her discovery with him. He certainly hadn't been accessible lately.

The look of misery on Davis's face must have kept Foss and Gus from saying anything critical. Davis was making a thorough enough job of beating himself up.

"We're all overworked," Gus said quietly, "and mistakes are easily made."

"Thank you," Davis said. "I'm not sure I deserve such understanding. And Gus, congratulations on your engagement. I wish you and Sheila every happiness."

Gus nodded and left the room, muttering that he was on his way back to Oban that evening.

"Well?" Davis asked, waiting for a sharp comment from Foss. The two men had often tangled.

"Just give Cat our thanks," he said, following Gus.

"I will." *And also my apology.*

One of the most important operations of the war. He wondered why he didn't know about it. Possibly because Welchman had been away. No matter. If he couldn't handle his own responsibilities, he didn't have a right to know.

Cat returned to the office, wishing it weren't necessary, but she needed to lock up her papers. Another dead end on this one, but something was wrong; she could smell it. Perhaps luck would be with her, and Dave would be gone for the day.

It was not to be. "Dave," she said. "You're still here."

"I was waiting for you."

"Oh?" She braced herself to continue the argument but then looked at him closely. This was a different man from the one she had left.

"First, I want to apologize. You were right, and I was wrong. Careful vetting does need to continue, and you're definitely doing a better job than I."

"Not necessarily. I seem to have struck out today."

Struck out? Davis couldn't help smiling at the expression. The Yanks were having quite an impact on the language. "Gus and Hugh Foss came by to thank you. It seems that you have hit a home run. Or perhaps you landed a big fish, if you want to switch idioms."

"I . . . What are you talking about?"

"Your suspect, Porter. Gus and Foss didn't give any details but said Porter's knowledge would have been devastating if he had been able to pass on the information to his Nazi control. They said you must carry on with your work. I am sorry, Cat, that I . . ."

"Oh, that is good news. No apology necessary, Dave."

"I disagree, and I'd like to talk more. Do you have dinner plans?"

Cat shrugged. "Not really, but I'm pretty tired."

"Perhaps tomorrow night?"

She nodded. "As long as it isn't the Eight Bells, although it has improved."

Davis laughed. "I found out something about that place. The original owner had eight daughters. The pub started life as the Eight Belles."

"Then it should be more friendly to women," Cat said.

Davis had found a quiet old-fashioned restaurant, out in the country—an ideal hide-away from the war, at least for a few hours. The food and drink were not ideal, but they had grown used to even worse and, with relish, tucked into their tripe and liver hot-pot and odd-tasting ale. No water, of course. Strangest spring ever, with its killing frost in early May, combined with a long-lasting drought. Over a fig-charlotte pudding, Davis resumed yesterday's discussion.

"Again, Cat, I'm very sorry I doubted you and the work you've done."

Cat shook her head. "It's all right, Dave, really. You always told me I should trust my instincts, and that's what I've kept on doing. Even when it seems pure malarkey."

"I wish my instincts were as good."

"They used to be. I'm wondering if you have too much responsibility right now. You're so over-loaded maybe you can't see clearly."

Davis took a sip of bitter tea and made a face. Tea lately was either too weak or too strong—no in between. What he wouldn't give for a cup of hearty Chicago coffee with cream and a sinful amount of sugar. "It's the petty chores mixed with serious business that's getting me down," he admitted. "It's being in charge of running BP, plus things I'm unable to talk about."

"Tell me about some of those chores. The stuff Holmes used to handle and that you probably shouldn't have to."

"Let's see." Davis used his fingers to itemize. "The loos need toilet tissues, especially the ladies. There are problems with heat in Hut 4. The canteen workers request salad ingredients, macaroni, sausages, and I don't remember what else, and maintenance is required constantly on certain never-to-be-mentioned, top-secret machines, now under armed guard in Blocks A through H."

Cat laughed. "Oh, my! Gramps would say you're covering everything from the Sublime to the Cor Blimey. I have a suggestion. Other than caring for the wretched don't-breathe-a-word machines, maybe you should delegate what anyone could do."

"Right. But everyone is busy already. Any suggestions?"

"Yes. Perhaps even for the machines. First, stop being one of those people who dinnae think a thing is done right unless ye do it yersel'. Then turn most of it over to Janet and Helen. Send them the supply requisition slips and trust that it will be done. Probably a lot of the requests come from them anyway. Items pertaining to Bletchley House could be handled by Lady Katherine."

"Not a bad idea at all. And the machines?"

"Sheila, once she returns. Gus has made it clear she must not continue whatever caused her so much distress, but couldn't she order and manage routine maintenance?"

"She could, but will she be able or even want to? Sheila even has the knowledge to handle some of the maintenance herself. But I don't know when she'll return, do you?"

Cat wasn't able to answer, for they were interrupted by their agitated waitress. "It's just coming over the wireless! Listen! I'll turn up the volume."

Cat and Davis, with their hearts in their throats, listened to Winston Churchill announcing the Allies' attack on the Normandy beaches.

> *This vast operation is undoubtedly the most complicated and difficult that has ever taken place. It involves tides, wind, waves, visibility, both from the air and the sea standpoint, and the combined employment of land, air and sea forces in the highest degree of intimacy and in contact with conditions which could not and cannot be fully foreseen.*

Would this mean a free France, or disaster for them all? And both of them wondered if Cat had helped make this happen. Could this be what Foss and Gus had alluded to?

His Cat was really quite wonderful, Davis thought. His Cat.

Sheila and Gus heard the news in Oban, where they were dining in a harbor hotel. She took a bite of her sausage and tomato pie. Funny, before the war, she couldn't abide sausages. Before the war. In the past, dates were determined BC or AD. Now it was BW or AW, before the war or after the war. She wondered if AW she would continue to eat sausages.

Sheila felt rested now. A very grown up Gemma had boarded the train and returned to Oxford by herself, in order to take an extra summer term enabling her to enroll in a higher form in the fall. Sheila would return with Gus to BP at week's end. But what she might do there was yet to be determined.

"Perhaps I'll go back to the Typex," she said.

"Or perhaps not," Gus said, picking up on her train of thought immediately. "Feeding misinformation to the Nazis using Colossus might be more to your liking and ability."

"Is that what just happened, Gus? Is that why you've been grinning since we heard the news? Did the Nazis think the Allies would strike somewhere else?"

"You know better than to ask that." But Gus winked at her, wishing he could reveal that Operation Fortitude, which used the Colossus computer to send Ultra intelligence to confuse the enemy, had proven a great success. Of course, the outcome on the beaches of Normandy would not be determined by the Geese at BP, but by brave soldiers, so many of whom would pay the ultimate price. At least Gus and his people had contributed in giving the Allies an opening advantage. But the Germans would extract revenge for being fooled. Even harder times most certainly were coming.

Letter from Maureen Bradshaw, soon to be RN
Simmons College, School of Nursing, Boston, Massachusetts
To Janet Hill, the best Gram in the world
13 June 1944

Dear Gram,

This letter is for you to share with everyone. I have very little time to write these days, but I do appreciate all the letters I'm receiving. They make me not miss home quite as much. I am so happy you have fully recovered and have returned to your many activities. I have seen a few plays here in Boston, but none of them, in my humble opinion, have been as fine as those offered by our own Theatrical Society.

I still walk with a slight limp, but my doctors are hopeful it will disappear in time. While I miss Millie and her family and the more pleasant weather of Baltimore, Simmons is an excellent school, and Boston is a comfortable city for me. In many ways, it reminds me of London before the war. Yes, there are blackouts and rationing, although not nearly as stringent as what we have in England. I live in a dormitory with other student nurses and have made a few friends. I suspect, though, I would be very lonely if I had time to think about it.

My nurse's course of study is going splendidly and, thanks to both Lady Katherine's and Gus's excellent preparations, I should complete it in good order. Whether or not the war has ended, I will be anxious to be of service. Everyone here is talking, of course, about the recent developments in France, and most believe all will be successful. Once I'm a registered nurse, any time I'm able to help a soldier, or anyone else, I will be doing it to honor Lee.

That's right, Gram. I have accepted that Lee is probably gone forever. I haven't given up entirely, but I'm no longer fooling myself. I guess I needed some denial just to keep on. Recently, a friend of mine arranged a date for me with her brother, and I did enjoy myself. But I doubt I'll repeat it any time soon. I still love Lee, whether he is alive or dead. Dead. There. I can actually say that word now.

I am thrilled with Mum and Gus's good news. Gus will be a proper husband for Mum, and I will be proud to have him as a stepfather. Please tell Danny I think of him as my little brother already.

Give everyone my best love, Gram—you, Mum, Pippa, Gemma, Danny, Gus, Lady Katherine, Helen, Cat, and Mr. Dailey. I miss all of you dearly!

Affectionately,
Reenie

CHAPTER THIRTY-FOUR

ONCE SHE WAS BACK AT work, Sheila realized that both Gus and the need for revenge would be her cure. Gus gave her joy and hope for the future. Revenge helped to erase from her mind, just a little, what she had learned of the war's atrocities. She would get back the only way she could, by following orders and bombarding the Nazis with coded disinformation—enough truth to be believable, but so misleading as to make the information, in fact, a lie.

Gus had been correct that the Germans would retaliate for what was referred to as D-Day. Buzz bombs, also called doodlebugs, rained on London, beginning one week after the invasion of Normandy Beach. Hundreds of the little fireballs exploded, killing untold numbers on the ground below. But Sheila and others had discovered how to use the German codes against them by giving false locations for airfields and military holdings. As often as not, the German V-1 rockets struck unpopulated areas.

V-1 stood for *Vergeltunswaffe*, meaning vengeance weapon, and seeking vengeance was Sheila's partial path to recovery. But Gus . . . It was becoming so difficult to conceal the truth from everyone. At least she would see him soon, and they would have a bite to eat at the cottage—he promised to bring something from the canteen—and then a sneak upstairs for a few hours. Janet and Helen were at a late rehearsal, as was Pippa, so it was unlikely they would be disturbed. Life would be so much easier if others knew her true identity—Mrs. Hamish Fergusson. Gus's reasoning for keeping the marriage a secret seemed sensible at the time—or perhaps she had been willing then to agree to anything he suggested. Their work came first, no place to live together, her family's feelings needed consideration—excellent arguments. But that was then.

She would talk with Gus. He needed to consider her feelings, too, and then, hopefully, re-consider.

Pippa was feeling rebellious, although she hadn't shared her thoughts with anyone. Studies were tiresome, and even Lady Katherine knew she had reached the end of her capabilities. Reading and writing were good enough, but maths was hopeless. Who cared? She was sixteen and ready for acting instruction at the Royal Academy in London. But Mum would not listen—just because the main theatre had been bombed and the school was in temporary quarters. She was too young—London was much too dangerous. When had Mum become so unreasonable? Gus and Mr. Dailey had promised to look into a safer place, perhaps a school in the country, but they had yet to keep their promise.

For a while, Pippa had had a crush on Sid, the young man who was now training dispatch riders. Sid had fancied her, and she fancied him—until she realized he fancied all the girls. And there were plenty far prettier than she among the newest crop of riders. Pippa had stuck her nose in the air, refusing to be one of many. But it did hurt and helped to make up her mind. She was an actress, and no mere boy was going to stand in her way.

Cat marked another day off the calendar—25 August 1944. She had arrived at BP exactly four years ago. She was twenty-seven now. A great age, indeed. A simple cryptic crossword puzzle had changed her from a happy-go-lucky, sharp-tongued wit to a sober, un-smiling, soon-to-be spinster. "Oh, get over yersel', Cat," she scolded herself. "It's nae sae bad." Then she forced a large grin—just as Davis entered the office.

"What's this?" he demanded. "A private celebration?"

Cat laughed, cheered by the sight of him. "No, I was feeling sorry for myself, remembering the silly, happy girl I used to be, so I decided to snap out of it, as you Americans would say."

"There's not much to be happy about these days. Don't worry, though. Once the war is over, the old Cat will return."

"Will she? We've all changed, Dave. Inside, parts of the war will stay with us forever. But you're right. At last, we'll give ourselves permission to be ourselves again."

"Permission granted right now—at least for tonight. Some good news on the war front—the liberation of Paris has begun." Davis didn't say that he thought the Nazis' now certain defeat would make them desperate and their last-ditch crimes even worse. Why dampen Cat's positive efforts? "To cheer you further, we've been invited to a party, and I've come to take you there."

"A party? Where?"

"Bletchley House, to be hosted by Lady Katherine and, I believe, Janet Hill. Something mysterious seems to be in the wind."

As it turned out, the true hosts of the party were not Lady Katherine or Janet. Gus and Sheila were in charge of decorating and supplying both food and drink: a plum cake, baked by Sheila herself, and whisky from Gus's own supply, sent from Scotland. Gus had listened, finally, to Sheila's pleadings and was prepared to announce their marriage. Having to make private assignations with his own wife had become wearing on him, as well.

The guest list was small, but those they cared about most dearly would attend. Even Gemma was taking the train from Oxford to spend the weekend at home. Gus had invited Hugh Foss, Alan Turing, and Gordon Welchman, his closest associates, while Sheila's guests included—other than Gemma and Lady Katherine—her mother, Pippa, Helen, Cat, Davis, and Danny.

Everyone gathered at nineteen hours. Lady Katherine smiled a welcome but informed them she was as much in the dark as they were. Clearing his throat, Gus took charge. "Thank ye all for coming," he said, nerves making his brogue more pronounced. "Ceud mile fàilte—a hundred thousand welcomes. You are our dearest friends and must be the first to know. I would like to introduce my bonnie bride, Mrs. Hamish Fergusson." Smiling, Sheila gave a deep theatrical bow.

"That's brilliant!" Danny yelled, causing laughter from all.

Davis shook his hand. "You were right all along, Danny. You have a new da, a mam, and three sisters!"

Cat looked carefully at Dave. He truly seemed happy for them. Perhaps he was over Sheila. Perhaps Millie was right, and she should still hope. Davis gave her a slight smile, but he wasn't thinking of hope. Eleven years, he thought. I'm eleven years older.

Lady Katherine insisted on champagne instead of whisky. "It's the only proper drink for toasting," she said. "And yes, Pippa, Gemma, and Danny, you may have a sip, too. Davis, as Deputy Commander, will you give the toast?"

Davis held up his glass. "Let's drink to the victory of our beloved countries and to the health and happiness of two of the finest people I know. To Mr. and Mrs. Fergusson. To Sheila and Gus."

"To Sheila and Gus!"

Then Gus announced they were starting a new tradition. Instead of receiving gifts, they intended to give them.

"Just like an American Indian potlach," Davis said, giving Cat a brotherly hug. "What have you got for us, Gus?"

"Sheila will do the honors," he said.

Most of the gifts were simple but precious offerings: packages of boiled candy, a bottle of whisky, a package of cigarettes. "Gus will give the last gift," Sheila said. "It's for Pippa."

Pippa had been wondering when her turn would come. Some sweeties would be lovely.

Uncertainly, Gus handed her an envelope. "I do hope you'll approve, Pippa. I have found a drama coach for you—a former teacher from the Royal Academy. She lives in a boarding house in Oxford, where there is room for you. After studying with her, you certainly will be qualified to enroll in RADA as soon as the war is over."

Pippa stood frozen. No reaction at all. The guests looked at her and Gus, worried. Was she displeased?

Gemma tugged her arm. "Aren't you happy, Pippa? Someday you'll be a famous actress, and meanwhile, you'll live near me."

Finally Pippa reacted, tears of joy streamed down her face. She threw herself into Gus's arms. "Oh, thank you, Papa," she sobbed.

Assorted letters to Maureen Bradshaw
14 October 1944 to 6 March 1945
From Hamish Fergusson and Danny Fergusson

My dear daughter,

Words cannot express our joy each time we receive a letter from you. My apologies that this is the first time I've written. So much is happening right now in our efforts to end this exhausting, heartbreaking war, and your mother and I have been kept very busy. I can't possibly thank you enough for making me feel welcome in my new family. I thought I was fated to live alone until I finally died alone. And now, I have my ready-made, off-the-racks family: a brilliant, caring wife, three beautiful daughters, and a young rascal of a son.

We are all proud of what you've accomplished and look forward to the day you walk through the gates, back with us once again.

Lovingly,
Gus

Dear Big Sister,

I fell down yesterday and scraped my knee. Please come home and put a sticky plaster on it. Lady Katherine says it won't bleed if I stop picking at the scab, and if I do it one more time, I will have to put the plaster on myself. I told her I would write to you about it. I think a nurse should be in charge of the case. Da will put this in the envelope with his letter.

Your brother,
Daniel P. Fergusson

From Catriona MacLaren

Dear Maureen,

I am pleased to hear you did well on your examinations and do not have much longer to go before you are our own Florence Nightingale. We are all looking forward to your return, although Dave says your journey back should be planned out carefully because of possible dangers. So many terrible things seem to be happening now—some we are only just learning about. Never a day goes by that we don't hear dreadful news about families of our Jewish volunteers. I do not know how they are bearing it. Your mother especially seems distraught, but Gus is watching her carefully. They are quite a wonderful couple.

Perhaps you've heard about all our billeting changes. We have been playing a game of Going to Jerusalem, or what Dave calls "Musical Chairs." I'm still in my small room at the cottage. Your grandmother and Helen are occupying the room you used to share with Pippa. Gemma and Pippa are both studying in Oxford, of course, but share a room in Bletchley House when they come home on holiday. Danny is remaining there under Lady Katherine's watchful eye. This means the newly-weds, Sheila and Gus, have Number Two Cottage all to themselves. Our other billet mates are in and out. We've lost some, and new ones have come to take their places. I don't know them well, but they seem a friendly lot. We are all U-boats that pass in the night.

Thanks to a recent doodle-bug, Janet has lost her house in Nottingham, so she and Helen will not be living there after the war. In truth, I believe they will remain right here until they are forcibly removed.

I wish I had better news about Gramps. His memory is dim, and his heart troubles him greatly. If only it were possible to make the journey north.

It will be a grand day when you return, Maureen. We will have a celebration to remember.

Fondly, Cat

From Pippa Bradshaw

Chère Mlle Maureen,

I hope you are doing très bien. I am studying acting with a wonderful coach, Mlle Lucille Lenoire. Yes, she is also French, so I am forced to learn some of the language. Actually, it is rather fun. Mlle Lenoire is very very old but also very very good. She is a famous acting coach and was once a famous actress. She is strict and keeps a fierce eye on me. She is on my list of people I love most in the world.

In case you think all I do is learn to act, I must tell you that I am also taking a few classes in literature and writing at Gemma's school. They are not as advanced as her classes, but Gemma is smarter, and I don't mind anymore. Gus says he will help me with maths when I'm on holiday. I am hoping he will forget, but that is not likely.

Mlle Lenoire has other students besides just me. Sometimes we come together for scene study classes. I have made a few friends. Often we go to the pictures together. My favorite was *Since You Went Away.* Shirley Temple was in it, and it was ever so heartwarming.

Reenie, I had a strange dream the other night. Perhaps I shouldn't tell you about it, but it seemed so real. I dreamed Lee was still alive. He came to the pigeon loft to make sure I was taking good care of the pigeons. I had to explain to him it was not my job any longer. Then I woke up. What do you think the dream meant?

Soon you will be a nurse, and we will all be together again. That will be a happy day.

Avec l'amour,
Philippine (That is my French name. Pippa isn't French.)

CHAPTER THIRTY-FIVE

A LONE SAILOR EMBARKED FROM the London train and started walking up the hill toward Bletchley Park. A short walk, if that were his destination, but obviously a difficult one, his every step belabored. Gaunt, almost skeletal, in a sagging uniform that might have fit once, he walked with a limp, leaning to one side as if the sling supporting his arm also carried great weights. Anyone spotting him might give a wide berth, not wanting his apparent war weariness to rub off on them.

Gus and Sheila, driving back from dinner in Oxford, approached the struggling stranger. At least, Sheila didn't think she knew him, but something seemed familiar.

"Gus, maybe we should offer him a ride. He's having a difficult time."

"I'm not sure that's a good idea, darling. If he's headed for BP, he'll need proper identification to enter. I've certainly never seen him before."

As they drove on past, it clicked. She knew. "Pull over, Gus. Pull over now!"

Before Gus had even fully stopped, Sheila leaped from the car and ran back. "Lee!" she shouted, throwing her arms around the sailor, nearly knocking him off his feet. "Lee, it's you! You're alive!"

The telegram, dated 10 March 1945, came after Lee's arrival. Sent to Davis Dailey, it said only that Lee had been liberated from the German P.O.W. Camp Marciano in Italy and was on his way home. The previous telegram had been a mistake. He had never been in Tunisia but had been captured in Gibraltar, a life-changing error for those who loved him and thought him dead.

Lady Katherine, appalled by his shattered state, insisted he convalesce in Bletchley House. Lee agreed, for that was truly where he felt most at home. Let everyone cluck around him as much as they liked, he thought, as long as he could eat and sleep until he couldn't eat or sleep anymore. First, though, he must call Reenie.

After joyous shrieks and tears, with Maureen insisting she would return home at once, Lee finally convinced her to stay. "Look, sweetheart, you're almost an RN, and Mr. Dailey thinks traveling by either ship or plane right now is far too dangerous. Finish your training, and then come home. With everyone here caring for me, I promise to be well and strong by the time you return."

The advice was wise, of course, and Maureen accepted it, even though her heart disagreed. Lee was alive. That was what was important. She had received perhaps the one miracle that would be allotted to her. It would be best not to tempt fate further.

On the very day a defeated Adolph Hitler committed suicide, 30 April 1945, a fully registered nurse, age twenty, left the railway station and walked the short distance to Bletchley Park. She was somewhat surprised that no one had come to meet her and wondered if her telegram had been delayed. After showing her identity papers, she hurried to Number Two Cottage Stable Yards. No one was home. Number One was vacant as well. Was everyone at work?

The stables, too, were empty. "Where is everyone?" she whispered. And then she grinned. "Don't they know there's a war on?" A rustling from the aviary caught her attention. Probably just pigeons, but she would check.

A thin, haggard man was feeding the excited birds and talking softly to them. Pippa's dream come true and Maureen's very own miracle.

"Lee?"

He turned to her.

"Lee, I'm home."

Telegram to Catriona MacLaren, WREN, HMS Pembroke V
From the Residence for Retired Gentlemen, Inverness, Scotland
6 May 1945

Douglas MacLaren dying. Come at once.

CHAPTER THIRTY-SIX

DAVIS HAD BEEN IN WORMWOOD Scrubs for a week, unable to contact anyone at Bletchley Park. No matter. They would learn the good news soon enough. Hitler was dead in an apparent suicide, all of Italy was in the hands of the Allies, and those in the know expected an unconditional surrender of German forces at any moment. England's war was essentially over, and so, he thought, was Bletchley Park's. And Davis had learned for the first time the possible meaning behind all those whispers in Chicago so long ago. He shook his head. "Madness," he whispered, "but if it must be so, it must."

Gene Bifford—Biff—caught up with him in the hall. "You still here, Dally? Thought you'd be long gone."

Davis smiled at his old chum, who likely would be promoted to head of MI5. Somehow the foolish old nicknames kept him grounded, taking him back to beloved Oxford days. "I'm heading for the railway station now," he said. "I was just waiting for permission to relate the good news to those back at BP."

"A wonderful day," Biff said, "but many difficult ones still remain. The Japs aren't beaten yet, you know. Then we'll need to rebuild. We'll need to rebuild this whole country."

"The whole world, Biff. But we'll do it. Never fear."

Davis reached BP early evening and went directly to his office, hoping to see Cat. She would be the first person he told. But Bletchley House was empty. Not even Lady Katherine was home. Was there a play rehearsal that night?

At Cat's cottage, only one of her billet mates was there, although about to leave. Dave wasn't certain of her name. "Do you know where I can find Cat?"

"Inverness." The girl giggled, and then stopped herself. "Sorry. It's not funny. Cat received a telegram saying her grandfather was dying. She left yesterday." Rudely, Davis hurried away, not responding to her foolishness.

Finally finding Welchman, Foss, and Turing in Block H, he tried to congratulate them but discovered they were hard at work analyzing the Japanese Naval codes just received from the Japanese Purple Cipher machine. They did stop long enough to shake his hand and to remind him the war wasn't over yet.

"I'll be back," Davis promised, before jumping into a staff car. Good. A full tank of petrol, and he had enough points to assure him of at least two refills. He had a long drive ahead—straight through the night, if necessary.

God bless you all. This is your victory! It is the victory of the cause of freedom in every land. In all our long history we have never seen a greater day than this. Everyone, man or woman, has done their best. Everyone has tried. Neither the long years, nor the dangers, nor the fierce attacks of the enemy, have in any way weakened the independent resolve of the British nation.

Cat and the staff at the Residence for Retired Gentlemen had listened to Winston Churchill on the wireless. But Cat thought only of Gramps. She would have given anything to tell him the great news.

But he had died earlier that night, amid joyous celebrations on the streets, on the sidewalks, in pubs all over Inverness and all of Britain. "It's over! We beat them! The Hun is destroyed!"

Cat wished she could have joined in, but her heart was too full and the rest of her too empty. The next morning, after giving instructions for a simple funeral service at the home, she left to seek out the pastor of Gramps's Scots Presbyterian church, located next door to their house on Ness Bank. For Pastor Black to lead the service would have pleased Gramps. The two men had been cronies. Perhaps Pastor Black would know of others who might wish to attend.

Walking along the river—alone—wondering what to do next. But someone was following her. Someone familiar. A tall, slim man with a chiseled face of sharp angles, dark hair graying slightly, and warm brown eyes, now more sensitive than she had ever seen them.

"Dave, you're here?"

"Yes, Cat. I've come to take you home."

"Home. Where is my home?"

At last, he gathered her into his arms. "Wherever I am. Wherever we are. Let's decide that together."

October 1994
Bletchley House
Bletchley Park, England

And suddenly it was over. House didn't notice the change for many months. It could see people carrying out office equipment and furniture amid the rustling of papers, followed by crackling sounds in the fireplaces. Outside, hammers banged loudly as both huts and the machines inside them were destroyed. But outside was of little concern to House. Then mostly quiet—days, weeks, months, years passed. Occasional voices: "It's an architectural nightmare, an eyesore, a wreck. It needs to go." House grew dormant, sleeping, aware of nothing, not even the aches and pains of growing older. It failed to notice peeling paint, rising damp, musty odors.

One day, an elderly woman and her younger sister, perhaps in her late forties, came through the front door. The older one seemed vaguely familiar—something about her tone of voice. "It is so strange to be back here," she said.

"I'm grateful just to be out of the cold wind."

"You don't know what cold is. It's only October and will be much worse soon. Oh, what grand times we had skating on the lake in winter. But surely, you, Moira Janet Maureen Fergusson, can't complain about the cold. Oban winters are brutal. I remember them well."

"Didn't you notice I left there as soon as I could? Show me around the house. It's hard to imagine our parents working here."

"Well, they weren't stationed in Bletchley House. Before we leave today, I'll show you Hut 8 and Block D, where Mum and Gus used to work on deciphering Enigma codes. Look, Moira, this is Lady Katherine's library, and across the hall is Davis's and Cat's office. I wish the stairs weren't such a problem for me. I would show you where my grandmother and Pippa performed their plays, and where we had many, many concerts."

"You make those days sound like fun."

"Oh, they were, at least for the children—most of the time. I had such freedom until Mum grew wise and sent me off to boarding school." She sighed.

"Practically everyone is gone now. Mum, Gus, Gram, Reenie, Lee, Pippa . . . Almost everyone I loved."

"I'm still here, dear."

"So you are. And Danny is close by."

"I'll take a quick peek upstairs, Gemma, and then you can show me the huts. I'll be warm enough soon. And I especially want to see the bookshop where our Danny will be working."

Gemma. That's who she was. No wonder she sounded familiar. House remembered a tiny girl, running up and down the stairs, playing hide-and-seek in its great rooms. And Danny. What a delightful rogue he was.

"Be patient, Moira. I will show you everything. You dash upstairs while I just sit here and look. All too soon, BP will be overrun with visitors, anxious to learn what happened here. And now, at long last, we're allowed to tell them."

But instead of looking, Gemma closed her eyes and breathed in familiar smells that time had not erased. And the room seemed full of remembered voices. Some might have been the same ones House still heard.

Me? Riding a motorcycle?

You have a great attachment for kitchens, Mrs. Bradshaw?

I can't emphasize enough the importance of your work.

By George, we did it! We sank the Bismarck!

Ice skating! I'm rather good at that.

I love you, Reenie.

They're not killing babies, are they, Mummy?

Many of the things we're doing would appall us normally.

Oh, no! Oh, dear God, no!

The love that makes undaunted the final sacrifice.

My goodness, what an enigma of a house!

House sighed, proud and content, remembering what Lady Katherine had said so many years before. "It's a grand old house. It deserves to live. We all deserve to live." House knew it was not *just* a house, not *any* home. It was no mere manor or mansion. Vital work had taken place here. It was Bletchley House, a war hero, ready to live again.

What's Real and What Isn't?
Fact and Fantasy About

THE GEESE THAT WON THE WAR

A LL OF THE LOCATIONS IN the novel are real, and so is the situation. In the war against Nazi Germany, Bletchley Park in Buckinghamshire, England was a vital station, where from 1939-1945, as many as 10,000 people worked tirelessly to crack German codes.

Every effort has been made to avoid anachronisms. The songs, expressions and, more important, what was actually happening during the war at the time has been carefully researched. The missions in the Huts and Blocks are accurate. Many of the people mentioned in the book lived, although they were not fictionalized or used as key players: Lady Fanny Leon, Lord Herbert Samuel Leon, Alan Turing, Hugh Foss, Gordon Welchman, Winston Churchill, David McLean, Rudolph Hess, William J. Donovan, and Alistair Denniston. Some license was taken with Alfred Dillyn Knox (Dilly), George Leon, and Admiral Hugh Sinclair. All other characters are fictional, though some of the experiences attributed to them are based on fact. I am especially indebted to the many fine books about Bletchley Park written by Sinclair McKay, Marion Hill, and others. Their true accounts tell of code breaking and spy detection which, along with concentrated "people power" from thousands "doing their bit," Britain was saved from Nazi domination and the world avoided two or three more years of war.

THE GEESE THAT WON THE WAR is fiction and may seem a stretch at times. Not exaggerated were the dedication, determination, and sheer drudgery of Churchill's "Geese," who guarded the secrets, selflessly performed arduous tasks, and helped save both lives and country.

*T*HE GEESE THAT WON THE WAR is Marilyn Ludwig's sixth book, the second taking place in the United Kingdom. Marilyn considers herself an Anglophile and has visited the island nation many times. She also has a strong interest in World War II, a period she just missed experiencing. Moving closer to home, although farther back in time, her next book is another historical fiction, set in her hometown, Downers Grove, Illinois, where she lives with her husband, Ed. The time: The Civil War. The place: Downers Grove's historic Main Street Cemetery.

CPSIA information can be obtained
at www.ICGtesting.com
Printed in the USA
FSOW02n0711150517
34274FS